Conquests: Hearts Rule Kingdoms

EMILY MURDOCH

ISBN: 149223420X
ISBN-13: 9781492235309

DEDICATION

To the loves I have lost – William "Billiam" Murdoch and Graham G. Thomas.
To the loves I have found – Joshua D. Perkins.

CONTENTS

ACKNOWLEDGMENTS

Thank you to Endeavour Press, who have taken a chance on me, and Richard Foreman who has been beyond helpful in the process to get this book from on my computer to you. Many thanks must go to my family, Gordon and Mary Murdoch, and Haydon Murdoch, who have always supported my writing, and with whom I had a lot of fun talking about titles. Georgia Bird was my early editor, and supported me when I was convinced I was in a rut. But without Joshua D. Perkins' encouragement to start writing seriously, this book would never have been written. To him I owe a ridiculous debt of gratitude.

PROLOGUE

The village burned in the darkness. Anglo-Saxon women crawled in the ashes and blood, crying, but quietly. They did not want to be found. They knew what would happen to them if they were discovered. In the light of the flames only one building could be seen left standing; the great manor house. None dared approach it. They knew that if the men returned, that would be exactly where they would go to. In the courtyard of this house, a shadow wept.

A young girl was crouched in a corner, sobbing. The stone wall behind hid her in its silhouette, and she tried to muffle the sounds of her cries. She did not want to be found.

A noise startled her; the sound of hooves on wood. They were coming.

Picking herself up and wrapping her long skirts around her, the girl ran – but she was not fast enough.

"Hie there!"

A whining man's voice rang out into the darkness and broke through the silence. It was the rider of the horse that she had heard, but now many more horses had joined him. It was a whole host of men. The girl gasped and tried to run faster, but there was nowhere to run to. Nowhere was safe now. Before she could reach the other side of the courtyard, strong rough hands grabbed her.

"Bring her here!"

The same gruff voice spoke, and the girl struggled. The man holding her had to drag her over to the horse of the speaker. The man had dismounted, and the girl caught sight of his broadsword. She gasped, and pushed backwards trying to stay as far away as possible from the blade. She had seen swords similar to that one. She had seen what they could do.

"Hold her up."

The man was older than her, probably as old as her father. He stank of sweat, and his mean eyes bore down into her. When he gazed down upon his captive, he was surprised. The lonely figure that he had taken to be a child was much older. The girl must be verging onto womanhood.

He leered at her.

"Do you have a name, my sweet?"

The girl stared back at him. Fear danced in her eyes, but also resentment. She knew why he had come to her home. She knew what he wanted.

"My lord Richard asked you a question!" said the man holding her back, twisting one of her arms so she let out a yelp of pain.

"Avis," she breathed, her arm searing and tears brimming in her eyes. "My name is Avis."

CHAPTER ONE

Avis leaned against the flint wall and looked up at the magnificent sky, and forced a blonde curl back underneath her veil. The sun was setting, and she could feel the cool of night descending quickly. The long summer was starting to cool into autumn, and soon winter would be on its way. As she sighed, her breath blossomed. A loud voice behind her startled her.

"Avis!"

She turned to see Richard walking aggressively towards her, and instinctively took a step back.

"Are you not coming?" The medieval Norman Richard stared down at her, panting slightly at the exercise. The running was unlike him, a man who spent his life swaggering from meal to meal. Rolls of fat were carefully covered by his tunic, but Avis knew that she could outrun him. A fact that had given her comfort over the long three years since he had first arrived. He sneered down at her, mentally undressing her in a way that was disgustingly apparent.

"I follow you, my lord." Avis attempted a smile as she spoke in the harsh Norman language that she had come to learn, and Richard seemed appeased. Offering her his arm, she draped her delicate blue velvet sleeve across and allowed herself to be led inside to the Great Hall. A feast had been prepared – in her honour, Richard had told her, but in the three years since the Normans had conquered England that she had been forced to share her ancestral home with Richard, nothing had ever been organised for her own comfort before. She was suspicious, and Richard knew it.

"Come now, relax." He sniggered, and she sat down gently at her normal place near the head of the table. The knights and other men that now lived in her home sat down at various points along the trestle tables. Richard took the seat at the head of the table, where her father had once sat. He clapped his hands, and servants immediately began bringing in food. Sizzling meats and sweet aromas soon filled the Great Hall, and the large dogs that had been snoozing by the fire soon jumped up and positioned themselves around the tables, hoping for scraps. Men began pouring ale, and soon the Great Hall was filled with the scraping of metal on plates, swirling goblets and belching. Avis ate silently, and many men's eyes flickered across to gaze upon her beauty.

Richard leaned over her, breathing in her scent as he poured her wine. He lingered just a little too close for comfort, forcing her to lean back in her seat to avoid him.

"The question is," Richard began speaking as if continuing an earlier conversation, "when are you going to realise that you must marry me?"

A few of the men nearest to Avis leered and chuckled, and she could feel her pale skin darkening red. How dare he!

"You have offended me enough with your constant disdain for my wishes." She managed to contain her anger. "Please do me the courtesy of never asking me again."

"No." Richard was forceful. "You have no land, no property, no wealth, no family. You lost all that three years ago."

Several men cheered, and one man yelled, "God bless King William!"

Richard chuckled. He had good memories of the Norman invasion three years ago in 1066, and gave no thought as to how Avis may feel. She gripped her knife hard, and tried not to speak. She had borne the indignity of being taunted by her people's defeat for the last three years. She could do it again.

"The Normans rule here now!" Food and saliva leapt from Richard's mouth as he shouted. Goblets were lifted in the air and men began giving speeches, praising themselves and their friends for the great deeds they had performed during the invasion. The Battle of Hastings, the Battle of London, the subduing of the Anglo-Saxon people, the murder of innocents, the ransacking of churches…

Avis felt hot and angry. Her father had been the Anglo-Saxon ealdorman of these parts – the local lord, a just, honest, kind man who had not wanted to go to war but had obeyed out of love for his King. And he had paid the price with his life. Now she, an Anglo-Saxon noblewoman, had nothing. No one to protect her, no one to care for her, and no options.

Richard cut across his men to once again speak to Avis. "Avis, I am getting tired – "

"As am I! Tired of your constant requests for a promise that I will not make!" Avis cut across him. She would not allow herself to be bullied.

Richard grinned at her. "And I am not getting any younger."

"We can all see that." Avis muttered under her breath. Richard's weight had only increased after William the King gave him her father's home, and the skin around his eyes had sagged and creased. He was losing time, and he knew that if he was to have an heir, it would have to be now.

"Quiet!"

Richard's shout had silenced the entire hall, and Avis blushed again. She knew that the whole household would hear his next words.

"You will marry me," Richard spoke with a hardness and finality. "William has ordered his Norman nobles to marry native women. He is going to create a new people, of both sides. You and I."

"Never." Avis stood up. "You may live in my home, Richard, sleep in my father's bed and give orders to my people, but you do not order me."

Sweeping her long blue skirt behind her, she walked out of the Great Hall. As she pushed the wooden door shut behind her, she could hear the beginnings of chatter – led by Richard, in an attempt to cover up the embarrassment of his ward once again defying him. She slowly breathed out, releasing the tension from her lungs and slowly calming her shaking hands. Avis knew that after three long years, Richard would not be taking no for an answer much longer. The trouble was she didn't have any other choices.

Seated at the top of the Great Hall, Richard stroked his greying beard as his men soaked themselves in ale and wine. He had never thought that forcing a lonely and unprotected girl to marry him would be so difficult. William had been insistent when he had given Richard this land that he must marry a local girl to secure it, and his time was running out. He leered at the thought of getting his greasy hands under those flowing dresses that he permitted Avis to wear, and his loins tightened – but then he sighed. He called a servant to him, who quickly retrieved a letter that had been delivered to him by a King's messenger that morning. Scanning its contents, he sighed again. But William's word was law, and if he decreed something, it was to be done.

He would tell Avis in the morning.

CHAPTER TWO

Avis awoke naturally before dawn. As she lay in bed, listening to the house stirring, she smiled. She could not help but hope that as Richard could not, he would not force her to marry him. All she had to do was wait, bide her time. Soon enough Richard would have no other choice but to marry another so that his heirs could inherit this land. Her land. Her smile flickered, and faded.

Forcing herself out of her warm covers and into the coldness of morning, she struggled to force her pale smooth figure into her bodice, and quickly tied the laces which held various garments together. When she was younger she had a servant girl to aid her in this monotonous task, but she had learnt quickly how to take care of herself after she was plummeted into poverty. Avis pulled on her leather shoes, and began the arduous problem of maintaining her hair. Golden blonde and full of curls, it constantly attempted to escape the veil that she placed on her head to protect her modesty. For her Anglo-Saxon people, one's hair was not seen, and so both she and her mother had always worn veils that covered their hair but left their faces free.

"Your face is important," her mother had always said, "because that is where people see the truth."

Even after her mother had gone, Avis always wore her veil. She knew that she was not fashionable – but then being of Anglo-Saxon stock automatically made one lower class in this new England that William had created. She frowned, placing the last wayward curl behind her ear. This 'new' England was not one that she particularly liked.

Avis wandered leisurely down the stone slab stairs into the kitchen, firm in the knowledge that none of the servants would be up yet. The blue sky that heralded her lifted her spirits. She had always loved the summer season the most. After passing through the long corridor, Avis entered the kitchen. Checking the fire by the spit was lit, she began to prepare dough for baking. She had loved cooking ever since she had been taught as a girl, but it was not appropriate for a noble woman to be seen doing servants' work. This was why she always worked in the kitchen in secret. Even the servants did not know who prepared the delicious bread that was seemingly delivered every morning.

It was hot work, and soon Avis had forgotten about Richard, and proposals, and invasions, and family. One could not bake bread and fret. She threw herself into the task, and before she realised it the servants were beginning to appear. Washing her hands briskly in the nearest ceramic bowl of water, she pretended to inspect the wooden tidy surfaces as men and women streamed in, ready for a new day of work.

"Oh!" The cook saw her and attempted a curtsey, almost tripping over her own feet.

Avis laughed. "It's alright, Æthelfreda, I just wanted to check everything was running smoothly down here."

"Oh." The cook attempted a smile, but was clearly terrified. "We're doing our best in preparation for my lord's guest, but I haven't – "

"Guest?" Avis stopped her, and nonchalantly began walking around the kitchen. "Who?"

"A man from the King, my lady. He brings a message about your marriage."

Avis stopped. Her eyes widened and she could see bright lights moving around her. "My marriage?"

The cook swallowed, suddenly aware of every other servant looking at her, horrified.

"Maybe my lady should speak to my lord about this."

Avis nodded, and collected herself. Walking serenely out of the kitchen, she broke into a run towards the Great Hall, the centre of the manor, where she knew Richard would be warming his back by the fire.

Pushing the door violently and neglecting to shut it, she burst out, "Richard!"

The short sweating man turned, surprised, and scowled when he saw her.

"Avis."

"I have heard tell of my impending marriage!" Avis was incredulous. "Pray do tell."

Richard opened his mouth to retaliate angrily, but stopped. He thought carefully, and then sat down in a chair by the fire.

"Sit." He ordered curtly. "I will tell you all."

Avis rushed to the comfortable wooden seat with several throws covering it that was opposite him, and dropped down, smoothly her skirt around her. Raising her eyes to him, Richard was reminded once again how striking she was.

"I have grown weary of this pretence," Richard began.

"It is not my choice to – "

"I know." Richard had been gazing at his feet, but now he looked up at her, the newly lit fire throwing his wrinkles into sharp relief. "But it must end."

He waited for her to challenge him, but she knew he was right.

"I received a letter from our King yesterday. William requires further marriages between my people and yours, to cement the nations together. He knows that I have been…unsuccessful with you."

Avis looked at him. She could not pity him – he was a Norman – but she could understand the pressure that he was under. Part of having noble blood was that certain things were expected of you. Marrying well was one of them. Richard was tired, and he looked it.

"And so William has chosen a husband for you."

Avis started. "A husband? He cannot choose me a husband!"

"He has." Richard was firm. "He presents you with a choice: to marry me, or to marry young Melville."

Melville. Avis thought hard, and translated the strange Norman word. Bad town. Not a name that suggested a brave, strong man. He was probably short and pale, like Richard, she thought miserably.

"Who is this Melville?" She said finally.

"He is a young nobleman of Norman stock. That is all you need know. He will arrive today, and then," Richard's gaze moved from her to the fire. "You shall make your choice."

"And if I choose none?" Avis spoke strongly, and Richard turned to look at her again. "If I choose not to marry at all?"

Richard smiled, bitterly. "That is no choice."

Avis was confused, and her small nose wrinkled.

"Everyone has a choice!"

"Not you." Richard stood up and began to walk away. "You are a Saxon."

He slammed the door behind him, echoing the Great Hall with a hollow note. Avis bit her lip. She did not know what William, Richard or this Melville would do to her if she tried to disobey, but she could imagine. She had lived but sixteen summers when the Normans had arrived in her village, and she could still recall the smell of burning and the screams of the women who had been taken. She shut her eyes, and tried to think.

There could be no harm in viewing this Melville. Perhaps he was old, like Richard, and required a companion in his old age. Maybe he is tired of this country, and could return to Normandy without her. She opened her eyes, and her face looked determined. Richard's passing insult had only revived in her the spirit of her people: proud, strong, and courageous. Anglo-Saxons did not give up without a fight, and their women were powerful. They had to be. She knew she was brave enough to face down this Melville, whoever he was.

CHAPTER THREE

Melville was tired and disappointed with this weather. Riding for three days towards a town which he had never heard of, to marry some wench that he imagined dirty and petulant, had not improved his mood. He swept his long dark hair out of his eyes as two of his men returned on horseback from a scouting trip on the area. Rain poured down his face, lining his jawline and causing his clothes to cling to his taut body.

"Nothing to report, my lord."

A curt nod from Melville was enough to prevent the man from speaking any longer. He was not in a temper to hear someone rattle on about pastures and woodland – not until he'd dried off and changed into clean clothes. This country, England. He was sick of it. He had been here three years too long.

Melville could feel his horse tiring underneath him, and patted his mane encouragingly. Melville's strong body was highlighted by the rain dripping down along the leather chaps and onto the ground. His horse twitched unhappily, and Melville reached down again to calm him.

"Nearly there," he murmured – but the platitude to his horse grated on his very soul. The horse could not understand why he was riding so hard and so fast towards a destiny that he did not want.

But William was the King, and William must be obeyed. The vows a man took when he became a knight were until death, and obedience was not required, but expected. Melville had known that when he agreed to come across from Normandy, to go over to the land where the savages roamed, he had not believed that he would remain there for very long. Now he had been given English land, and land needed heirs.

A man near the front of the party hallooed, and Melville started from his reverie, enjoying the time spent with his own thoughts. Looking up, he saw a large manor house. He had arrived.

A short balding man was waiting outside the building to greet him. As Melville pulled up and dismounted, the man came towards him.

"Richard, at your service."

"Melville, at yours."

The two men briefly embraced, and then began to talk about the weather. Anything to pretend that they weren't two men at a meeting, forced to be there against their will and better judgement. Richard looked over this youth. He was tall, and had clearly fought in many battles. You could tell by the way that he held himself that until he knew he was safe, he would never truly relax. Melville's dark features gave him the appearance of distrust – but then, Richard thought, Normans did not expect trust in this foreign land.

"Come inside. We have warmth, and food, and cheer." Richard gave the offer with a watery smile, and Melville matched it with almost less enthusiasm. They walked into the Great Hall, their men and servants following them at a respectful distance.

As Richard indicated where Melville was to sit, he called out, "bring in Avis."

Avis? thought Melville. It was a Norman name, but an uncommon one. Was Avis a servant girl? But the young lady that gracefully walked into the Great Hall was no servant girl. Her face was frightened, but determined, and it was obvious from her luxurious and tasteful clothes that she was a woman of high standing. A strange veil covered her hair in a manner that Melville had never seen before, but it was not unattractive. He wondered why she covered what was such a beautiful part of a woman, but was pulled back into the moment by Richard's booming voice.

"Avis!"

The girl increased her speed, arriving at a brisk walk in front of Richard. He lowered his voice to speak to her, and she began replying with hurried tones, both of them glancing nervously at Melville. He began to feel uncomfortable, especially when her frosty eyes landed on him. Her frantic but quiet words were spoken in a manner devoid of panic – but her calm words were clearly not being well-received by his host.

Avis could not believe that this man – this tall, dark man standing but paces away from her already viewing her home as if he owned it – was her intended husband. How dare this William, this King, dictate her life to her! How dare idiotic Richard agree to this pathetic charade! As Richard tried to placate her, and remind her that she always had another option, she repeatedly glared at this stranger. At least Richard over the years had come to appreciate and almost love the surrounding area. This man was an outsider. He could never understand the beauty of her country, and the nobility of her people. The strange man stood there, stock still and straight having refused the seat offered to him, and his muscular thighs strained at the leather hosen, and under the soft white linen shirt, muscles rippled. He must be a great deal taller than her, Avis surmised, glaring at him under her blonde lashes.

Eventually Richard grew tired.

"Food!" He shouted, gesticulating that nourishment should be brought up from the kitchen to the trestle tables. His men and the men that Melville had in his service gave a cry of appreciation, and Avis was forced to sit down on the left hand side of Richard, with Melville on his right.

The conversation in the hall was so loud and the men so enthusiastic in their eating and drinking that Avis could not hear what the two lords spoke of. She ate her chicken meekly, trying to ignore the occasional glances that the newcomer kept shooting her way. The man called Melville seemed uncomfortable, and Richard appeared to be attempting to convince him over something.

But Melville would not be convinced.

"I refuse to marry a woman at the order of my King!"

Richard's eyes narrowed.

"Then that is treason, my lord."

"Sir," Melville took a deep breath, trying to quell the anger rising up inside him. He was a long way from his land and the men that were loyal to him, and he could not afford to start a real argument here. "I love the King as much as any of his true and honest followers. But I love not his desire to design my marriage!"

"Marriage is not an individual matter." Richard said curtly. "It is a matter of state when a nobleman decides to wed. When I marry, I shall be at my King's disposal."

Melville looked at the older man, and pitied him. It was plain that Richard would never marry. He had run to fat, whereas Melville was nothing but lean hunger and fierce power.

Choosing his words carefully, Melville began again.

"It is not that I would not lay down my life for my King. I just don't want to have to lay down my life for my King every night!"

He threw a glance at this girl who the King had chosen for him. She had taken a brief peek at him, and he looked away quickly, furious with himself that she had caught him.

Even with that quick glance, it was difficult not to notice her supple figure, and the rigid way that she held herself allowed his gaze to see all of her. She had scrunched up her nose when she caught him gazing at her, clearly unimpressed but nervous. Even in her shyness, she was beautiful.

"Do you not want success?" asked Richard. "Do you not want land, and fortune, and children?"

"I want to go home," said Melville shortly. He stood up. "Forgive me, my lord, but I am tired and require rest. I will see you on the morrow."

He strode rudely out of the hall, aware of two pairs of eyes following him out – one much clearer and more dazzling than the other.

After Richard had watched him go, he turned to Avis.

"Well?" He said abruptly. "What do you think?"

Avis hesitated. All of her assumptions about Melville – old, haggard, ugly – had been destroyed when the young man walked into her home. Why, he could not be that much older than she. His dark long hair often covered his moody expressions, but she could not help but feel that he was just as uncomfortable with the situation as she was. If he had been Anglo-Saxon, he would probably have been a family friend, someone that she could have trusted and relied on – as it was, he was a Norman. A man that she could never trust.

"You ask me to try and make a very sudden decision," she murmured, unwilling to commit herself to a decision so quickly. Richard nodded.

"Our King does not wait, he acts. And so must you. Who is your choice?"

Panic flooded through her veins: but not a cold panic. A hot panic filled her as she considered the curt, sturdy man that had just left the hall. Melville, her husband? She could ignore the fact that she physically warmed to him – wanted to know just how strong he was. He was her natural enemy, but in a country devoid of friends, that was not unusual. Her isolation forced her to make the only choice that she could.

Avis looked up at Richard boldly, determined to meet her fate in the decisive style of her heritage, afraid of nothing and no man.

"I shall marry my lord Melville when it suits the King."

Richard looked disappointed, but not surprised.

"And so be it. I shall send word to Melville and the King, and you shall be wedded."

He made a movement away from the table, suggesting that he was leaving, but Avis swiftly put a hand on his arm.

"My lord?"

Richard lowered himself back down, startled at the fear and discomposure in her voice. He had never seen her so unsure of herself, not since he had first ridden towards the gates of this place to take residence after the invasion.

"My lord, I wondered…I wondered if we may have a betrothal, in the style…in the style of my people."

Avis' eyes looked up at his, clear and stunning but full of tears. He remembered that for the people who had once lived in this land, it was not merely the wedding but the betrothal that held great power and hope over people's lives. It was a time when the families of each of the couple came to celebrate their joining together, with much feasting and joy. The Normans had spoken about it with both awe and derision. Richard was curious, and he knew that this would be the last step in Avis' Anglo-Saxon path. When she married, she would be leaving that behind and become Norman.

He smiled. "Make your arrangements."

Avis nodded. She was so grateful to Richard for allowing her this last rite of passage that she almost regretted not choosing him to be her husband. But she recalled the constant groping, the sweat that poured off his nose on a summer day, and shuddered. She would never have been able to keep her marriage vows to Richard, and for her a failed marriage was worse than death – even a marriage without love was kept. Melville looked a man that understood the power of an oath. He would be a more apt partner for her.

Richard continued speaking.

"Let this mark your entry into our society. Let no expense be spared, and arrange it for three nights hence. A week today you shall be married."

CHAPTER FOUR

A flurry of busyness and organisation overtook the manor house as preparations were made for the wedding between Melville and Avis. Avis managed to avoid seeing her future husband by spending the majority of her time in the kitchen, supposedly watching others prepare food but also helping by baking and roasting along with the servants. She threw herself into the work, hoping to forget that it was all for her wedding. Robes were ordered, candles delivered, foods that Avis had never seen brought from far and wide. As she decorated the Great Hall, she remembered the betrothal of her friends and family, back before the Normans had conquered in 1066. They had been such glorious affairs, full of laughing and merriment. The old days, those days that Avis ached and longed for every waking moment. The characters that filled these happy thoughts were no longer around her, and she was desperate for them.

These recollections of her old Anglo-Saxon life made her all the more determined to avoid Melville. The only time that the two had to face each other was at meal times, but Richard carefully placed himself between them. He knew that for Anglo-Saxon nobility, prolonged dialogue between a couple intended for wedlock was not only frowned upon, but actively discouraged. He did not want to put Avis in the difficult position of having to ignore Melville's conversation – though, he thought drily, she may even enjoy the chance to insult him.

Melville was not enjoying himself either. Stuck in the middle of nowhere with nothing to do, he had taken to riding all day with a select group of friends. They did not stop teasing him about his marriage, but he was more inclined to allow them their mockery than to seriously consider the consequences of his actions. While he was riding, seeing the rolling downs of southern England burst slowly into reds and scarlet, it was as if nothing else existed. This part of the country held nothing of beauty for him: the land that William had given him here in England reminded him of his Normandy home, and Melville was surprised how much he missed his English manor. He knew that once he consummated his marriage with Avis, he was as tied to this country England as he would be with a chain. His greatest wish was to return to his homeland, back to Normandy, back to where he belonged. And he would take no wife with him, and allow no wife to prevent him from seeing his birthplace.

Before either of them realised, the day of their betrothal came. Haughty Melville sat at the head of the table for the first time during his visit, and looked out over the Great Hall. He had not really noticed the individual changes that had been made over the last few days, but was in awe of how warm and inviting it had been made. He was the guest of honour tonight, and was afforded every consideration, with spices and salts surrounding his plate, and each dish offered to him before all others. Musicians were carefully placed at regular intervals behind the revellers, and exotic incense was burning along the tables giving an air of mystery and suspense. He could smell rosemary, and expensive frankincense. Melville inhaled slowly, drinking in the atmosphere: but his breath caught in his throat as he remembered that this was to celebrate his betrothal to a woman that he had barely spoken to. Despite his irritation at the whole farce his appetite was not diminished, which meant that when Avis entered the Great Hall he had his mouth full of salted chicken and a handful of bread mopping his lips. The room fell silent, and Melville looked up.

Avis was standing there, in a cream gown that floated over her subtle curves. Long sleeves hid her hands, and her hair was loose. Gentle streams of blonde curls showered her back and her shoulders. The men and servants closest to her stepped back in awe. Melville realised that he was dripping chicken back onto his plate, and quickly snapped his mouth shut. He had not expected this. This woman was not the child he had seen on the night of his arrival. This was a lady: of noble or even royal birth. She exuded power and elegance, and Melville was intoxicated.

Richard walked forward to meet her with a smile on his face that made it clear to Avis that he had completely ignored the carefully chosen dress she was wearing and was seeing her naked. Avis begrudgingly gave him her arm as the highest ranking lord in the room. He walked her slowly towards the table at which Melville was eating. Melville stood up so quickly that he knocked his plate to the floor, drawing muffled guffaws from the men. Ignoring them, eyes transfixed on Avis, he walked around the table towards her, unable to remove his eyes from her, though she would not look at him. The three met in the centre of the room, and according to the Anglo-Saxon custom that Avis had explained to them all the day before, all of the others in the room formed a ring around them.

"I, Richard, offer this woman for marriage to my lord Melville." Richard began in what he considered to be his booming voice, which always sounded weak and timid to Avis' ears.

She sighed. It was not as she remembered her cousin's betrothal; but then, how could the Normans understand?

Their idea of a wedding and a marriage was one of convenience, and the bringing together of wealth and property. Love did not enter into their minds. For her family, marriage had always been a matter of the heart. She was the first in her line to agree to wed a man she had no compassion for, and she felt the dishonour strongly.

"…agree to give your consent to this man?" Richard finished, and turned to look at her. Avis had been so lost in her thoughts that she had not realised that he had finished his first portion of the ceremony. She met his eyes, and saw the hardness there, and the lust. Her soul recoiled at the thought of him becoming so important to her. She would do anything, anything to rid herself of this man who had taken everyone from her. Even if it meant marrying this stranger Melville.

"I agree to give my consent to this man." Avis spoke clearly, but with no emotion. Richard now began to recite the male counterpart of the betrothal ritual, a ritual that Melville could not understand – and did not particularly want to. This old fashioned nonsense! It belonged to the Anglo-Saxon past: something that was dead and gone. No wonder William, his King, was discouraging the whole culture. It was enough to drive a man insane.

"…and protect her honour and her name?" Richard looked to Melville. He looked at his future bride, who was slightly perspiring under the gaze of so many people. Her full red lips were slightly open in expectation, and her clear eyes glanced up at him, waiting for his reply. Melville's lip curled. This Saxon girl had no honour. She had no family name of repute. She had a Norman name anyway – chosen to convince this Richard to take her in as his mistress, no doubt. He shook his head, and looked down at the floor. He heard an intake of breath from around the Great Hall, and saw that Avis had almost stepped towards him, hand raised to strike him.

Richard moved violently towards him, shielding him from Avis' menace.

"Goddammit man!" he uttered through clenched teeth. "You dishonour me by refusing her now, here, in this manner!"

All in the hall murmured, astonished at Melville's response. Several heads were shaking, and he could hear tutting and clicking of tongues.

"I have not spoken." Melville's voice rose clear over the hubbub of sound, which died away instantly. He fixed his eyes on the person in front of him: his bride.

"I swear to take, marry, and protect this woman. To keep her as my bride, and tend to her as my wife." He spoke clearly and loudly, and although the words that he had spoken were not the usual response, all could hear the power and determination in each word.

Melville stared at Avis with penetrating eyes, and Avis knew that he was speaking directly to her and to her only. She tried to look away, but could not. Those dark eyes swallowed her clear ones as a peat bog refuses to release its victims. She could hear that Richard was speaking, but it was a long way off.

Melville broke the moment between them when Richard congratulated him, and he looked away from her. When he turned back to look at and speak to Avis, she had gone. He swung around, looking at the crowds in the busy Great Hall to find her, but he could not see her.

"Custom." Richard said matter of factly, slapping him on the back. "The woman doesn't speak to her betrothed until after they are married. Anglo-Saxons. It's their funny odd way of doing things."

Melville felt disappointed, and then surprised. He did not want her – so why was he saddened that he would not have the chance to speak to her? The look that they had shared had gone beyond two strangers; had linked them in some way that he could not understand. He shivered. Melville did not like to be out of control, but Avis pushed him out of his self-control, preventing him from knowing exactly where he was.

"Come – sit, eat." Richard seemed completely unaware of the inner turmoil that Melville was experiencing, and sat to begin tearing into his plate of food. "Plenty of time to tumble that slither of a thing."

Before he knew what he was doing, Melville had drawn his silver dagger and pointed it at his host's throat.

"Mind your words, sir! That is my intended wife of whom you speak, and you dishonour her!"

Men turned in astonishment, and Richard grew red. All knew that he should have held his tongue, but the bitterness of losing the prize of Avis to this young thing had bitten him too deep.

"I apologise, my lord." He muttered. "I spoke carelessly."

The blinding rage that had swept through Melville died instantly, and he felt just as embarrassed as Richard.

"Speak not of it." He held out a hand. "I was rash."

The two Norman men shook hands resentfully, and feasted long into the night – but Melville could not shake the feeling that Avis had affected him in some way that he would not be able to escape.

CHAPTER FIVE

The day that Avis was to lose her Anglo-Saxon identity and became Norman dawned early, and she stared at the sky from her bedroom. Winter was approaching: a new season. A season of coldness. This would be the last day she awoke in this room, the last day she would eat in her home, the last day she would retain that identity which she had learnt to suppress. She stroked the familiar wall. Avis knew how every nick and groove that had been made, and smiled as her fingers brushed a small carving that she had once made herself – a small cross with the initials ANS. She had grown up in this room, and had thought at one point that she would one day die in this room. The invasion of English shores by the Normans had been long expected but badly prepared for, and when the Normans entered her village…

Avis shook her head, and her hair gracefully followed the movement. She could not dwell in the past. She decided against sorrowful memories. This was to be her wedding day, and even if it was a wedding she had not chosen, to a man she knew she would despise, it was still a triumphant day. For the Anglo-Saxons, the day a girl married was the day that she became a woman. She would now make decisions for households, and bear heirs, and have a significant amount of power in the local area. Avis did not know what marriage meant for these Norman men, but she could not imagine it was as important and as celebrated as it was for her. Men did not understand marriage.

As she dressed, a thought struck her: a painful one, one that seared through her. Children. She had always wanted children but now she was entering into what the Normans were laughingly calling a 'mixed marriage' it altered everything. Avis looked around the room that had sheltered and nursed her as a child, and knew that she could not have a child with Melville. She refused to bring children into a world that lived in a divided household, to dwell in a nation where hatred was the currency and spite was the language. Avis also shuddered at the thought of baring herself in the most vulnerable way to that man. No – she would not consummate the marriage, she thought wildly. He cannot force me. Surely taking me in marriage is enough for him.

As Avis made this decision, she wandered to the window to brush her hair before taming it behind her veil. Displaying it at her betrothal four nights ago had been reckless, and she regretted it. Never again will she so wantonly reveal herself, that inner part of herself.

Melville walked across the courtyard below whistling, and she watched him. It was but small recompense that her future husband was nothing like Richard. Energetic and enthusiastic about the outdoors, she had noticed his penchant for riding and admired it. Her horse had been taken away from her when the Normans had invaded, as had all of her worldly goods, and she missed the freedom that it brought. Gazing down, she absentmindedly brushed and untangled her hair, humming a folk song that her mother had sung to her.

As he walked, Melville could feel someone watching him, but was convinced that he had risen early enough to get a quiet ride to himself. He could not shake the feeling of being watched and halfway across the courtyard towards the stables, stopped. He turned slowly, but could see no one behind him. Then he looked up, and saw Avis.

By God, she was beautiful. She stood there at the open window, allowing the sun's meagre rays to illuminate her. He could feel her beauty affecting even him, a man who had decided that he would not desire this woman, and felt traitorous to his finer feelings. To have such a wife, to hold her, to know that none other had touched her in the way that he had – but no. She would be his wife in contract only, not in act.

Avis had seen him. She looked down at him with no shame, or affectation of pretending that she had not noticed him. They gazed at each other, and the power of their mutual look stunned Avis. She had never expected to find a man who was so willing to match her, and yet this man obviously felt no shame in gazing up at her. Just as their look at the betrothal had taken her breath away, almost causing her to faint when she thought that he was going to reject her, so again his eyes snared her in a trap which she almost enjoyed. An emotion tugged at her heart that she did not recognise. The power of this feeling stunned her, and she withdrew, unsure why her heart was beating so powerfully.

He was the enemy, she reminded herself. He was one of that army who came and destroyed everything you knew, everything you cared for. He will destroy you. If he doesn't marry you first.

CHAPTER SIX

A flurry of excitement filled and seeped into the manor. Today was the day that Avis and Melville were to be married. Excited preparations by the servants had culminated in an elegantly decorated Great Hall, covered in flowing silks and rose petals, with trestle tables buckling under platters and platters of lovingly prepared meats and glazed vegetables. Different sauces and stuffings were dotted about, and there was an abundance of fruit cascading down from red glazed vases. A variety of wines and ales were ready in caskets at one side of the hall, and goblets enough for all were stacked beside them. A man was tuning a gittern, a stringed instrument that was incredibly intricate and needed a highly skilled player. The musician had been brought in from the nearest town to play at the wedding. Three jugglers rehearsed near the top table, throwing small balls over the chairs in which Melville and Avis would be seated at the feast that evening. All was prepared. Richard nodded appreciatively as he crossed the hall. His servants had surpassed themselves. Everything was ready, and everyone was in their place. All except one.

Melville was missing. The man who tended his horse had readied it extremely early in the morning as was his custom, but neither horse nor rider had been seen since. Richard was trying not to panic, but he knew that the King would not look well on him losing the groom. The servants had been doing their best to keep the fact that Melville had not been seen for hours from Avis all morning, who was wandering around the place in her bridal gown, unsure as to why her morning wedding had been postponed to the afternoon. After searching for her along the many corridors and chambers in the manor, Richard eventually caught up with her in a passageway.

"Flaunting your wares this early in the morn?" He remarked snidely, grinning at the smooth skin on her shoulder that was just about made visible by the speed at which Avis was moving.

She could smell his stale sweat, and she leant away from him – difficult in the confines of the corridor, but necessary if she was not going to gag.

"Good morrow my lord," she said stiffly. "And when will these bridal trappings be put to use?"

"When we can find your husband, I suppose." Richard spoke viciously, and was pleased to see Avis' countenance drop.

"Find my husband?" Avis looked confused. "What on earth do you mean?"

"Just what I say." Richard relished in her discontent. "Melville is missing."

Avis clenched her fists. It was bad enough that she was being made to marry this man, but did he need to continually insult her? No wonder the wedding ceremony had been postponed this morning. She had been waiting all day for an event that may never happen.

Richard smiled at her, enjoying her discomfort.

"Who knows," he said carelessly. "He may not return. He may not have liked what he saw."

A pale hand moved faster than he could, and a resounding slap filled the corridor. Richard's cheek smarted and began to colour red. He stared, shocked, at

Avis. She was breathing deeply, trying to regain control of herself, but could not.

"Filthy man!" She spoke calmly but with real hatred in her tones. "You have attempted to make my life a misery since you arrived here, but you do not own me. This Melville may be a swine of a Norman, but if marriage to him means escape from you then so be it!"

Turning wildly she strode away from him, but Richard followed her, calling out.

"Avis! Avis, how dare you!"

But Avis didn't care. Years of anger and resentfulness had finally burst upon the unsuspecting Richard, and Avis did not care how violently he was offended.

She shouted behind her shoulder. "Where is he?"

"Melville?"

"Of course Melville!" She snapped. "You are a very stupid man Richard."

The very stupid man was panting, trying to keep up with the fuming girl.

"He went riding." He gasped, sweat dripping from his brow. "Towards the north."

Reaching the end of the corridor, she threw open wide the wooden door with both hands, and turned the corner into the stable yard.

"Horse!" Avis shouted.

Stable boys and groomsmen stood up hurriedly from their game, counters scattering across the cobbles, and began yelling further orders. In but a short moment, a horse had been prepared for Avis, but her impatience overflowed. Ignoring the helpful arm of the man beside her who was attempting to help her mount the horse, she kicked back her heels and vaulted onto the box beside the horse. In an elegant leap, she mounted the huge beast.

Accompanied with cries of, "my lady!" she forced the horse into a gallop. As Richard watched her expertly turn her steed northwards, he thought about the unsuspecting groom.

"God help him," he muttered as he turned back inside, away from the stares of his servants. "God save him from her wrath."

CHAPTER SEVEN

The cooling ride and time alone gave Avis the ability to collect her thoughts. She felt slightly embarrassed about the way she had behaved. She had always sworn to herself that she would never let her temper control her, but the last three years had been a torturous lesson in keeping one's comments and thoughts to oneself. Without a friend or confidant, it had been a relief to finally strike back at the man who had continually insulted her since he had taken her house from her. But as she slowed the horse that was breathing heavily after the intense exercise, she reflected on what lay before her. Gazing around the land that she had known from birth, she saw piles of dead leaves lining the road. Autumn was here. It marked the end of a glorious summer, and an unknown winter was approaching.

Avis looked around her, but could not see another rider, or any evidence that a horse had passed by here. Where could he be? Closing her eyes, she pictured the local landscape and tried to guess where he could have gone. The woodland was too far away, along a treacherous road. She had already passed the small village, and it would have been obvious if a horse had been there – there were few buildings tall enough to hide a horse. The houses here were partially dug into the ground, giving them a huge amount of space, but not challenging the natural landscape. A horse would be high above the roofs of the village, but she could not see one. Snapping her eyes open, she glanced to her left, where the river was. That was the perfect place to relax. She would try there first.

The horse snuffled, enjoying the experience of being ridden by a gentle but firm hand. Avis dismounted, slightly sore from the reckless journey that she had undertaken. She slipped her shoes off, and smiled at the glorious feel of the grass underneath her toes. Meandering slowly down towards the river, as she turned a corner another horse became visible. A horse carrying a livery that she recognised.

Lying on the bank was Melville. His eyes were closed, and he was humming quietly to himself. It was not a tune she recognised. The horse was untethered, but was happily grazing around his master. As Avis came closer, the horse looked up, startled. His gentle whinny alerted his owner, who languidly spoke.

"Yes?"

His voice sounded bored, and he didn't bother to open his eyes. Avis did not trust herself to speak until she was much closer – she did not want to begin the conversation shouting. Although it was not the custom of her people for two betrothed people to talk before the wedding, she had had enough. Something had to be said.

When she had reached Melville, she sank down beside him without a word. Melville spoke again.

"What is it?" he asked testily, eyes squeezed shut.

He thinks that I am a servant, Avis thought. Come to summon him. Her rage grew again, and before she realised what she was doing, she had aggressively pushed him over and started pummelling his chest with her fists.

"Where have you been?" she shouted. "Why have you not returned?"

Melville opened his eyes in shock under the onslaught from this unseen woman. He had been pushed away from his assailant, so he could not identify her, but her punches were not tender and her shouts were unabated.

"Have you no honour? Keep you not your promises?"

Melville forced himself up and tried to pin the thrashing arms to the sides of the strange woman. He could feel the tension in her delicate limbs. She continued to scream at him, and he shouted over her desperate voice.

"What do you want, woman? I have no quarrel with you – "

And then he saw her face. Her cheeks were covered with a deep blush and her eyes flashed with anger, but it was definitely her. It was Avis.

Melville stopped protecting himself. Before Avis could realise his weakness, he stood up and took a few paces back, thrown by the fact that it was not a random peasant but his betrothed. Avis did not follow him, but raised herself up also, panting slightly but holding herself up high.

The two of them gazed upon each other. The river slowly continued behind Melville, lending its sweet tune to the atmosphere. Melville could not believe that once again, the calm and meek girl that he had seen on his first night in this horrible land had given way to such a passionate woman. Despite himself, and despite the bruising that he could already feel under his linen shirt, he was impressed.

"My lady," he managed, in a voice that he wished was a bit stronger.

"I am not your lady!" Avis countered violently, tossing her head to shake her hair behind her. She scrunched her nose at him, and scowled. "Perhaps if you had bothered to attend our wedding I may have allowed you to address me in that manner."

She drew a lock of hair back into the confines of her veil, which she had managed to keep on during the scuffle.

Melville swore under his breath, and stared upwards into the sky, looking for the positioning of the sun. He had not realised how late it was in the day. His wish to be free of this constraining marriage had led him to take what he considered to be his last free ride, but the enjoyment of the open space and the restfulness of the river had clearly kept him away for hours. The chaos that he had probably left behind was unimaginable.

He shuffled from foot to foot, unsure as to how to placate this livid lady standing in front of him.

"My lady…" He began again, awkwardly, but Avis would not allow him to speak.

"No," she said, the heat in her voice lessening. "Listen to me, my lord. Either this marriage takes place today, or it does not take place at all. No," Avis' interjection prevented him from speaking again, and he bit his tongue furiously. "You made me a promise. A promise amongst witnesses. If you are truly a man of honour, you would keep to that oath."

Avis looked strong, but she had never felt so weak. For the Anglo-Saxons, an oath was something that bound two people together forever. It was stronger than birth-brothers, and lasted beyond death. For this, this *Norman* to make an oath to her and then break it…it was unthinkable. It did not happen. It would not happen.

Melville looked at her determined face, still flushed, and then looked down at her hands. Although they were clenched into small fists, they were shaking. It must have taken her much effort to come here. And probably the loss of much pride, he thought to himself.

Avis turned away from him, and Melville took his chance to speak.

"My lady, I swear, if I had realised the hour – "

She pivoted to face him once again. He broke off, hoping for reconciliation – as much as he hated her, he would rather enter into an apathetic marriage than an acrimonious one. He could hear the song of a bird in the tree behind her. She began to walk towards him, and Melville took a step backwards. As much as he would like to mend the disagreement, such intimate physical contact was not something he had expected or wanted. But then Avis began to run, and raised those fists, and Melville suddenly realised too late what her intentions were.

Avis reached Melville at speed and pushed him backwards, straight into the river. The loud splash resounded around them, and caused the two horses to revolve around, looking for the source of the noise. Melville sat on the shallow riverbed, weeds rushing around him and mud seeping into his clothes. He was soaking wet, and Avis looked disdainfully down at him from the bank.

"When you return," she said haughtily, "you may want to change."

She strode away with her horse, and within moments was out of sight.

For several minutes, Melville remained sitting in the river. The cold began to sink into his bones, but he did not move. He was stunned. Such a thing a woman had never done – not in his knowledge. Ladies simply did not act in this way. A cynical smile broke across his face, and he hauled himself, dripping, onto the grass. Maybe the majority of women did not ride miles alone, physically attack and then push into rivers their betrothed, but Avis certainly did. Melville chuckled as he gathered his belongings and placed them into the packs attached to his horse. This woman was clearly not what he had assumed her to be. But then his face darkened, and the smile disappeared. Despite this new revelation of her character, he still did not want to marry her. Raising himself onto his horse, he sighed. Not that he had much of a choice.

Avis dismounted as a servant came running towards her.

"My lady," he panted. "My lord Richard requires your presence in the hall."

Avis groaned. Must he intrude on every part of her life? Was she to have no time to herself?

"Tell my lord I shall join him shortly." She tried to speak graciously.

The servant looked uncomfortable.

"Now, my lady. My lord was quite insistent."

Avis took a deep breath, and looked heavenwards. Living here, in her home ran by another, was akin to being a prisoner in a palace. Beautiful, but terribly dark at the same time.

Casting a brittle smile at the servant, she said, "I follow you."

The two of them walked into the Great Hall just as Richard was chuckling with one of his retainers.

"And here she is!" he turned to her and beckoned her to come towards him. The servant melted away from Avis' side, and she wished he had stayed. She would have liked all the company that was not Richard that she could get.

"So," Richard beamed at her, wickedly. "Did you find your husband to be?"

"Indeed I did, my lord." Avis answered quietly. The knight retainer guffawed, but froze when Avis' venomous eyes turned to him. Making an excuse, he left, leaving Richard and Avis alone.

Avis also made to depart, but Richard grabbed her arm with one of his fat fists.

"Could not persuade him to return, eh?" He breathed. "I suppose it's just you and me then."

Avis tried to prise off the unwanted hand, but he was too strong.

"I have waited for you," Richard moved closer, and Avis stumbled away from him, unable to catch her balance because he had such a tight grip on her. "And now you are mine."

"Never." Avis exhaled.

"Now."

Richard lunged towards her, but as he moved there was a noise behind her and he halted.

"Melville is on his way!" A herald shouted.

Richard released Avis, and she spun around to see the man who had just spoken. He looked hot and flustered. "Melville's coming! We must all to church!"

Richard muttered oaths under his breath. Deep down, he admitted to himself that he had been hoping that Melville had decided against taking this delicate creature for his bride – leaving her for himself. Turning to Avis, he plastered a false smile across his filthy beard.

"Ready?"

As the wedding procession left the manor house, Avis glared at Melville. How could he embarrass her – again! The silence and hesitation at the betrothal feast had been terrible enough, and she knew that she would never forget the laughter and taunts for the rest of her life. But to be late for his own wedding? So late in fact that the entire celebration had to be altered, occurring in the afternoon instead of the morning. So late that the bride herself had ridden out to demand that he return? Avis had never heard of such a thing happening, and she was ashamed to her very soul.

Avis turned her eyes furiously towards Melville, walking alongside her, but he seemed totally unaware of the malice that he was stirring up inside his future wife. He was sweating, but none could tell through the damp patches still covering his shirt. He had been unable to change into clean clothes after his long and difficult ride, and Richard had sworn at him when he arrived, not giving him any time to organise himself.

Melville was decidedly uncomfortable. He knew that he smelt very slightly of river. He felt dirty and disgusting, and surrounded by so many elegant people dressed in their finest, he felt incredibly out of place. Looking across to Avis, he almost jumped back at the vehemence in her eyes. He was not surprised though – if she had arrived at their wedding in a similar state, he would have refused to marry her. His brow deepened as he frowned. It was her own fault – if she didn't want her husband to smell of dank water, she should not have pushed him.

Richard had warned him again that Avis would be unwilling to speak to him. Melville was not sure whether Richard knew of the events down at the river, but he prayed that he did not. There was only so much humiliation that could be experienced in one day, and Melville felt that he had achieved his quota for today.

Melville turned away from Avis and looked ahead, at the small wooden church at which they would be wed. As they arrived, the local villagers cheered and threw down blackberries on their shoots and old-mans-beard across their path. They were the only living things of beauty that were still in bloom at this time of year, and so it was the best that they could offer. Avis was grateful to them. They had known her as a babe; had watched her grow, and learn, and struggle to accept her place in this world in which women so rarely had a voice. They had remained loyal to her when the Normans had arrived ready for battle and thirsty for blood, and they had paid the price for that loyalty – some of them with their lives.

Glancing sideways at Melville once again, she wanted to point out to him the people that she knew, and ask him where their husbands were, where he thought their sons had gone, why there were so few young women living in this village, and why each pair of eyes that rested on him were filled with fear. But there was no time for that.

Richard came up behind her and grabbed her arm suddenly, causing Avis to jump.

"It is time to say goodbye to your past." Richard could not have looked more delighted. "You are a Norman now."

Snatching her arm away, Avis and Melville walked towards the church, towards their fate.

CHAPTER EIGHT

The priest of the village met them at the door of the church. Avis saw that his usually sunny smile was overcast with concern. Perhaps he had been warned that Avis had not exactly been willing in this arrangement. Perhaps he had been threatened if he did not perform the marriage. Avis' heart ached; another person who may suffer because of her, because of what the Normans had made her become. She tried to reassure the trembling man with a smile, but he did not return it.

Avis and Melville stood before the priest with everyone else behind them. Avis caught the women of the village humming softly under their breath, in the traditional way of their ancestors. Unbidden tears began to rise in her large eyes.

"I bring notice to all," began the priest in a quiet, yet determined voice, "of these two people here before me. They have declared their intent to wed before you all in their betrothal, which none can destroy in all honour. They have understood the decision that they made to come to this door. They are, before us all, to become one."

A man behind Richard snickered, and Melville turned to glare at the unfortunate man, who cowered under the incensed gaze wrought upon him. He soberly looked at the ground, ears a boiling red. Melville shifted his feet to once again face the priest.

Goodness, how did it come to this. Right now, right at this moment, he was getting married. And not to some woman that he had chosen, that he thought may bring him delight and comfort in his youth, and joy and relaxation in his old age. No, to some ridiculous Anglo-Saxon girl, who had hardly the look of comfort about her. For all her looks of meekness, she evidently had a wild temper – a temper that he would have to quash at the first opportunity.

But as if she had heard his thoughts, Avis turned up to look at him, as the priest droned on about the joys of marriage. Her eyes…they were full of something that looked like fear, but was not quite that cowardly emotion. Melville almost took a step away from her when he realised what it was. Hatred.

But the priest had finished his introduction now, and Melville had to pay attention.

"Who supports this marriage?" The priest called into the crowd gathered behind the couple, a worried expression on his pale face. "Who supports them in their marriage?"

There was not a sound. Avis was convinced that she really would cry now. At all the weddings she had been to, this had been the moment when a huge cry and cheer had resounded from the couples' friends and family. But at her wedding – not a whisper. None of the villagers could bear to agree to this charade. So why could she?

"Humph," Richard coughed, awkwardly. He was not sure what was meant to happen at this point in the wedding proceedings, but he was certain that what had just happened, was not it. "I do. I mean, I support them."

The priest looked at him gratefully, but was forced back into a look of fear at the anger emanating from Richard's face.

"Good," he managed. "That's good."

The man of God was sweating now, despite the chilly breeze that tangled around the branches of the trees around the church. Avis pitied him. It was not his fault that he was under pressure to wed a woman that he had baptised as an infant in this very church – to wed her to a brute, a man that they all despised.

"My lord priest," she said to him deferentially, as was the custom. "You do me a great honour to wed me today. Please, do not hesitate."

Melville's eyes widened. All that he had seen from this woman indicated that she was a great noblewoman, of high birth. But here she was, touching the sleeve of a plebeian priest?

But the priest smiled. His hand covered hers, and he murmured something that only Avis could hear.

"Bless you, my child," he whispered. "And may God forgive me for what I do."

Avis nodded, but before their hands separated, Richard marched forward and pulled Avis away from the old man.

"Do nothing," Richard hissed, furiously, "but marry this hussy," flinging her towards Melville, "to this man."

The priest wavered, and was about to speak to Richard but Avis stopped him.

"Please." And now the tears were visible. "Please, my lord. For my sake. Do not anger my lord Richard. For it will do none of us any good."

The priest looked around at the frightened villagers standing around the church. At the way that the old women clung to each other. At how mothers pulled in their young children closer. And he realised why Avis was paying such a high price.

He swallowed, and continued.

"God brought Eve to Adam, and He knew that it was good. So too do we, in God's stead, bring forward the lady Avis to this man Melville. We know that this is good."

The last sentence brought a choke to his voice, but only those that knew him well would have noticed it, and none spoke of it. Within moments, the wedding would be complete.

"Therefore," resumed the priest, "I consider these two people to be married and one in my eyes, and in the eyes of God. I call you all to recognise them as such. Melville and Avis."

This time the villagers did speak up in their traditional manner, unable to help themselves.

"Melville and Avis."

The three words echoed around the crowd like a summer's breeze. But it was a sad echo, and an echo that died quickly.

"Do you have a token?" The priest muttered to Melville.

Melville looked blankly at the holy man. Token? What on earth did he mean?

Avis sighed, and pulled a delicate gold ring out of the pouch attached to her belt.

"Will this suffice, my lord?"

The priest nodded. "Very well, my child."

"What mean you with this token?" Melville asked roughly.

The priest blushed in fright, but said nothing. Avis tutted irritably.

"At a wedding, the groom presents his bride with a token," she explained hurriedly under her breath. "It is a sign of their marriage, and of his provision." She shot a scornful look up at him. "Although now I have supplied it, I am not sure what this wedding will suggest about our marriage."

"I did not know!" Melville exclaimed quietly, with resentment in his voice.

"You should have asked!"

"And so," the priest interrupted, panic now approaching his worried face as he tried to bring the supposedly happy couple to order. "I offer you, my lady

Avis, this ring, on behalf of your husband, my lord Melville, as a sign and reminder of this day."

Avis accepted the ring back, rather ungraciously, and slowly slid it onto her left hand. It shone there, a repugnant reminder of this ridiculous charade.

With the look of a man who has just seen the light of the dawn after a very long night, the priest spoke for the last time.

"Melville and Avis."

"Melville and Avis," came the answering reply of the crowd, and this time even some of the Normans joined in.

Richard remained silent. He was not going to condone one moment of this shambles of a wedding. But, what was done was done.

Taking Avis by the shoulder, Richard somewhat roughly turned her around to face him, and the other people who had witnessed their wedding.

"And now you are wed!" He said.

"Yes," Avis replied dully. "Now I am wed. And now I am going home."

Sweeping her skirts around her, she started to push her way through the throng of people, but once again a hand on her shoulder stopped her. But this was different. This was not the lecherous hand of Richard. This was someone different.

"If you don't mind," said a strong voice, "I think we'll go together."

Melville took her brusquely by the arm, and began to march her towards the manor.

CHAPTER NINE

The musicians were incredibly loud and the fire too hot as the merriment of the wedding celebration in the Great Hall continued late into the night. Avis could feel her tight bodice pressing into each of her ribs, and the lace at the back of her spine pressing deep into her flesh. The jewels that adorned her neck flashed in the candle light, reflecting around the room and drawing the gaze of many revellers to her eyes, which perfectly matched the diamonds gently resting on her décolletage. Her eyes stung from the smoke issuing from the huge fire, and all she wanted to do was rest, but still she could not get away. She was a wife now, and it was her obligation to remain at table as long as her husband chose.

But then, Melville did not look as if he was enjoying himself either. She studied her husband who sat on her left hand side; a man that she was now legally tied to for the rest of her life. His left arm rested heavily on the wooden trestle table, toying with a pheasant bone, his other hand tangled in his own dark hair. Melville looked worried, and his eyes were focussed across the hall. Avis looked, but could see nothing that could have attracted his interest to such a degree. He did not seem to be present in the room, and Avis was offended. Could he not at least try and concentrate at their wedding feast?

"My lord?" she ventured to speak, hoping to force his attentions on her. Despite their argument at the river's side, she could not help but notice that he was the tallest, most attractive man in the Great Hall. As his wife, she could not help but wish he could be focussed on her.

He grunted at her, not looking away from whatever was fascinating him at the opposite end of the hall.

"My lord, are you quite well?"

"What?" Melville eventually turned to her with a face of contempt. She blushed, and felt the temper that she had inherited from her mother rising up within her. She had never seen her parents argue which she was thankful for, but she knew that her mother's temper had been a fierce one to behold once it was unleashed on an unsuspecting victim. It had always been her greatest difficulty, keeping her own temper under control, and as a child she had often been punished for not being able to contain it – but then she was sorely tried by this brute of a Norman!

Avis took a deep breath, and spoke again.

"I was merely enquiring, my lord, if you were well. You do not seem to be enjoying the festivities."

Melville's eyes flickered from her face, giving her entire body his full attention for the first time. Avis' feeling of discomfort increased. He's judging me, she thought. He's examining me to see whether the wares that he has purchased are of the highest quality that he is used to! Well, it's too late for that now. If he didn't like the look of me, he should have mentioned it before the priest declared them man and wife.

"Thank you." It clearly pained Melville to make such a concession to her. "Thank you for your kindness. But you are astute. I am indeed unused to such merriment and jollity. I think it is time that we retired."

With these few abrupt words, Melville rose and pulled her right arm with a strength and force that surprised her.

She stood up hastily, unable to control her balance due to the swift movement, and had to lean on him completely. He did not buckle under her weight, but supported her easily, forcing her to walk. Unnoticed by many of the dancers and cavorters in the hall who were too busy enjoying themselves to notice the silent couple, Melville half pulled, half dragged Avis towards a passageway that would lead to her – their bedroom.

Panic arose in Avis. In all of the chaos of the day, she had forgotten to think about her wedding night. She knew that the most intimate acts that could happen between a man and a woman occurred after the marriage ceremony, and she knew the basic details of what it would entail, but she had never given much thought to the act itself. Making love, in her mind, could only work between two people that were actually in love. Avis did not love this man! Could Melville, this husband of hers, demand such attentions so early on in their marriage? But I am his now, she reminded herself, desperately trying to keep up with his large stride. I am his property. He can do what he wants with me.

As they reached the door of her chamber, her only thought was confusion – how did he know where she slept at night? Little did she know that he had paced outside her room the last few nights, driving himself mad.

He thrust the heavy door open with one arm, and pushed her onto the bed before slamming the door shut and bolting it. Towering over Avis, he gave a threatening aura of desperation and anger. She could not help but let out a whimper of protest and fear.

"What?" Melville seemed distracted, and indeed he was. He could not help dwelling throughout the wedding ceremony and feast on his intense dislike of this woman before him – this woman who would by her blood and by her ring tie him to this land. He felt that she was purposefully trapping him. But the idea that he would hurt her, force her in any way, was repellent to him, and he could not ignore her heady scent of rosemary which had been taunting him throughout the feast.

"Be calm." Melville had little experience with women, but knew enough that his domineering height and masculine presence was probably not helping. Kneeling at the foot of the bed, he attempted to quiet her worries. "I am not going to hurt you."

Avis pulled herself up in the bed to face him.

"You had better not," she said angrily, adding a, "my lord," at the end to appease him and to give the impression of feminine submission and obedience.

A brief smile flashed across Melville's dark features, and he almost chuckled.

"I give you my word."

Throwing off his embellished jacket and belt, he dropped into a chair by the window – her chair – and looking out of it rather than at his bride, continued speaking. It was clear that he had no appreciation for her home as she did.

"I feel that it is only fair and reasonable to explain to you, my lady, the circumstances of this marriage."

The circumstances of this marriage? Avis remained silent, unsure what this unpredictable man would say next.

"I am a Norman." Melville began. Avis scoffed silently. By aligning himself with the people that she hated, he sealed his own fate. I will never trust you, she vowed to herself.

"As a Norman, I owe my life and allegiance to my King, William." The monotone of his voice belied his boredom, but it was a soft voice and Avis against her will began to be reassured by it. He was certainly capable of great violence, but she believed that he would not hurt her – at least not purposefully.

Melville continued speaking.

"My King has requested – nay, required – his followers to support him in his efforts to colonise this country – "

"My country." Avis could not help the interjection.

"The new Norman country."

"That you took from us."

"That has been taken." Melville reluctantly withdrew his gaze from the window to scowl at her. "And the way that William will perfectly and completely conquer this land is by marriage. Norman and Anglo-Saxon marriage. Such as our marriage."

"And so, I am a prize?" Avis spoke, less in anger than in wonderment.

"No." Melville stared at her, expressionlessly. "You are a punishment."

Avis' jaw dropped. How could he offend her so openly?

"I did not want to marry you." Melville spoke darkly. "If I could have chosen, I would not have married you at all. But now we are married, and so my obedience to the King cannot be besmirched."

There was a silence. Avis could not take all of this in, and Melville was tense, waiting for the tirade of her anger to attack him.

Avis began to laugh.

Melville's scowl turned to puzzlement.

"You mock me, my lady?"

Avis smothered her mirthless laugh. "No. I laugh merely because I too am unwilling in this ridiculous charade. I too am married against my will. I was given the choice of yourself or my lord Richard."

Melville was horrified.

"Your actions at the riverbed would have suggested otherwise, my lady!" He said accusingly.

"I have honour," Avis declared haughtily. "Once I have made my promise, there is nothing that can prevent me from breaking it. From the moment of our betrothal, I was to become your wife."

Melville's head was reeling. To think that both of them had been individually despairing at this marriage! That neither were willing, that both had separately and unknowingly desired freedom!

"Do you mean to say that if both of us had made our causes known, we could have worked together to prevent this?"

Avis shook her head, sadly. "I know not the King personally, but from what I have heard of him and his character, I do not believe he would have allowed two people's personal preferences to interfere with his goal." Her voice spoke of bitterness and hardship, but Melville ignored it. Whatever sob story this Saxon girl had, he would not be taken in by it.

"I must admit, I am relieved." Melville spoke slowly, taking this new knowledge slowly into his plans. "In that case I will have no fear in applying to our father, the Pope for an annulment."

He had expected her to be relieved, to be grateful that he was to spare her the marriage bed and free her from her promise – but as soon as he mentioned the idea of annulling their marriage, Avis started up where she sat in the bed and shouted, "my lord!"

"Quiet, girl!" Melville returned fiercely. "Or do you want the household rushing to our chamber?"

"I will not be quiet!" Avis rose from the bed, walking towards him, dress slightly slipping on her shoulder revealing indulgent skin. "This marriage is not one that either of us would have chosen, but it is done! And what is done is done, and must be dealt with."

"You would choose a marriage of apathy?"

"This is a marriage of hatred!" Avis' clear eyes had darkened to a deceptively brilliant green, and she had once again unconsciously clenched her fists as she moved towards him. "You are Norman! What makes you think that I can feel only apathy in your presence? You disgust me."

She drew closer and made to spit at him, but Melville rose swiftly and clasped her arms to her side.

"Woman!" He whispered deeply, with venom in his tones. "I swear by God if you cross me you will suffer, my wife though you are."

Melville and Avis stood there, in the middle of the room, clasped in a wedding embrace unlike that of any other newly married couple. There was anger and resentment deepening between them, an almost palpable tension that could not be resolved. Avis knew that he was stronger than she, and that she was tired. This would not be the time to begin her fight against this man. As much as she wanted to throw him off her, to release herself from him, there was a magnetism about him that dwelt in the core of his being. She could not ignore it, and she fought against it with all of her soul.

As they stood, Melville became aware of his breathing: deep and fast. But there was more – he could feel Avis' ribcage moving in a fluttering motion as she attempted to catch her breath. He looked down at his wife. His Anglo-Saxon wife. Hatred flooded into his lungs, so that every breath that descended from his lips down onto the top of her hair covered her in his loathing. But then Avis looked up. Her eyes widened when she realised how close his face was to hers, and he was struck by her beauty.

A desire to protect her rose unbidden from a deep place within him. This girl was his wife. He involuntarily began to lower his face down to hers – but then just as involuntarily released her and stepped back, almost pushing her away back onto the bed. This was not the time to lose control.

Avis stood where he had left her, gradually catching her balance from the force that he had pushed her with as he moved away. Her gaze followed Melville, waiting for him to make another move – away from her or to bring them closer together.

Melville swallowed, refreshing his dry mouth. His vision was blurred by the lust that had suddenly ascended, and he needed to create as much distance between them as possible.

"We are tired." He managed. "Rest."

"You lie not with me." Avis spoke quickly and surely, determined to force her point across to this strange man. "Not tonight. Not any night."

She was sure that he would refuse this suggestion, and was prepared to fight him – physically if necessary – to prevent him from taking her innocence. But a small smile danced around his lips, and she felt embarrassed, as if he was privy to a joke that she was unaware of.

"If that is what you desire, my lady." Melville strode towards the bed, pulling off one of the ornate covers and began making himself a bed by the warm embers of the fire. Avis was surprised. She had not expected him to be so quick to agree with her, but was too tired to question him. Unsure that Melville would keep to his word, Avis crept into bed after quietly secreting a dagger under her pillow. No surprises.

CHAPTER TEN

Avis woke up with her left hand clasped around the handle of the dagger, the sharp metal clinking metallically when she moved her finger with her wedding ring. Wedding ring. She turned quickly towards the fire, and was relieved to see the covers were vacant. Melville must have risen early and left without stirring her.

After dressing and moving towards the Great Hall, she could hear sounds of shouting and chaos emanating from the stables just at the side of the large room. Altering her course to discover what the disturbance was, she walked into what seemed to be every person of the house rushing around carrying chests and bags and completely unsure where they should be going. Weaving her way through the crowd, she eventually found Richard, watching all that was going on with a mocking laugh dancing across his features. After a short curtsey as greeting, Avis ignored all polite conversation and enquired immediately.

"Good morrow, my lord. What is happening?"

Richard looked amused.

"You are leaving."

"Leaving?" Avis was hungry, and still tired from the day before, and not in the mood to be teased and bullied by this foreign man again. "Leaving to go where?"

"You and your husband, when he returns from his ride, are going back to his land and property."

"Where is his land?"

"In the North."

Avis had never been in the North. She had lived all of the years of her life in the South, and had never ventured far from her home. She had heard terrifying stories of painted men and women who could tell your fortune by looking at you. The land there was said to be barren and miserable, with constant rain and few people at all. But she had also heard about the wilds – huge amounts of land where no people lived and folk told stories about magical creatures and deadly caves in which demons lived. She had been told about mighty rivers, and deep forests. She shivered, not only with fear but with excitement. Finally she was leaving Richard. A tear rolled down her cheek as she surveyed the building that she would be leaving. This place had been her home for almost two decades, and the home of her ancestors. With it she would be leaving scores of memories – not all of them happy.

Richard evidently was hoping that she would be overcome with fright, but she would not give him that satisfaction.

"I will await my husband in the Great Hall." She stated firmly. "He can come to collect me when all is ready."

Sweeping away decidedly, Avis walked away, not noticing the horses arriving with great noise in the courtyard behind her. Melville and two of his men were sweating and smiling after their ride – their hunting trip had been successful. A brace of pheasants swung down from a tight leather cord strapped to one of the horses. Melville's face fell, however, when he saw the back of his new bride in the courtyard. It had been easy when away from this depressing house and miserable inhabitants to forget his concerns, but now he had returned he had a duty to return home and take his men back to their families – and to become accustomed to the new family that had been formed.

"Avis!" he called across the courtyard, his deep voice resonating over the noise, calling for silence. She stopped, and slowly turned, a smile plastered on her face. Melville could see that she was attempting to be brave and self-confident in front of his men, and he could not help but begrudgingly respect her for it.

"Yes, my lord?"

"Make ready a horse." He spoke curtly. "We ride immediately."

Avis bowed her consent, but turned seething. He had clearly decided to humiliate her in every way possible, beginning with not allowing her respite to eat before their long journey to the North. She drew herself up, and concentrated. She was a woman. She was an Anglo-Saxon. She smiled. She could do anything.

The journey was long and arduous indeed, and it seemed to last a month to Avis who had never travelled such a long distance in her life. Every muscle ached, and her shoulders kept dipping under the strain of remaining on a horse for hours on end. For Melville however, a man from across the sea, it was but a short time until they had arrived at what he resentfully termed 'home'. Avis drew in a quick breath. The manor had been built near the bank of a deep river and was not only beautiful, but domineering. The manor dominated the landscape in a very powerful way – just as the Normans now own us, she thought angrily, lessening her appreciation for the structure.

"Where are we?" Avis had lost count of the names and locations of the towns and villages that they had passed, and many of the names had been changed since the Normans had come. Places that she thought she had known were no longer there, and they had passed the remains of many a village that had been destroyed, and whose inhabitants had not returned. Avis had not asked whether this had been out of choice. She was totally at a loss as to where she was.

"Just south of York. My village is Ulleskelf, under the jurisdiction of Copmanthorpe."

"Copmanthorpe," mused Avis, her nose scrunching as it always did when she tried to understand something. "I know that name."

"Indeed you should," Melville spoke carefully. "I believe that a man of your family once lived here."

"Yes!" Memories were slowly dripping through into Avis' mind, and she could picture her distant cousin now. "Gospatrick. He was the lord of Copmanthorpe – a brave man."

Melville was silent. He knew that Gospatrick had died on the same field that he had fought on, but was not sure just how aware his bride was of the battles that had been fought over this land that she pined over so.

"He was replaced." Melville was careful with his words. "I am lord now."

Avis flung a look over her shoulder as her horse moved gently on the spot to counter the movement.

"You?"

Melville laughed indignantly at her disapproval. "Am I such a bad choice?"

"What was wrong with the original?" Avis countered. "From my meagre memory, Gospatrick was a good man. A loyal man, who took care of his people."

Melville sighed. There was so much that she did not understand. It would certainly take a long time for Avis to accustom herself to the 'new' England.

Avis saw his disappointment with her, and flushed. It was not her fault that she could not comprehend the removal of a good man for a stranger. Melville obviously underestimated her. She knew full well what had happened to Gospatrick.

"You must be tired." Melville cut across her thoughts.

"I am." Avis was loathed to concede weakness, but was afraid that he would suggest another long ride as he had two days ago when she had tried to pretend that she was not exhausted. "I would appreciate a rest."

"This is your home now." Melville could not have sounded more unhappy. "Treat it as your own."

She bowed her head in thanks, and they rode the last mile towards the manor at a slow pace. As they entered the large open courtyard, Avis brought the horse to a stop, and then slid off the panting horse with relief. Her old horse that had been plundered by the Normans had been so used to her that they had moved in one smooth stream, and she did not exactly agree with this creature's understanding of a calm ride. Checking that her veil was in place – an object that she had refused point blank to leave behind – she strolled curiously into the manor.

As Melville watched Avis go, he let out a strangled sigh. It had been agony watching this delicate girl put herself through such pain in order to retain the appearance of strength before him. The conversation about her new home had been the first time that they had spoken openly since that wedding night when she had thrown the fact that he was a Norman back in his face. His hand tightened on the reins as he remembered the hatred that was clear in her face, and then loosened his grip. She was but an Anglo-Saxon, he reminded himself. She could not understand.

Giving out instructions to the many servants that began teeming out to see their master's return, he organised the removal of his new wife's belongings and began to prepare himself for another ride. Anything to put space between him and that woman.

CHAPTER ELEVEN

Avis had been worried that she would not feel at home in this foreign land, in an odd manor, amongst strangers. After all, this was a land that she had only heard talk of in dark tales, around a smouldering fire from elderly men whose eyes flashed as they spoke. Avis was sure that there would be many customs and routines that she would not understand, and all who saw her would quickly mark her as an outsider.

But she could not have been more wrong. After she had explored parts of the manor, she realised that she would very quickly get lost in the passages and rooms that she was unaccustomed to. Having never lived anywhere else, she was unused to finding her way around a new place. All of the walls were bare, and the rushes on the floors were patchy and dirty in some places, and simply absent in others. Many of the candles attached to the walls had burnt out. It gave the corridors a dark and gloomy atmosphere.

After a quick lunch in the hall at which she didn't see Melville, she began to venture outside the manor, to meet the people of whom she was mistress. She had been raised by her father to value and respect the people of her home, and she wanted to know these new people just as intimately as she had done the people in the south. Avis almost tripped on the uneven bridge, and she continued on painful feet.

The people in the village just across the river from the manor welcomed her as a friend, recognising in her the beauty and stateliness of an Anglo-Saxon noblewoman. They were all Anglo-Saxon, as she was, and she felt a familiarity with them that she had never felt with Richard. She chattered away to them in her native tongue, grateful to stop speaking the uncomfortable Norman that she had had no choice but to learn and speak with Richard and Melville. She learnt that the Anglo-Scandinavian village that was a thriving part of the area had been destroyed, leaving these Anglo-Saxons who were refugees from the south as the major group under Melville's rule. Avis shuddered at the thought of an entire village being destroyed. It was not unusual, but it struck deep into her heart every time.

It was not until the evening of Avis' arrival that she returned, as the sun went down behind the high manor. She began to feel the northern chill, and shivered. Summer was definitely fading, but she could feel winter more strongly here, far from the temperate climes of the south. As she entered the spacious entrance hall, she slid gratefully into a chair by the fire. It was threadbare and stiff, but anything that could hold her weight was a welcome relief.

A servant girl rushed to her side.

"Can I get you anything, my lady?"

"No, thank you," Avis replied, grateful for a caring voice in her mother tongue. "Could you direct me to…my chamber?"

The question was asked awkwardly. Avis could not help but feel embarrassed that she did not know the way to her own room. But the servant girl brushed away the uneasiness with her chatter.

"This way my lady." She gestured forward, and began talking happily. "There are so many corridors, aren't there? I remember when I came here from Ulleskelf, I didn't know where I was going for weeks! And then when I did…"

Avis smiled as she followed the prattling of the girl. She was very similar to a friend from Avis' childhood who she had not seen for many years. It was comforting to have somebody so friendly in such an empty, cold manor house.

The girl led her into a large chamber with an elaborate carved wooden bed taking centre stage in the room. A small fire was crackling, and the few trunks of her belongings that had survived the long trip sat beside it.

The girl made to close the door behind her.

"Your chamber, my lady."

"Wait," Avis spoke, and the girl paused. "Where are my lord's possessions?"

Now the girl was overcome with mortification. Her cheeks blushed a deep red, and she moved backwards, wishing to leave the room without replying. But she could not ignore her mistress' question.

"My lord," she finally said, "does not sleep here. He has his own chamber. You are not required to share with my lord."

Her last sentence finished, she closed the door with a creak as the rusting hinges moved at speed.

Avis sank onto the bed. Melville had organised two different sleeping chambers for them. His presumption evidently knew no bounds – but at least this did aid Avis in one way. The problem of consummating the marriage was therefore ignored by him, and she saw no reason to challenge him on the matter. She was relieved. On the road there had been no privacy, and therefore no expectations. During her travelling musings, she was unsure as to how she would have fought him off, here in his own home with no one else looking on to judge his actions either right or wrong.

She looked around her. This was her new room. There was little in the way of comfort anywhere, from the sparse blankets on the bed, to the lack of chests to place her clothes in. Avis sighed. There was much to be done here.

It only took one week for the lives of Avis and Melville to settle into a routine, but they were two very separate lives. Melville would rise early and go with his men riding and hunting, or preside over the local court, settling disputes between the peasants. Avis was pleasantly surprised. She could not help but be impressed at his dedication to justice and truth – though she probably would have been less impressed if she knew that his dedication had increased since her arrival in order to avoid her. Melville could not stand being in her presence for too long. She reminded him of his undesirable imprisonment in this country, and she was beginning to play havoc with his dreams.

With her husband gone for most of the day, after two weeks and darker weather Avis began to despair. She had had no intimate friends after the Conquest, but she felt the lack of one all the more strongly in a strange place. Boredom seemed to be her only constant companion. She missed performing her small culinary tasks, even though no one appreciated her input. Avis was unused to having nothing to do, and was growing frustrated. On a day when autumn winds had settled in, she was sitting on the bank of the river singing gently underneath her breath when she saw a man on horseback. His shoulder length dark hair framed his strong features, and the way that both he and the horse appeared to move as one made her smile. Her husband may be a Norman and a brute, but he was certainly skilled.

Avis sighed. Melville had such purpose here: as lord, he had responsibilities that she could not help but know that he did well. But she was alone, with nothing to do and nothing to be accomplished. Avis decided to meander down to the manor kitchens: just, she resolved to herself, so that she could see what they were like.

When Avis ducked her head under the door, she gasped, transfixed. She had never seen such large kitchens, with so many fires and contraptions for creating the most delicious food that had been brought up to her each of the days that she had been here with Melville. It seemed that his disdain to invest in the furnishings of his home did not descend to the kitchen. Contraptions that she did not recognise lay on tablets of stone, and herbs that she could not place hung from the ceiling. She longed to push up her lavish sleeves and experiment, and seemed to be unnoticed amongst the hustle and bustle of a working manor kitchen. Boys were roasting birds on one fire, while a pot on another was tended by a sullen girl, also seeing to a small toddler. Shouts and orders were thrown about, and she got a thrill of excitement. Every scent and every sound that she could conceive surrounded her, and it was painfully hot. This was where the heart and soul of a manor was! She began to move about, but was startled by a loud voice speaking her native Anglo-Saxon.

"What do you think you're – "

Avis turned to find the voice, and saw the face from which it issued: a round man with wild tufts of hair, slightly damp from the sweat of his brow. He started when he realised that he had been shouting at his mistress.

"Erm…sorry, my lady," he reverted immediately to patchy Norman. "I am sorry…"

He tailed off. The poor man clearly had no more knowledge of the strange sounding language, and Avis immediately reassured him.

"Do not be afraid," she smiled, in the language that he would understand. "I am Anglo-Saxon. And I do not mind."

Her bright smile and unworried air calmed the nervous man.

"I am surely glad, my lady." The man broke into his broad local accent. "I am most sorry about shouting, but you'll find many of my lord's men will sneak in here and try to grab some food. Ruddy Normans."

"I understand." Avis smiled again at the look of hope on the man's face.

"May I show you around?" His face brightened at the thought of proving to his superior just how wonderful his skills were. Avis laughed, pleased to see such enthusiasm.

"Only if you would be so kind."

The cook introduced himself as Bronson, and spent a full hour showing her the new innovations that his lord had brought – his gratitude stifled slightly by his admission that a Norman seemed to have a good idea of how a kitchen should be.

After that day, Avis spent most of her time down in the kitchen. She befriended the women there, hearing tales of dirty men, crying children, and laughing at their stories about managing a home. The men there considered her a daughter, and taught her tricks that improved her bread immensely, and one elderly woman explained herb lore to her that she had never before fully understood.

A week passed, and Avis began to feel that she belonged somewhere. Her mother had always worked with their kitchen staff – she never thought that it was beneath her, and her father had always chuckled that the kitchen was the place that both his wife and daughter would rather be. Here, in this kitchen, even though she was hundreds of miles from home, Avis felt at peace. That she was part of a family.

When not in the kitchen, Avis had begun to transform the cold and uninviting manor into a true home for herself – ignoring the needs or desires of Melville, which she did not know. Each room was individually attended to and cared for, bringing light and laughter into every space.

Orders were made to York, where some of the best merchants had gathered, and every day new deliveries brought new joy. The servants identified in her someone who would care for the place, and did everything that they could to aid her. The only real complaints were from Melville's men, who did not appreciate the almost constant disruption as she re-laid rushes and threw corridors into brilliant light as the candles were slowly replaced.

But the majority of Avis' time was spent in the kitchen. She lived in constant fear that Melville would discover that she had sought shelter with people that she knew he considered beneath her, and definitely below him. Being Anglo-Saxon was to be a second class citizen in this new Norman land, and to be Anglo-Saxon and poor was almost a crime. He would not be able to appreciate the kindness that these people had given her. But her happiness radiated through her into the whole manor, and she began to finally treat this place as her home. Her alterations did not go unnoticed.

"This bread." Melville one night snapped at a servant. "Who made it?"

Avis froze, dripping sauce as her eyes caught Edith's, the girl that Melville had barked at.

"Me. My lord." Edith managed to stutter out in Norman. Melville's eyes narrowed, and with a hand waved her out of the room.

Avis breathed a sigh of relief, but then Melville turned to her.

"Avis."

"Yes, my lord?" Their interactions had been so few over her first week fully established as his wife that she was surprised at his speaking to her.

"You have been making many changes here."

Avis braced herself. She knew that this conversation was coming, and she was secretly glad that he had chosen to do it in public.

"And why not indeed?" Avis was not going to be bullied. "This place needed them."

In this hall, unlike her previous home, the majority of the servants ate with their master, at lower tables than him admittedly, and with less extravagant food. There were chuckles along the table from anyone who could follow the foreign Norman language that Melville and Avis were using. They were proud of their new mistress, and knew that she would not let their Norman lord off lightly.

Melville bristled with anger – and embarrassment.

"Is my home not fit for your ladyship?"

Avis swallowed a mouthful of food, determined not to rise to the bait that Melville dangled in front of her.

"Perfectly," she declared clearly. "But it is my home now too."

"You belong to me now!" Melville almost shouted, and his dark eyes met Avis'. He could see her enjoyment of his temper, and it did nothing to lessen it. Muffled laughs up and down the hall caused his temper to deepen, and rage bristled with every moment.

"Yes!" Avis stood up, in order to make her voice carry across the entire room. "And with that ownership comes responsibilities. The duty to keep me warm, for example! Did you know there was no system here for ordering firewood? Or to keep me clothed? Half of my belongings were abandoned on the way here – or did you not know that? If you cannot care for me, my lord, I have no choice but to do things myself!"

"Do you think I am ignorant?" Returned Melville. "I know how to care for a lady, but I do not see one when I look at you!"

"Because I am slovenly, or dirty?"

"Because you are Saxon!" Melville spat at her, standing up and staring at his wife. His height did not frighten her. Avis stared at him, shaking in anger, and stared at his blatant anger – but instead she was drawn even more strongly into his orbit, unable to escape how small he made her feel, but also the feminine force that he drew from her with his strong arms and powerful gaze.

"Will you ever look past that, Melville?" The words had escaped her before she realised. Her eyes flickered down. One moment of weakness.

"Will you ever forget that I am Norman, Avis?" Melville countered.

The two of them stood there, a force between them simultaneously pushing them apart and bringing them together. Avis looked up at him, and saw the desire in his eyes – and she matched it. Never had a man drawn such emotion and such feeling from her. There were parts of her that were stirring that she did not previously realise she possessed, and she swayed slightly towards him.

Melville saw the movement, and his heart leapt. He knew that he could tame this timid and yet terrifying beast if he chose to, but he did not know if he could match her passion. She was so young, and so precious, and so angry. He could see the movement of her breast, and the desire that overflowed from his eyes was met by a similar lust from Avis. But suddenly he realised: she was Anglo-Saxon. She was probably taught to please – and by God, she would certainly please – but he would not give himself to a woman who would refuse to work with him. It would have to be a partnership, or nothing at all.

Avis took a step backwards. Silence coated the atmosphere in the hall. All of the servants and Melville's men had stopped eating, forks halfway to mouths, to watch the argument at the top table.

Collecting her blood red robes around her, Avis slowly and gracefully walked its length and left quietly. A murmuring from the servants erupted as soon as she was no longer visible.

"Silence!" Melville demanded. Fearful eyes turned towards him, and then looked quickly down at their food. Melville sighed. That woman! She knew exactly how to frustrate him, pointing out his faults in front of Anglo-

Saxon servants, bringing herself closer and closer to him, taunting him with her very presence. How dare she! He had not realised how susceptible he clearly was to her charms. Pursing his lips, he knew that he would have to conquer her – just as her people had been conquered.

CHAPTER TWELVE

Avis was angry. She was often angry in this new life of hers, but she was learning to channel it. Always a passionate child, she knew that the deep emotions that often stirred her could be used to do great things – and she was determined to do just that, whether Melville approved or not. As she almost ran away from the hall, she could feel her cheeks burning. To start considering this man as a man, as her equal, and not as a Norman, would be a mistake. She must not forget herself. By the time she had reached her bed chamber, she was resolved. She was going to continue to do exactly as she had been doing. Melville and his posturing be damned.

The next morning saw her organising many servants, all busily working to change the hall in which she and Melville had had their last passionate but restrained encounter.

"Higher!" she called to a male servant. "Higher up!"

When she had arrived the high walls of the hall had been bare and unwelcoming – but now they were covered with tapestries and hangings of bright colours and golden silks. The light from the hundreds of candles reflected brightly on the expensive twists of thread, and in turn illuminated Avis' golden hair, only just visible beneath her veil. She smiled.

"Perfect." Avis turned on the spot, taking in the beauty and elegance that she had created. She sighed, smiling. This was now a hall worthy of being her home. Already she felt more comfortable, and it showed as she relaxed and flexed her aching shoulders. There was little that women like her could do, but in this small way, her acts of rebellion were mounting.

Shouts of men and barks of dogs heralded the entrance of Melville, who had once again been hunting all day. Avis surreptitiously caught the tangles of hair that had escaped her veil and trapped them once more in its folds, preparing herself for the verbal onslaught that she had come to expect from her tall and brooding husband. She had not seen him since their last, very public argument, and she would be astonished if she survived punishment.

"Out." Melville ordered the servants, not even looking at his wife. They obeyed him, terrified of his shouting voice, but Avis stood her ground. Once all others had gone, he slowly walked up to her, stopped about a foot from her, and lowered his deep voice.

"What do you think you are doing?"

Avis wanted to hate this man, but found that she could not. Her dislike was still strong, of course, but she could not hate a fair person. He was a just man, and his dark eyes were never happy but always sad. She had known much sadness, but could not comprehend how a Norman could know the pain that she did.

"Making a home, my lord." Avis spoke softly, hoping not to arouse his anger which – although she had never seen its full extent – she imagined rivalled hers.

"This is my home, Avis." His voice gently caressed her name, and she shivered. How could this man have such a physical effect on her?

Melville noted the shiver, and strove with himself not to take this luscious woman into his arms. He had been watching her the few weeks that she had entered his life, and had been amazed at the strength and resilience that she had shown. Ever since their encounter at the river, he had observed Avis, and noticed many instances of kindness towards these people, and many times he had caught her smiling.

Many people were afraid of him, and his coarse manner of speaking, and this did not surprise him. But she had matched him – and always with that subtlety and beauty that in his mind was found nowhere else. He watched the flutter of her throat. She was frightened of him. He was almost glad; glad that he seemed to have just such a strong effect on her as she did on him.

"My home also," she replied. "Whether you enjoy that fact or not, my lord, you are married. I live here too, and I prefer to live in somewhere more…" she savoured the moment of offending him, "refined."

This cut Melville more than she could know, and the light in which he saw her extinguished. He would not be taken in by her tricks, and her beauty.

He laughed. "You don't know the meaning of refined," he spat. Saxon."

Melville turned and strode out of the room, laughing. Avis sat down suddenly on a nearby chair, and put her head on her hands. Why was what she considered to be a badge of honour suddenly the best insult that any man could throw at her? How much longer could she continue in this tortuous marriage?

But she shook her head, and stood up again. No matter what happened, no matter what this brute threw at her, she was married. Nothing was going to change that, and all she had to do was survive.

The next day was Sunday, a day to go to the local village church. It was built in the new Norman style, a style that Avis was not familiar with but sadly admitted was indeed beautiful. The priest was also Norman, but mass was given in Latin – a language that none but Avis knew.

She relished this refinement that Melville lacked, and made sure each time after church to explain the meaning of particular phrases, watching his annoyance rise but unable to act with such distinguished company.

"And of course there's *spiritus sancti.* That's the Holy Spirit."

Avis flashed a look of mirth across to Melville, but his face was as determinedly blank as ever. She continued.

"Another word you probably didn't understand was *Deus*. That translates as God."

Melville did not reply, and she eventually fell into silence also.

Avis could not understand why Melville, as a nobleman, had not been taught the sophisticated language of Latin as she had been, even though as a Norman he was only slightly better than a savage. But Melville had never risen to her bait, and at times she felt childish for constantly forcing him to maintain his calm demeanour when she knew he would rather shout at her.

Having returned from church, Avis was enjoying a lavish and thankfully solitary meal while Melville presumably was dealing with the affairs of the estate. A noise startled her, but turning she could see that it was only a messenger, holding a scroll.

"My lady?"

Avis stood up, smoothed down her green gown and smiled. "Yes?"

"My lady." The messenger looked nervous. "I bring a message from my lord Melville."

"Yes?"

"My lord Melville would remind you that his comrade and friend, Hugh le Blanc of Flanders will be visiting us." Avis had not heard such news, and was angry that Melville had neglected to mention it when he had brushed past her so cuttingly after they had left the church that morning.

"Visiting?"

"Yes, my lady. He will be arriving today, and staying but one night."

Avis cursed under her breath, an old Anglo-Saxon curse which allowed greater vehemence and expulsion of feeling than these tame Norman phrases. Another Norman! Would she never be rid of these marauders?

The messenger was waiting nervously for her reply, and she realised that he would not leave until she had given him a missive for his master.

"Please thank my lord," Avis said graciously. "Tell him I will see him later at the feast."

After waiting for the messenger to leave, she rushed to the kitchen, shouting out orders in Anglo-Saxon and forgetting herself in her hurry to encourage the servants.

"Bread! We are going to need much more bread. Are there any chickens left? Good, kill three. We shall need everything we've got on the table; my lord is expecting a great visitor."

People rushed around her, and further orders were given. As Avis threw herself into the task of baking as much bread as she could muster, she tried to remember who Hugh le Blanc of Flanders was. She knew that he had come across with the other Normans, but no more details could she recall. He was probably a man of low status, she gritted her teeth, and yet here I am, slaving away! But as she kneaded bread, wearing down the skin on her knuckles and causing her slender back to ache, she realised that she would gain nothing from impoliteness. The best way, she smiled to herself, to prove to Melville just how noble her blood really was – her Anglo-Saxon blood – was to be the perfect lady of the manor. She knew she had it in her. She would prove to him that the Normans did not have a monopoly on gentility.

CHAPTER THIRTEEN

Trumpets heralded the arrival of Hugh le Blanc of Flanders. Avis rushed out into the main courtyard, glad that she had had just enough time to wash the dough off her hands before coming out to greet their guest. Beside her stood Melville, silent as ever. As Hugh le Blanc dismounted, she rushed towards him and curtseyed low to the ground.

"May God find you well," she began, "and bless you at our humble home."

Avis smiled up at the man, and was surprised to find a smile in return.

"A welcome indeed!" beamed the man, whose blond hair and pale complexion explained his name immediately. "Melville, you had not told me your wife was so beautiful!"

Moving forward, he clasped his host into a large hug, which Melville returned gruffly.

"Hugh, if I had told, you would have married her yourself! Come, into the warm where food and entertainment in your honour awaits you."

Arms around each other, the two laughing warriors were drawn into the hall where splendour and spectacle awaited them.

"Melville!" cried Hugh le Blanc, shaking his head in wonder as he surveyed the hall. "Everything is so altered! I am mightily impressed – what convinced you to finally add some life and space into this place?"

"It was my wife," Melville was quick to pass the blame. "It has all been her doing."

Hugh le Blanc turned to Avis. "My lady, I congratulate you. You have created a magnificent home."

Avis blushed, and curtseyed once more. It was unusual for any of her hard work to be recognised in a positive manner, and it was heartening to hear – even if it was from a Norman.

As the three of them feasted, along with their servants and retinues, Avis turned the full strength of her charm on their visitor, who responded as if he had never met a woman before. Melville could only sit back, amazed, as the woman that he had considered cold and hard towards all Normans flared up into flames of joy. She laughed, she shared Norman riddles which had Hugh le Blanc in stitches; she listened to his war stories and gasped in all of the right places. She made sure that his plate was never empty and his cup always overflowing.

Melville watched her. He saw as she threw her head back in unashamed laughter how the light gave a perfect shadow onto her cheek, and how a wisp of refined gold hair gently rested alongside her ear. He noted the delicate and careful fingers caressing the table covers, and suddenly wished that he knew the touch of those elusive fingers. His gaze travelled upwards along her tight sleeves, perfectly encapsulating elegant arms, leading to her bodice, and a waist that –

"Melville?" Hugh le Blanc's voice shook him back to concentration. "Can you hear me, old friend?"

Melville flung his head back, as if to loosen water from it.

"I am quite well, my friend." He smiled weakly. "I was…distracted."

He looked directly at Avis, who coloured. She knew exactly what had distracted him, and was suddenly very aware of her fitted gown and revealing cut.

"I am to bed," she announced, in the vague hope of cutting short Melville's predatory gaze. Turning to Hugh le Blanc, she spoke in a gentle tone with soft eyes. "Forgive me, my lord."

"No forgiveness necessary," Hugh le Blanc gave a wide smile. "It was my honour and joy to spend such a long time in your presence."

Rising, he kissed her hand. Melville's hand moved towards his dagger, but then stopped himself. If the little self-control he had had gone, he would have easily killed Hugh le Blanc. It seemed ludicrous that this stranger had touched more of his wife than he had – but then he had organised separate sleeping quarters for a reason. He watched his wife leave the room, glorifying in the sway of her hips and the minuteness of her waist. As Hugh le Blanc seated himself, Melville let out a staggered sigh.

"You," Hugh le Blanc raised his goblet, "are a lucky man."

"Luck has nothing to do with it." Melville replied in clipped tones. "She was not my choice."

Hugh le Blanc's eyes widened. "You cannot mean to tell me that you have ever laid eyes on better?"

Melville laughed, but without mirth. "I would choose not to marry at all, my lord. It is not my preferred path."

Hugh le Blanc looked puzzled, but then comprehension dawned. "The King."

"The King indeed." Melville drained his goblet and slammed it down. "Our King. Long may he live." He stood abruptly. "And if you will excuse me, I must go and see to my wife."

"Oh." Hugh le Blanc was startled by his host, but was too much a man of the world not to be surprised. He could see the lust in his host's eyes, and knew that the display of affection for him from Avis was primarily directed at her husband. "I wish you a good night."

"Not good enough." Growled Melville, as he stalked out of the room.

Thrusting open the door, Melville stormed into Avis' chamber. She screamed, unable to see the intruder through the curtain of her bed, but calmed slightly when he threw open the hangings to reveal himself.

"Melville!" Avis gasped, suddenly very aware that she was only wearing a linen shift, which threw into sharp relief the contours of her body. She clutched the nearest blanket to her breast, hoping that he had not noticed.

He had. Melville stared at her as if he had never noticed her existence, and his heavy breathing from running the length of the outside corridor did not lessen.

"What do you want?" Avis asked.

Melville knew that the honest answer to that would terrify her, so satisfied himself with, "to talk."

"Talk?" confused, Avis brought her knees up, curling herself up into a ball far away from the threatening stance of Melville. "What do you want to talk about?"

"Let's start with Hugh le Blanc!" Melville spat. "What do you know of him?"

"Nothing!"

"Liar!"

"I swear, I knew not of him before this day!"

Jealously bit through Melville's veins, jealously that he knew was absurd because he did not care for this woman. He was sure that he did not.

Avis' eyes were fearful, and he realised just how terrified she must be, seeing him burst into her chamber like a raging bull. He stepped away from the bed, and tried to steady his breathing.

"You must accept my apologies, my lady." He muttered. "I did not mean to startle you."

Avis looked at him properly for the first time since he had stormed into the room, and saw a man in torment. It was clear that little thought had gone into this bursting entry into her chamber, and he would very soon be regretting his decision. Warmth crept from her, towards him, and she reached out a tentative hand.

"My lord?"

Melville saw the smooth, soft skin move closer, and fought the instinct to take it in his rough hand, to caress it and luxuriate in her. He looked at her, and saw an openness that she had always hidden from him. Dropping to sit at the edge of the bed, he took her hand in his.

Avis gasped. Shivers of surprise echoed through her body as their skin touched. Nothing had ever been like this before, never had she felt so bare. His fingers gently traced the lines of her fingers, encircling her knuckles and resting for a moment on that slight part of her wrist where her pulse beat. She breathed an unwitting sigh of pleasure, and drew herself slowly towards him so they sat opposite each other, but side by side, on the bed.

Melville was looking down at their two hands entwined. He had never known a feeling of possession like this. He wanted to somehow remove the kiss that Hugh le Blanc had imparted on this perfect hand of Avis', and did so in the only way he knew how: by lifting her hand to his lips and slowly imparting a chaste kiss into her palm.

Avis rocked slightly as emotion flooded her veins. Unbidden and untaught, she lifted her other hand to cup his cheek, forcing his face towards her. He looked utterly confused – and in her power. Neither of them thought, they just acted, moving closer and closer together until Avis could feel Melville's warm breath on her cheek. She exhaled quietly.

"Melville…"

This calling of his name brought him to his sense, and he froze. How did he get to this place? The wine that he had drunk at the feast must have been stronger than he thought. Untangling himself from her willing arms, he stepped away and repeated his last words.

"My apologies, Avis."

Melville left the room as quickly as he had entered it. Avis sat in shock, not entirely sure what had just happened. It had looked as if Melville was envious of her attentions to Hugh le Blanc – and they had come close to finally breaking that invisible barrier that always seemed to prevent them from understanding one another. And that was not possible, she reminded herself. He is a Norman.

CHAPTER FOURTEEN

By the time that Avis was ready to go to the hall the next morning, she discovered that Hugh le Blanc had already left. She was disappointed – despite being one of the enemy, as she had mentally labelled him, he had been a witty and enjoyable companion. Now she only had Melville, moody and mysterious, as her evening conversation. After a few quick words with a servant, she learnt that Melville had left as Hugh le Blanc had, but had travelled in the opposite direction.

Avis saw Melville at midday returning from business for a quick meal, and tried to fade into the background, unwilling to meet him again after the events of the night before. She cursed the blood red dress that she was wearing. It was one of her favourites and she had wanted Hugh le Blanc to see her wearing it, but it had never been more badly timed. It was completely impossible for anyone to avoid seeing her, and as Melville walked towards her he placed his hands around her waist and pulled her without speaking towards the corner of the room.

"My lord!" she tugged at his arm, hoping for release, but he only increased his grip.

Her back touched the cold stone of the wall behind her, and with the bulk of Melville before her, she was completely trapped. Her frantic eyes met his.

"Hugh le Blanc greatly enjoyed his stay here." Melville told her, in the manner of relaying a bereavement.

Avis looked confused. Had she not done what was expected of her – as a gracious 'Norman' hostess?

"Is that not good my lord?"

"Good!" Melville spat. "I want to be left alone! I want to be left in peace! He has informed me that he will be telling all of our wonderful hospitality – and especially the regal manners of my manor's lady! Soon half of Norman nobility will be here!"

Avis paled. "No."

"Agreed!" Melville finally released her arm, but only to fix her more tightly in the corner of the room with his magnificent gaze. He could smell her scent of rosemary once again. "Do you not recall how I did not want this marriage?"

"Ha!" Avis laughed. "Do you not recall how mutual that feeling was?"

Her clear eyes bore into his, but he maintained the gaze, trying not to forget the speech that he had so carefully prepared while pacing up and down his room after his potent encounter with her in her chamber. An encounter which he wished he had not cut short.

"I want to be left alone." Melville repeated.

"And I want to be free!" Avis' lips broke into a smile: but a smile of anger. "I do not wish to be paraded up and down for Norman enjoyment, like a trophy prize – but sorry, my lord, I forget myself. I am a punishment, not a prize."

Melville winced as his own words were flung back at him. He wished he had not been so hasty in speaking on that wretched wedding night.

"Can we at least agree to portray the couple that is enjoying a happy marriage?" He begged her. "If reports of our…disagreements reached the King – "

"You are right." Avis glared. "Best save your reputation at all costs. That is what you Normans are good at."

She pushed at his shoulder, trying to break free, and was surprised when he gave way. Avis strode past him, the feeling of entrapment whilst in the corner that he had forced her into overtaking her better judgement. Without looking back, she marched out of the room.

Melville leant forwards against the wall, fists above his head. That girl! She tried and tested him more than anyone he had ever met, and yet still she got the better of him. He could not understand her dislike of him – she hardly knew him. Raising himself, he looked outside. The sun was still up; he had time to go down to the village and check on these people that were now apparently his.

Ordering his horse, Melville and several of his men rode across the river to the village of his people. They spoke loudly in their strange words which he had not bothered to learn. Norman was so simple, he reasoned. They could learn it themselves, and then counteract the problems of translation. Only one man in his retinue spoke the local dialect, making him invaluable.

"Robert!"

A young man rode to Melville's side. "My lord?"

"Enquire about the rents and taxes due me. I want it all collected. No excuses. And remind them of my orders about the fallow land – it must be part of the harvest this year."

"They will not like it," Robert, a young man whose potential Melville had realised early, spoke earnestly.

"The tradition of fallow land is a good one, it protects the land – "

"I am lord here," Melville cut across him, and Robert shut his mouth with a red face. "When they are lord, they may decide how they feed their people. But today, the decision lies with me. And it has been made."

Robert nodded and dismounted, searching for the local priest who was the man that the Normans spoke to when dealing with the Anglo-Saxons. Melville's eyes scanned the crowd: and stopped dead at one. A woman, with long flowing blonde hair flying about in the wind. Curls were tugged by the breeze around her, creating a natural halo, and she laughed as she played with some of the local children. The tallest one threw a rough leather ball towards her, which she caught, fingertips outstretched, to the sound of cheers.

It was Avis.

"Avis!" he called out, startling her and causing her to drop the ball that she was carrying.

"Melville!" She was clearly horrified, and turned to run. Melville urged his horse forward, and caught up with her behind a small dwelling.

"What on earth are you doing here?" Melville dismounted hurriedly and didn't bother keeping his voice down, reasoning that none close by would be able to understand the clipped Norman tones. "Among these people? You dishonour me!"

"It is you who dishonours me," Avis did not try to avoid Melville now, but took a step towards him, her face close to his. "These people know how to tend the land, and you ignore them! These people know the way the land breaths and lives, and yet you in your arrogance dictate to them their own harvest!"

"This is not about harvest!" Melville argued. "This is about you – you fraternising with these people!"

"Fraternising?" Avis moved closer to Melville, and reached out her hands to place them on his chest. "Fraternising?" Encircling his waist with her arms she gently rocked towards and away from him, turning him around to face the other way, her back to his horse. "Fraternising?" Slowly she lifted her lips to his, and he unwillingly looked down into her face, and her red, inviting lips.

Before he could lean down and take what was rightfully his, she leapt backwards, mounted his horse, and laughed. "It's difficult to fraternise with your own kind, my lord," she giggled. Forcing the horse into a gallop, she left Melville standing in the middle of the village.

CHAPTER FIFTEEN

The next week was cluttered with visits from varying Norman nobles, and although they were unwelcome, they thankfully left Avis and Melville with very little time in which they had to bear each other's company. Each visitor was given the show of a happily married Anglo-Norman couple, but behind closed doors they had nothing to do with each other. Not a word was spoken – though Melville sent more than one sneaky glance her way.

It was not until the following Sunday that they really spoke at all, and once again it was an argument. They had just returned from church, and were as was their custom having a small meal alone. As according to church custom, Sunday was a day of fasting – not completely from food, but from rich nourishment such as meats and wine. As they ate their meagre portions, Avis was painfully aware of Melville's gaze upon her. Eventually she raised her eyes, and spoke.

"Do I displease you, my lord?"

Far from it, thought Melville. He replied, "I am curious."

"And where does your curiosity lie?"

"In your prayers."

Avis had not been expecting such a personal statement, but resolved herself. She had known that her mocking over his lack of Latin knowledge would eventually be countered. A servant entered to light the candles. Their afternoon church service had been long, and now the early evening was casting shadows across the room. Avis blushed. She just had not expected so private an enquiry. She put her bread down.

"My…my prayers?" She faltered.

"Indeed." Melville poured another goblet of ale, and smiled at her. "Your prayers."

Avis had no idea how his plan of attack was to progress, but braced herself. Waiting for the servant to leave, she did not speak again until the door had closed after him.

"I do not know what you are referring to, my lord."

Melville smiled again. "You do not pray in Norman."

"I pray in Latin! You remember, that language of culture that I have in charity been trying to teach you – but then, you Normans cannot bring yourselves to learn!" She laughed, confused but relieved his comments were not any worse. "After all, my lord, I am not Norman."

"Melville."

"What?"

"Call me Melville."

"Why?"

His smile broadened. "It is my name."

Avis swallowed. Her husband was playing some sort of game, and she did not like it.

"Melville. I am not Norman."

"But I am Norman."

"I had noticed." She said, drily, picking up the bread again and starting to eat.

Melville continued. "And now we are married, you too are Norman."

Avis choked, and in trying to reach some wine, accidently knocked over a goblet in her large gesture. A dog leaped forward to lick up the spilt liquor.

"Never. I am Anglo-Saxon."

"With a Norman husband." Melville reminded her. "In the eyes of God that makes you Norman. I wonder," he smiled maliciously, "if God understands your prayers, when He is expecting the pure Norman tongue."

Melville leant back, obviously pleased with himself that he had dealt her a blow that she could not recover from. And indeed, this was not a progression that she had expected. But that did not console Avis; it enraged her. Did he know nothing? How can he know so little? Could he really be so stupid?

"What language do I speak, Melville?"

He blinked, perplexed. "Norman."

"Wrong."

"Avis," Melville tried to stay in the realms of reality. She has drunk too much wine, he thought to himself. "We are speaking Norman now."

"*Eallwealda*!" Avis' eyes were lifted to the heavens in her appeal to God in her native tongue, and Melville raised his eyebrows in shock at the strange term. It was definitely not Norman.

"What was that?"

Avis sighed, and looked at him with eyes that glowed as the candlelight reflected on her welling pupils. She was not going to cry, but it was an effort to contain the tears that were at every moment threatening to escape. All anger had rushed out of her, and she was full of nothing but sadness. Her shoulders slumped down, and she looked utterly defeated.

Melville immediately felt regret; he wanted to rush over and comfort her, pressing her small body to his mighty strength, but knew that this was not the time. She was not ready – and neither was he.

"Melville." Avis began gently. "Think about where I was born."

Melville could do nothing but look at her.

"I was born here – here in England, of noble Anglo-Saxon stock. I grew up in the downs of the south, gathering harvest with my people and taming the seagulls on the beach. I saw the sun go down, and I saw it go up, and for almost sixteen summers I spoke only the language of my people."

There was a pause as Melville took this information in.

"You…you can speak as they do?" Melville was amazed.

"I am one of them." Avis reminded him. "And until the Normans, you, arrived in my country, I had no need of any other tongue. But then…"

Avis' voice trailed off. She could still hear the screams, smell the scent of burning wood, of burning flesh. Her mother's cries were right behind her, and she couldn't look round, she must not look round…

"Avis?"

Her eyes were blank, and she began to slip sideways as the tears overcame her self-control.

"Avis! Avis!" Melville rose and came towards her, pulling her into him, hoping to shield her from whatever it was attacking her in her memories. "I'm here, Avis."

At first she struggled against him, unwilling to be confined, but as her hands reached tentatively out, she discovered a strength more potent than anything she had ever known. She grabbed the folds of his shirt, and buried herself in his intensity, knowing that nothing could reach her or harm her when she was enwrapped in his powerful arms.

Melville tried to sooth her, stroking her face and keeping her close to him. He had never known fragility and force combined in such small a frame. He cursed himself for not thinking more about how his taunting would touch her at her core. He could not believe that he had just assumed that Norman was the only language that she spoke – he was so stupid! An idiot, not worthy to be called a lord, if that was the height of his intelligence. It had only been three years since he and his countrymen had conquered this land, and still only babes in Norman families were blessed in being taught his great language.

"Avis," Melville murmured gently by Avis' ear. "Avis."

Deep in that quiet, safe place, Avis heard her name being called – and with a jolt of recognition, she realised that it was Melville that was calling her. She was in his arms. He was comforting her. She must get away, she thought. I cannot stay here with him.

Eventually Avis calmed herself, and tried to escape from the strong arms of her husband.

"Please, do excuse me," she murmured.

"No," Melville countered, speaking softly. "Excuse me."

Avis looked up at him, aware of how close they were – closer than they had ever been before. She could not help but trust this man that held her close and comforted her in her time of weakness. Part of her – a small part of her – wanted to stay. But she could not forget that this man had contributed directly to her father's death.

"No," she said, half to herself, pushing away from him and standing up. "I am sorry, my lord."

Melville rose also, moving towards her, but she pushed him away. She could not accept this man, this Norman man, any closer.

"I am Anglo-Saxon." She stated bleakly, gazing at him with dead and tired eyes. "You are Norman. And there it is."

Avis walked purposefully out of the hall, leaving Melville alone. Once again she was angry, but this time she was angry with herself. She must not let her guard down, she must not let him see her true self. Without her emotional armour, she would not be safe – and not being safe around the heady masculinity of Melville could only end in tears.

Melville sank to his seat, and brought a goblet of wine to his lips, wishing it was more intoxicating. He was beginning to understand this complication, this paradox of a woman. Or at least, he was beginning to see just how much he did not understand. He had always seen himself as a warrior, as a brave man, as a man seeking his fortune – but he had never really noticed that by seeking his fortune, he must necessarily take it from another. Melville shook his head. Try as he might to avoid the truth, he could not help but admit to himself that he was beginning to fall in love with this girl, and he knew that she would never be able to see past his Norman beginnings. If she knew his entire history…well, maybe then she would see him in a different light.

But Melville knew that was not good enough for her. Avis deserved the best, and she needed the best that life – that he could offer her. And he knew what the best he could offer her was.

He called for his scribe, and began to dictate a letter: a letter to the pope, requesting the annulment of his marriage.

As he spoke, he clenched his fists. He didn't want to lose her, but he knew that unless he let her go, she could never choose to stay.

CHAPTER SIXTEEN

For the first time since she had arrived in his life, Melville began to seek Avis out. She drew him to her, in a way that he could not describe. All Melville knew was that he felt safer in her presence. Avis calmed him like no other, and he craved her, as a man craves a soft embrace after a long day at war.

As Avis thought, she frowned, unconsciously crinkling that perfect forehead in her intense concentration. She was finding it more and more difficult to go down into the kitchens, because Melville kept appearing at her side just as she was about to walk down her preferred corridor, requesting her opinion of the next harvest, or asking her what her plans for the day were. Despite her brief and occasionally rude replies, Avis could not shake him. Day after day she was obliged to answer his questions, and to change her direction in case he suspected her destination. Her frustration deepened as she received only titbits of gossip from the kitchen whenever she pretended to complain about the food to Edith during a meal – but with Melville's close eye on her, there was little that she could do.

Avis altered her tactic. She longed to spend some more time with the villagers of Ulleskelf; to speak her native language, tell the old stories, and laugh at the same jokes. It would almost be like being back home, although she knew that she could never truly go back. But again, Melville seemed determined to prevent her from doing anything. As Avis walked into the entrance chamber with her fire and chair, she began to move towards the door that would release her: but there he was. He smiled at her, and she returned the smile with a haughty look, changing her direction towards her chamber. As Melville watched her go, he smiled wryly. Neither of them was winning this battle of wits.

It was probably the last warm day of the year before winter captured the isle. Melville had not appeared at breakfast, probably taking advantage of the last good conditions for riding. Avis could not help but smile to herself. She knew that today would be the day that she could escape the manor without his notice.

Grabbing her long blue skirts in her left hand, she crept along the north wall until she was close to the bridge. She took a deep breath, and ran. Sharp air filled her lungs, but she kept running, and as she did a smile broke out onto her face. She had not run so hard since…well, she had not sprinted for pleasure in many years. Her leather shoes bit at the bridge's wooden slabs, and she was across.

Avis slowed down her pace, catching her breath. She revelled in the freedom of it all – the open grassland, red and golden leaves raining down upon her in the breeze; the cloudless sky beckoning her on further; the swifts looping over her head, ready to begin their long journey across the sea to warmer climes. All cried out with her, the longing to be alive.

Avis wandered to her special oak tree, and dropped down by its trunk, drawing out her billowing skirts over the seat of leaves that had been formed. She sighed, happily. There could be no greater joy than this.

"Good morning."

Melville's voice was clear and close. Avis almost tipped over in her fright, but managed to contain herself.

"My lord!" she gasped. "What a pleasant surprise!"

She frantically looked ahead of her, trying to make out where his voice was coming from. Melville chuckled, walking around the wide tree trunk where he had been hiding, and casually sat beside Avis.

"Not by the look of it! I seem to have given you quite a shock."

Avis collected herself, and sat stiffly upright. "I was not expecting company."

"Well then, I apologise for disturbing your solitude," smiled Melville good-naturedly.

Avis pursed her lips. She had hoped that her cool demeanour and pointed wish to be alone would have had greater effect on her husband, but Melville was settling himself down quite comfortably. When could she be rid of this troublesome man?

"How have you been, my lady?" Melville began. "I have not seen you much this last week."

Avis' anger finally broke through her determined silence.

"And why do you think that is, *my lord?*" she said scathingly.

Melville smiled, leaned back and pulled out an apple.

"Hmmm?" he shut his eyes, basking in the newly-returned sun that would soon be disappearing.

"Melville!" Avis shouted, unable to help herself. "Would you do me the courtesy of listening to me?"

Melville's eyes snapped open, but he turned a lazy head to face Avis, unwilling to sit up.

"I am listening."

Avis snorted.

"I am, indeed!" Melville rose now, turning to directly face her. His smile fell. "I promise you. I am listening."

Avis looked at him, anger fading as she saw how earnest he was. This is a man who will truly keep his word, she thought. A man whose word I can trust. His dark eyes met her clear ones, and she looked away, unable to face their intensity.

Melville spoke more gently now.

"What was it that you wanted to say, Avis?"

Avis considered whether pretence may be a more favourable option, but she realised that she was Melville's wife. Marriage was not a short term venture. There was no escaping from him, and sooner or later he would have to know how she truly felt. But it would be difficult: more difficult than any of their previous conversations, and none of them had been simple.

"Melville," Avis said awkwardly. "You may not have noticed, but I am not entirely happy with…" she trailed off, realising how ridiculous she was sounding. "With our marriage."

She glanced at him nervously under her long light lashes. The state of female happiness was never a concern of most menfolk, as she knew, and there was absolutely no reason for Melville to care how she felt.

But it was Melville's turn to snort.

"May not have noticed? Avis, you don't stop thrusting that fact into my face!" His voice was incredulous, but without malice. His gentle smile reassured Avis, and prompted her to continue speaking.

"I have been avoiding you." Avis confessed. Head low, she glanced once more through her fair lashes to see how Melville had responded. She was shocked to see him bowing his head in – was that disappointment dancing across his attractive features?

Avoiding him. Melville had hoped that his cynicism had been misplaced, but he was right: she had been purposefully avoiding him. Melville could not help but feel disappointed – but then he was not in love with her, he argued with himself. There were no expectations between them; they knew that neither of them had chosen this sham of a marriage. Then why did the fact that she would rather spend time alone rather than with him cut him deep, and stung like a scratch in salt water?

Avis' voice cut through Melville's deep reflection.

"I mean no disrespect, my lord," and she was surprised to find that her words were true. "It's just…"

"Yes?"

"I want to feel free." Avis stared up at the sky rather than face Melville's stare. She tucked a wayward curl behind her ear. "I was so used to organising each one of my days on my own behalf. Being kept in like an animal…it is difficult."

Avis wetted her dry lips, and Melville was drawn to their fullness, and had to deny himself the pleasure of taking her into his arms. Another swift dipped to the ground in front of the couple, and Melville sighed. Who was he to cage such a beautiful creature? In spite of what his time in combat around hardened warriors had taught him, he knew that he did not own Avis – he could not truly own any woman. She was her own person, and should be able to make her own choices.

Melville resolved himself to speak a statement that he knew he may regret.

"Avis?"

She turned her face from the sky to gaze upon his tanned face, and tender smile.

"Avis, this is your home now. You should feel as free here as you want."

Avis' eyes widened. "My lord?"

Melville sighed. "I cannot tell you where to go and what to do – or who to be." He shrugged his shoulders. "That is your choice. Make it."

Melville rose, and walked away from Avis without giving a backward glance. Avis surprised herself in hoping that he would, but he reached the manor door and entered it without turning. It had been one of the most difficult walks in Melville's life, and after he had passed through the door he leaned against the cool entrance hall wall, breathing deeply.

It had been torture being there with Avis, unable or reluctant to reach out and touch her. She challenged him in a way that no other woman ever had – but he could not force her. Not only was he unwilling to force her, but he suspected that she was stronger than he thought.

Avis sat underneath the oak, unsure what had just happened. Was she ever to truly understand this husband of hers? Melville seemed to have a respect for her unlike any other Norman – any man she had ever met. His last speech had reminded her so strongly of her father that she had to brush away a few tears. She had cried enough over the life that she had lost – Avis would not let anyone else force her to tears ever again.

CHAPTER SEVENTEEN

No more did Melville make Avis feel uncomfortable for leaving the manor. This for Avis was a great improvement. Now she was able to spend more time in the kitchen, with the other Anglo-Saxon residents of the household, and happy afternoons in the village relaying news of their family members scraping a living inside the manor walls. She felt so much more open with them than she could be with Melville, and she developed an unlikely friendship with Edith, the kitchen servant girl. Having lived so long without a true friend, and still unable to be honest in any meaningful way with her husband, it was wonderful for Avis to finally have someone to whom she could open up. The two of them often chatted as they kept themselves busy, but it was a difficult and at times awkward friendship. Both of them could not lose their awareness that they walked on very different paths, but their shared identity of being Anglo-Saxon held them together as nothing else could.

Winter by this point had settled into the land, and the stable boy came shivering into the kitchen with a request to Bronson to help the spit boy.

"You just want to keep warm!" Scoffed Bronson. "You don't want to work!"

"I will work," chattered the teeth of the little boy. "I swear."

"Let him," Avis called over, and Bronson turned to look at her. She shrugged. "Poor mite. And Ælfthrup could do with the help."

Ælfthrup, the spit boy, scowled at the suggestion that he was not strong enough to do his job. He usually guarded his place by the fire aggressively, as only a small boy of eight or nine could. But today, he begrudgingly made way for the little Norman boy to sit beside him by the roaring flames.

The boy smiled. "I'm Felix."

Ælfthrup threw a glance at Bronson, who frowned at him. The Anglo-Saxon boy sighed.

"Ælfthrup." The word was spat out, but good natured Felix persevered, and within minutes the two boys were chatting away in a mixture of the two languages.

Smiles were sent around the kitchen as the servants watched the two children, but they were wry smiles and sad smiles. Many parents remembered their children, similar ages to the boys, who were taken. Many remembered brothers that they had lost.

Avis turned back to her work, and Edith with a sigh joined her.

"What did you do before?" Avis asked her, breaking the silence. Edith did not have to ask what Avis meant by 'before'. They both knew.

"My father was a *ceorl*," Edith explained, brushing away a fly that was buzzing around her head. Avis knew the word – it was an Anglo-Saxon class of men – fairly wealthy, with responsibility in the community and generally well respected. "But he died when the Vikings came over the water." She bent her head over the bowl of herrings that she was marinating.

Avis shook her head sadly. Living so far south as she had done, she had only heard brief accounts of the Battle of Stamford Bridge. The Viking King, Harald Hardraadar had thought he had a claim to the English throne, and had clashed with King Harold just before the Normans had invaded. Hardraadar was a man feared in many countries, and the fighting had been fierce, bloody, and agonising for the local people. Harold had won, but then had the long march down to the coast to confront the challenge led by William. That southern battle had been brutal, but the Battle of Stamford Bridge had already become a legend. Many good and noble men had died there when Harold's brother, Tostig, had betrayed him and joined the force of Vikings led by Hardraadar. Widows across the north had let out a wail of distress that day, and it was but days later that Avis had released her own cry, hundreds of miles away.

Avis placed a comforting arm on Edith's shoulder. A quick hand swept the tears from Edith's eyes.

The two women kept working together to prepare the meats for that evening's meal until Edith spoke again.

"It is Æthelfrith that I miss the most," Edith confided to her mistress.

Avis had heard her friend mention the name before, but had been wise enough not to enquire. Too many brothers had been lost to the Viking and Norman hordes in that terrible year.

"Who was he?" asked Avis, nervous of the answer she would receive, and worried that she may have overstepped the elusive lines of new friendship.

Edith looked straight at Avis as she said, "my betrothed."

Avis drew in a horrified breath. Every death was a tragedy, but for each death there was the tragic story of those that had been left behind. It was bad enough that these Normans had forced her into marriage, but by their invasion they had prevented Edith from marrying at all.

"That's awful," she murmured. There was nothing else to be said.

Edith nodded matter-of-factly. She had done her grieving, and was now bound by her numbness.

"It was." She said bleakly. "But I was not the only one."

Avis knew that she was right. The year 1066 had brought to England two invasions and the loss of not one, but two generations of menfolk. Honoured and respected men such as her father, and Edith's father – men who had thought to put their fighting days behind them but had been called to arms by their loyalty to their King. And then young, untried and excited youthful men like Edith's Æthelfrith, ready to prove themselves on the battlefield. Villages once full of laughter and honest labour rang quiet as women wept for the loss of husbands, brothers, fathers, sons.

Avis was forced out of her unhappy reverie by Edith's warning.

"My lady!"

Avis ducked behind the worktop as the heavy steps of Melville echoed on the stairs. Although Avis had been flattered by his speech the day before underneath the oak tree, she was sure that he would not appreciate the sight of her working, elbows deep in cooking grease and the stench of chicken guts on her hands.

"Bronson!" thundered Melville. The small man rushed up, brushing the cheese gratings from his sleeves and wondering in panic what part of last night's meal had offended.

"Yes, my lord?"

Robert appeared behind Melville, ready to translate his master's orders.

"Be aware that I want local and traditional dishes served from today." Melville muttered quietly to the shaking man, with Robert rapidly making Melville's order understandable to the terrified cook.

"If possible, some southern dishes as well – though I'm not sure how far your expertise goes. Whatever you can manage. Do you understand?" Melville finished.

The cook looked from his translator, to his master, and back.

"My lord would prefer…Anglo-Saxon food?" he asked incredulously.

After Melville had been told of Bronson's question, he nodded.

"Primarily Anglo-Saxon food from now on," he repeated. He turned and had almost exited the kitchens when he paused. "And try to make it palatable," he said, as if asking the heavens for rain in a drought.

He left, causing the silent uproar that he had created to be released – and no one's voice was as incredulously as the one that emitted from Avis.

"Anglo-Saxon food?" Avis said in disbelief. "He must be confused. A rock must have hit him on the head – it is the only explanation!"

Edith grinned at the other servants. They had all been watching Avis and Melville over the weeks since they had arrived, and although none of the glances that he had sent her way had been noticed by her, they had been seen by the servants. It was hilarious to see the two of them try to avoid the ever deepening tension developing between them.

"It appears he wishes to sample our food," stated Bronson, beginning to shout orders to the servants.

Edith grinned slyly at her mistress.

"Or, he is trying to please a certain someone."

Avis coloured at the suggestion. This change in diet could not be on her behalf, surely. Melville was not that thoughtful. But she remembered the delicate kiss he had pressed into her palm, and his understated passionate speech under the oak tree. She could feel his arms encircling her as he comforted her, and could imagine the heat from those arms if –

Quashing such thoughts, Avis began to help the preparation of the new menu. She had no time, and no business thinking such thoughts, she chastised herself. No business at all.

At dinner that night Melville's hand hovered undecided between several dishes and platters that he did not recognise. He was already beginning to regret his hasty desire to please Avis. Glancing at his wife, he saw her plateful of the food that looked so distasteful to his eyes. Foreign food. He scrunched his nose in disgust, but then reminded himself that to many, he was the foreigner.

Picking three foods at random, he piled them on his plate and forced himself to try each one of them. His childhood had taught him to never leave good food untasted – a habit which he had struggled and failed to shake off. He gathered some of the stew on his bread, and together with some chicken covered in an unknown glaze, he filled his mouth.

Unknown textures and flavours burst across his palate, and he was shocked to discover great enjoyment. Melville took another mouthful, suspicious that the first bite had been a fluke. It was delicious.

Melville turned to Avis.

"This is incredible!" His face was so openly filled with pleasure that Avis allowed herself to smile in response.

"I am glad my lord approves."

"Approves? To what end do your people hide such delicacies?"

Melville had meant the statement to be a compliment to her heritage, but Avis turned away.

"You Normans did not cross the water for our recipes," she muttered.

Melville bit his lip angrily. It seemed that he, a Norman, would never have the skill and finesse to treat Avis as she required – as she deserved.

Avis chewed on her favourite foods determinedly, refusing to allow Melville's harsh comments to infringe on her enjoyment. She had missed honest Anglo-Saxon food for the last three years, and she was not going to talk to Melville if he was only ready to mock her.

Melville racked his brains to find something that he could say to raise Avis' humour. He would do or say anything to see her smile, but he felt immensely stupid sitting beside her as she gracefully reached out to pour herself another glass of wine. Remembering their bitter and distant first meeting, it seemed ridiculous to him that within the space of a handful of weeks, he was now trying all he could to please this woman.

"What has occupied you today?" he ventured, hoping to encourage her to speak – but he could not have chosen a worse topic.

Avis froze, panicking that he had discovered her secret past time. She would not give up her hours in the kitchen for anything. It was the one place where she felt at home. She did not answer, and Melville grew angry.

"Will you not speak to me?" He barked.

"I will speak when I choose!" Avis returned. "I am not your servant, to be ordered when to speak and where to go!"

Suddenly Melville threw back against the table, throwing all a-top it onto the floor. Platters clanged as food splattered against the rushes, sinking into them.

"Can I do nothing that pleases you?" he thundered, eyes flashing. "Can you never be satisfied?"

Avis had jumped up to prevent herself from being covered in a particularly gorgeous sauce that had fallen forward. She took steps backwards as she attempted to dodge the food scattered floor.

"You forget yourself my lord!" she hissed, eyes glancing at the men and servants lining the hall, all who had jumped at the loud clamour. "Attempt to keep your anger to yourself!"

"Just as you keep your life to yourself!"

"It is my life!" Avis smiled angrily. "Or so I was told underneath a certain tree. But I suppose I was wrong to have thought that such pleasing words could be trusted."

In three short strides Melville had closed the distance between them. He stood as close as he dared to the trembling Avis, who rocked unwillingly towards him. She felt dizzy. His musky presence confused Avis, causing her to forget they were in a crowded hall. Unsure but summoning his bravery, Melville drew her closer slowly by encircling her waist with one hand. Her bodice brushed his chest, and fire burst into his veins. Avis refused to raise her face, but a hand reached to lift her chin. Melville.

"What can I do?" he whispered softly. "What can I do to please you?"

Avis could not reply, unable to speak. Her anger dissipated as quickly as it had risen, but the emotion that remained was unknown.

"Command me," Melville spoke slowly and quietly, so that only Avis could hear him. Avis could feel his heart beat against her breast, and the hand placed in the small of her back felt comforting – it felt natural. There were many things that she could command, Avis thought wildly. He was at her mercy.

Melville was at her mercy. Avis gazed into his dark fervent eyes and realised that her husband was completely in her power. This was not lust, but something softer that drenched her from his eyes. Avis knew that she could not be so heartless as to manipulate him when he was making himself so vulnerable to her.

It was difficult, but she broke free from Melville's tight embrace.

"I'm sorry," Avis looked into his startled face, and felt terrible for the words she was speaking – but knew that she was speaking the truth. "Do not ask me."

Avis began to walk away, but Melville took her hand and pulled her back.

"Command me." He groaned.

Avis pulled her hand away, terrified at the rush of emotions that spread from his red-hot touch.

"Do not tempt me." Her voice was hoarse, startling her, and she ran from the room.

Uncomfortable chatter had filled the hall whilst Melville and Avis had been speaking, and so Melville stood alone in an embarrassing silence. Her rejection had been clear – but he had seen the desire in her face. Melville smiled wryly. Progress of some sort, at least.

Avis had retired to a small room which preceded her private chamber. It was intended as a place for her to receive important guests and visitors, but there had been no need for that during her marriage, and she used it more as a place to sit and think. A large fire warmed her shaking hands, and she sunk gratefully into a large chair, snuggling into the furs that draped over her back. She shivered, despite the heat of the room.

"I cannot explain him!" she muttered to herself.

And this was the problem. Avis had been quick of thought since her childhood, and there had been no person that she had been unable to understand – even if she disliked them. Avis had been very ready to dislike Melville when she had married him, and indeed his haughty, superior manner had aided her in this feeling. But here, and more frequently now, were glimpses of a different Melville. Avis brought her feet underneath her, curling herself up into a ball. This different Melville was a confusing, vulnerable and yet strong man – a man unlike any she had ever known.

Avis sat by the fire, and began to doze. She was so unaware of her surroundings that she did not notice a solitary figure leaning against the door frame.

Melville stood there, contemplating this tantalizing woman that was his wife. She had wrapped herself in the furs like a small child, and a smile danced across her features as she slept by the fire.

Melville walked silently into the room, and settled in the chair opposite her. He studied her, marvelling at the gracefulness of her features: her clear expressive face, soft skin, and the reams of golden hair that had escaped its veil. Melville longed to know more of her – to see more of her. But as Avis slumbered, he allowed her to rest. Their lives had become so angry and on edge, he mused, she must need the sleep and relaxation.

Avis was dreaming. She could see Melville rushing towards her across the bridge, and she was completely unable to move. She tried to open her mouth to speak, but before a word had been uttered, the dream-Melville placed his closed lips powerfully onto hers. Tight arms drew her to him, and she initially struggled against the intoxication of it all.

But the dream-Melville was so careful with her, allowing her to keep her lips closed as he tenderly massaged life and vigour into her mouth. Avis could not help but respond, clutching at his linen shirt, unable to feel her legs, weightless in the experience of his kiss.

Avis could smell that elusive fragrance that announced Melville's presence, and in her sleep she moved – and realised that the tight clasp of her dream was no fantasy. She could feel strong arms underneath her knees and neck, carrying her. With a great effort, she forced her eyelids open, to discover that she was nestled into Melville's neck as he lifted her. Not the dream-Melville with whom she had been sharing such an intense experience, but the real Melville. Her physical husband, a very definitely tangible man.

"Melville?" Avis said drowsily.

"Hush," he replied softly. "Sleep. You are safe."

The veracity of his words lulled her back to sleep, revelling in the safety of his strong and sturdy body. Melville cautiously placed her gently onto her bed.

Asleep again, she reached up for his comforting touch, murmuring, "Melville?"

He gritted his teeth. Avis was so unaware of herself, even of the chaste but powerful kiss that he had devotedly placed on her inviting lips, that he knew he could remain in her room. Spend the night. Share her bed. But it was not a choice that Avis had consciously made, and Melville bristled at the idea of taking advantage of any woman – especially Avis.

Silently he left the room, calling a servant to fill the copper bath in his chamber with ice cold water. He was going to need it.

CHAPTER EIGHTEEN

When Avis woke up, she at first could not recall how she had travelled from the chair in the outer chamber to her bed. Blurred images and sounds crowded her mind, and she tried to organise them into a coherent order. She had sat by the fire – had slumbered in the balmy air. She had fallen asleep. She had dreamt…

Avis sat bolt upright, horrified as partial memories flooded into her consciousness. The intimacy in which Melville had lifted her, had carried her! The care and concern in his words! Avis' lips seared as she recalled the kiss, which she hoped beyond hope had been part of her strange yet intoxicating dream.

Shaking away the remnants of such thoughts, Avis arose and dressed quickly. She hoped to go down and speak to the villagers before she broke her fast. There were concerns amongst the peasant Anglo-Saxons that Melville's agricultural decision about the fallow land would ruin next year's harvest, and she prayed that she would be able to bring the two opposing views together without much discord – and before planting began.

Although she reached the village of Ulleskelf before the sun had arisen, the situation was more complex than Avis had previously thought, and it was near midday when she finally reached the familiar hall of the manor. Bronson would be disappointed that she had missed one of his sumptuous breakfasts, but she had been given a wonderful meal by the baker and his family.

But when Avis arrived in the entrance hall, she was surprised to see no Melville. He did not appear throughout the afternoon, and she began to half hope that he would appear without warning – but when she ventured down to the kitchen as the lazy sun was setting, Bronson informed her that Melville had ridden off to York early that morning on a judicial matter. Powerless to decipher her own confused feelings, Avis settled into the soothing routine of bread making.

Relaxed chatter surrounded her, and Avis poured out her intense unknown emotion as she kneaded the dough. The servants gave her a wide berth; it was always obvious when Avis wanted to be left alone. A sudden end to the noise was ignored as Avis focussed on creating the traditional Anglo-Saxon loaf – but a gasp and the sound of a bowl breaking caused her to turn around, ready to scold the clumsy servant.

Melville was standing by the kitchen door, mouth open, staring at Avis in blatant and terrible disgust. Servants backed away from his threatening powerful authority, and Bronson rushed forward, hoping to distract his master from the flour streak in Avis' uncovered hair.

"My lord, my lord…" Bronson's voice trailed away, his knowledge of the Norman language almost exhausted.

Melville stepped forward and effortlessly pushed Bronson out of his path. When he spoke, it was a deep but bitter voice that the servants heard, but could not understand.

"Leave us."

No one moved. Melville repeated the words in a shout.

"Leave us!"

No translation was needed. The kitchen emptied, leaving Avis to face Melville alone and unprotected. But she needed no protection. Just as they had in their last confrontation, her fists clenched unconsciously as she prepared herself for the fight.

"You." Melville made no attempt to say anything else, his piercing gaze reaching down into Avis' soul itself.

"Me." Avis' reply was quiet, but strong. She would not allow herself to be bullied – and after all, she reasoned, shuffling her feet from side to side as if preparing for battle, she knew that she was not in the wrong.

"You – here!" Melville shot out. "What did you think you were doing?"

"Cooking. Baking today, actually." Avis said coolly.

Melville barked out a sad laugh.

"Cooking? You don't know how to cook."

Avis' cheeks burned, and she moved to face Melville, keeping the wooden trestle worktop between them as a shield.

"Don't know how? Don't know how to cook? Who do you think has been baking your bread every morning? Who was it that organised your wedding feast? Who ordered the betrothal menu? Who taught the servants in her own home – a home stolen from her?"

Melville's face drew back in horror.

"It was I! I am not as talentless as you would assume, my lord!"

Avis' hair had been flung back in her anger, and despite Melville's wish to tangle his long fingers in her tresses, he tried to think. Avis – a cook? Where he came from, it was a servant's role. A derogatory role. The role of a slave.

"You lower yourself in this manner?" Melville confronted her, walking around the table to stand beside her. Avis backed away from him, moving towards the spit which had been left untended by Felix and Ælfthrup.

"I see no such lowering of my status because I have more knowledge!" she cried. "Beside the fact that I love it, is it not my place? It is my duty as a woman, as your wife to make your house – ”

"Do you know nothing?" Melville shouted, following Avis as she backed away from him. "Can you not comprehend that to work with your hands is to immediately align yourself away from your noble blood?"

"What you mean is, to ally myself with the servants!" challenged Avis.

Melville's frustration grew. "Yes!"

"I am them!" declared Avis angrily. "What difference is there between them and I save wealth?"

Melville had no answer, and instead increased his pace, forcing Avis to increase her pace. She was now running backwards to avoid him. She hit her wrist on the hot metal spit, bringing it to her tongue to sooth the dreadful pain. Avis began to run around the side of the kitchen in panic, the agony of her arm and the shouting of Melville combining to create a haze in her mind.

"Run not from me!" thundered Melville.

He followed her across the room and caught up with her quickly. With his broad shoulders and strong hands he pinned her against the wall, and although Avis struggled he was careful not to hurt her. Her eyes darted around the room, looking for a way to escape him, but the weight of his body prevented her from moving.

A small whimper – partly from the pain in her wrist, partly in her vexation at being prevented from escaping the argument with Melville – was uttered by Avis. Both of them panted slightly at the effort, one of trapping and the other of being entrapped. Melville gazed at Avis, and at the radiance that illuminated her beauty when passion fuelled her, even when it was passionate anger against him.

A hand rose to slap him, but he captured it and brought it close to him as Avis struggled to strike him. He dipped his face down to her, but only to whisper quietly into her left ear.

"I am your husband, and with no father to keep you in order that task sadly falls to me!"

Melville felt Avis' face drop also, and turned his to the right to meet hers in the kiss that he was sure would follow. But he tasted salty water. Straightening up, he saw that his brave Avis had finally succumbed to tears.

The mention of her father from that callous mouth had almost stopped Avis' heart from beating. The show of weakness that she considered her tears to be were not checked as she gave in to the weariness and fatigue that had been her constant companion since her unwanted marriage.

Avis spoke softly, and it was difficult for Melville to catch her words.

"If you had known my father," she said shakily, "you would not…you could not have spoken about him in such a way."

Melville wanted to interrupt her, to prevent her from making herself more vulnerable to him when she clearly did not want to, but no words appeared.

"My father," Avis' eyes glazed over as she remembered the most important man in her life, "*wuldorfæder…*"

Melville caught Avis as she collapsed. Frantically checking her breathing, he was relieved to see that she had merely fallen into a deep faint. He gathered her many skirts around her, and lifted the delicate and slight weight into his arms. Melville left the kitchen, and pretended not to notice the line of servants lying underneath the windows of the kitchen, hoping to catch a glimpse of what was happening inside, unable as they were to follow the rapid speech in the strange language.

Melville took the unconscious Avis to his outer chamber, the room in which he entertained. Or at least, the room in which he would have entertained if he had intimates that he could invite to the manor. In a strikingly similar way to Avis – although neither of them were aware of this – Melville had little use for such a room. His friends that had accompanied him to his sham of a wedding had departed to their own land and families, and he could not feel more isolated – but Avis had to be taken care of. In the room there was a soft chair stuffed with down that he had recently bought himself, and as he laid her gently down onto it, he chastised himself for not having it placed in Avis' quarters instead. But then, thought Melville as he covered her with a soft rug and sat by the roaring fire, there was much that he could chastise himself about tonight.

Melville sighed and shook his head. Was he ever to understand this woman, this delicate and elusive creature? It seemed that no matter what course he took, he could have no part in her life – she refused him entry at every point. But what did she think she was doing, working down in the kitchens with the servants? If any of his peers had heard of such things, their respect for him would not diminish but decease! He considered whether any of the peasants that lived in his village knew what their mistress had being doing in her leisure time. Melville remembered their mocking smiles and laughs, and kicked forcefully at the leg of the chair. Of course they knew.

The sound of the kick had roused Avis. She stirred, and upon opening her eyes, frantically looked around the unknown room until they rested on Melville. The frantic look did not leave her.

"Be calm." Melville tried to reassure her quietly. "You are in my outer chamber. Rest."

Avis tried to sit herself up, but did not seem to have the strength. The pain by her wrist was a dull stabbing ache now, and she tried to ignore it. She would not admit to the weakness. She dropped back into the luxurious seat, and fixed her eyes on her husband, glaring angrily. She had clearly not forgotten the argument in the kitchen.

"My lord, I would prefer to be in my own chamber."

Melville smiled wanly. "I have ordered food to be brought here. Once you have eaten you may of course retire to sleep." He had done no such thing, but wanted any excuse to keep her quietly. He was desperate to talk to her.

Avis glared at him. He seemed to control her in a way that she did not like, and did not understand. He continued his smile, but it wavered as he spoke. As he spoke words that he was sure he would regret.

"Avis. Tell me about your father."

Avis desperately did not want to cry again, but she could feel the heat of tears behind her eyes. She dug her nails into her palms as she spoke.

"My father was a very good man."

Melville said nothing, and she felt obliged to fill the silence.

"He was the *ealdorman* of our area. Similar to your *dux*," she explained to a confused Melville. "He was the overlord of many noblemen, and all who knew him cared for him and respected him. My father was of mild manner, and gentle spirit."

She smiled, unwillingly, at the memory of her caring father.

"Where is he now?" Melville asked, hoping that the answer that he foresaw was the not the right one. But how could it be anything else? He had heard no word of him, seen nothing of him. Surely, if it had been possible, he would have come to his daughter's betrothal, her wedding. But Avis' words affirmed his fears.

"Father died." Avis knew that she had not been the only daughter orphaned that day, but the pain did not lessen with that knowledge. "He had fought as a young man and his debt to the King – our new King, Harold – had been paid. But then…"

Her soothing voice trailed off, and Melville swallowed.

"The Normans."

"You Normans," Avis agreed, bitterly. "We always knew that you were going to come, you know." She finally looked up at Melville. "But the war-season was over."

Melville knew what she meant, although the way Avis spoke of it was strange to him. Wars and battles in most places were only fought at certain times of the year, according to the seasons. No sane man would fight after September had arrived, for the harvest had to be brought in and the winter prepared for. The Anglo-Saxons had prepared for the invasion, and waited for the Normans to come all of the summer, but had then begun to return home at the beginning of autumn. Only then had the Normans finally invaded.

Avis was speaking again.

"Father was one of the last to remain. He wanted to be sure, and so was closest when you Normans landed on our shores."

Melville remembered that landing well. Onto a beach of a foreign land, with unfamiliar smells and a coastline he did not know. Panic filled him as he paced with the other men, waiting for the glory of battle or the emptiness of death.

"I am told that he died well," Avis drew her lips together, forcing her face into a frown. "We never received his body, but I am sure that he received a Christian burial. But he died in battle, as a man defending his people. Honour and glory is everything to my people, and when we received the news of his death, my mother was comforted. For a time."

Melville was listening, but another part of him was also on the battlefield. He could remember the cut and thrust of battle. Jump to the left – parry. The sense of a blade, just out of sight. Turn and stab and duck an arrow. And run, run, run for your life. The exhilaration had been mingled with fear and sweat, but now he wondered with a sickening thought whether he had been the man to destroy the bond between an unknown man and this beautiful woman. The realisation that every man he had killed that day probably had mother, father, wife, child hit him with a force that caused him to jolt in his chair.

"Melville?" Avis had noticed the yellow pallor of his skin.

"Continue," Melville managed to say, wading through his memories to the present.

Avis nodded.

"Father's death left my family isolated and unprotected, but as we waited for the men of our village to return…" her voice trailed off. "No one came back. Suddenly every child had lost its father. Every wife was a widow. Sons and brothers that you had thought you had valued when alive became priceless and unreachable now that they had been taken from you. Arguments that had been left were bitterly wailed, and discussions not finished were never mentioned again."

Melville looked at Avis, and cursed himself silently. How could he be so unfeeling. She had known real pain and real loss, and here he was, lecturing her about cooking! But she had more to say, and now she had started to speak, she found that she could not stop.

"We had thought that you Normans would be happy with the spoils of war!" Avis laughed drily. "The claims of William for the throne had never been taken seriously by my father, and so I watched and waited for the ships to leave our land. But…"

Her eyes moved from Melville to the fire. The large, destructive fire.

"You Normans came to the village. To my village." Avis whispered as her eyes drank in the sight of the flames, but saw other fiercer flames. "Every home was burned. Every child over the age of five, slaughtered. Blood pooled in houses and covered the grass. And the young women were all taken – they were taken and they were…"

Avis stared at the fire, unable to blink. Melville knew with revulsion what the Normans had done to those innocent Anglo-Saxon girls. He had heard talks of such occurrences, and had been disgusted then – but to hear it from an onlooker…it was more than he could bear.

"You weren't – " Melville spoke hoarsely. "They didn't – "

"No." Avis answered without looking around at him and without blinking. "I had been in the village but had run with the others. I was one of the eldest. I had run the fastest. I and a few children had climbed a tree unseen, but we had to wait up there for hours. I was there for hours and hours."

The smell of burning filled her lungs as she recalled the devastation that had swept through everything she had known.

"The church was burnt. And the fields, full of life, that should have been harvested by those that now nourished far off fields. Everything that I knew and loved was gone. The altar in our village was destroyed, and I cannot tell even to this day whether the women wept more for the death of our church than the death of their children."

Melville was horrified, but he could see that Avis had never spoken of such things before. Fain would he prevent her from speaking what must be purged from her heart.

"And then," Avis spoke so pragmatically that it tore at Melville's soul. "They went to my home. And they killed my brother, and dragged my mother out into the remains of the village. I could see her. They were right underneath my tree. They tied her atop a horse, and they rode off with her."

Avis breathed out a great sigh. "And then the King arrived. William the Bastard, he was then, on account of his illegitimacy. He looked at me, and I felt hatred like I had never experienced before. I did not believe that such hatred was possible against one man, but I surprised myself. I loathed him. He had begun a *cyninggeníðla* – a great feud. He had wronged my people, and I swore that I would have my revenge. He looked at me, and he laughed, and he rode away with my mother amongst his men. And one day I will have my revenge."

Avis spoke herself into silence.

Melville finally understood why to be married to him was to curse her. Why, she had vowed to punish King William, but instead she was forced by him to marry one of the people that had destroyed her life. To be allied in marriage to one of the men that had caused her such pain – that had caused her entire country such pain – must be a daily burden that she must bear alone.

"By then Richard had been given my father's land and home," Avis was forcing herself to keep speaking, knowing that if she stopped she would cry again. She never wanted to revisit this part of her life again, and so she had to tell the complete story now. "I could see that he was meant to be my husband. The King had sent him to take my father's land so that he could breed heirs with me. He said so, many times. But I refused. I had to learn Norman quickly, but every word was bitter wrath on my tongue. And I was alone, so alone. My father dead, my brother killed, none of my friends had survived the attack on our village. And my mother. My mother…"

Avis finally turned her eyes onto Melville. "I never saw her again."

CHAPTER NINETEEN

Melville swallowed. He knew exactly what would have happened to Avis' mother – to many of the widows of Anglo-Saxon noblemen after the invasion. But how to tell Avis, who was only just hanging on to her self-control?

"I cannot say for certain," he began, in a quiet voice. "But I know that many Anglo-Saxon women were taken back to Normandy."

Avis' eyes widened. "Normandy?"

"Yes."

Avis sighed. "At least the chances of her being dead are lower. I could not imagine…I was not sure what could have happened to her."

Melville was glad to see her wipe away some of her tears, but he wished that the rest of the information that he could give was happier news.

"My understanding is that they will be by now the wives of many Norman lords."

Avis trembled, and she finally released the nails that were drawing blood from her pale hands.

"Like mother, like daughter."

In a swift movement, Melville rose and knelt on the cold floor by Avis.

"If I could have done anything to prevent it – if I had known!"

He gabbled nervously. Avis smiled wryly.

"I do not believe you to be a dishonest man, Melville," she said gently. "Do not remove that belief from me by claiming intentions that you could not have kept."

Melville fell into silence. He knew that Avis was right – there would have been no way in which to prevent these events, and he could still not promise himself that he would have made a different decision. Acts of war such as those were expected, and it would not have been in his power to disobey his King.

"I have never defied my lord before." Melville admitted with a sad smile, looking full into Avis' face. "I was raised to believe that any man put above me was put there by God, and to disobey him would bring disrepute upon my household."

Avis smiled. "I too. But then, these matters are easier for us to say, being the ones above the people in question. There are but a few that we must obey."

Melville stood up, and lightly lifted Avis' legs up so that he could sit on the seat with her, with her legs resting over his lap.

"You have a great lineage." He stated, looking at Avis. She had been shocked at his moving so close to her, and could feel the muscles of his thighs tense as she spoke.

"Indeed. A long, noble, and honourable one. But I am the last."

Melville took one of her hot and bleeding hands into his. He examined it, and saw that it was the wrist that she had burnt in the kitchen. It was beginning to blister now, and Avis winced as he skilfully put slight amounts of pressure on the flesh around it, to check for poison in the blood.

"Perhaps not the last."

Avis tried to pull her hand away from him, but he gently restrained her, and she quickly gave in, too exhausted to fight him.

"Perhaps." She said, sadly, but ignoring the pointed reference that he made to the possibility of their children. "I have not received word from my cousin since the Normans came here, but I live in the hope that he escaped to Ireland. Perhaps he has married and had children that will continue the nobility of my family."

Melville looked deep into her eyes. "You take much pride in your family."

Avis smiled. "I am at the bottom of a long line of proud people."

"And I am the first." Melville said bluntly.

Avis was puzzled by this peculiar pronouncement.

"My lord?"

Melville wrenched his gaze from her injury, and looked shamefully into her open face.

"I am not of noble blood, Avis."

She pulled her hand from his.

"Another lie?" she said erratically. "Another pretence?"

The distrust in her tones tore Melville apart. All he wanted to be was open with her, to be honest. And now was the time to finally be truthful.

CHAPTER TWENTY

"You have given me such honour," Melville said, "in speaking of your life to me. I wish to share part of my personal history with you."

Avis glanced again at the fire, avoiding his intense gaze. She could never be sure of Melville's intentions, but he had seemed truly shocked to discover how the Norman invasion had been perceived and felt by the Anglo-Saxon inhabitants. Despite her tiredness, she knew that she owed it to him to hear what he wanted to say. Even if it caused her more pain, which it undoubtedly would.

She could not understand how he could offer her an explanation for what had happened – it would be offensive to try and pretend that the pain that she and countless others had experienced could be explained away. But he had listened to her. She would not be so discourteous. And part of her was indeed most curious to know more about this brooding and usually so silent husband of hers.

She smiled at Melville through her tiredness.

"It would be my honour, my lord." She replied formally, and then added, "if you don't mind."

Melville returned her smile. He drew in a long breath, preparing for the difficult conversation he knew that he was entering into. Whatever her reaction, at least he was finally being honest with her.

"With your skill at languages, you have probably ascertained the meaning of my name." He began.

"Bad town."

"Indeed. In fact, it was a name given to me by my father – a man I cannot exactly remember. He…he was a…he seduced my mother and then abandoned her. She was a lowly peasant near Calais."

Avis almost drew her legs away from him, but desperately prevented the instinctive movement. This she had not expected. The idea that this man was of peasant origin, and an illegitimate son astounded her. To think that her noble line was now irrevocably linked with his! But then she recalled her most recent and most passionate statements. Her nose unconsciously scrunched as she tried to think quickly. She could not disapprove of Melville due to his blood and then challenge his assumptions of the Anglo-Saxon peasants in their village.

Melville continued.

"Every word is difficult for me to say," he said awkwardly. "I have never spoken to anyone about this – indeed, I had promised myself that I would never recount such painful things. Even those who became like brothers to me on the battlefield do not know about my troublesome past."

About his past, and sad and lonely childhood. Melville tried once more to explain to this noblewoman just what it was like to live as he did.

"To be illegitimate to the Normans was to be born half-dead."

"I know," whispered Avis. "At least, I understand. It is the same with my people."

"Then you comprehend," replied Melville. "You know then, the sort of life that I have lived – that all people of my birth will live."

He fell into silence, and Avis did not know what to do. There was no point in trying to comfort him – what could she say? She could not alter the circumstances of his birth. She wanted to reach out a consoling hand, but did not know how, and after a moment he continued speaking.

"I was raised in what I know you would call poverty, and I must admit I still retain the traits of one used to daily hunger. Lack of food was not unusual, it was the norm. The town that was closest to my village was one not unlike some I have seen here, but my home village is completely different to the village here. It was set upon a mountain side, with tall pines lining the way and each house a different shade due to the oils we used to paint them. Ours was a deep red, a burnt red that glinted in the autumn sun."

He smiled down at Avis, and she returned his smile. It was evidently helping Melville speak about his childhood, despite the effort that he was undergoing to tell it. Avis could not help but be intrigued. Melville continued speaking, his voice low and soft, and Avis was once more calmed by his tones.

"The birds are not of your kind, and the songs I think are sweeter. The air there is clearer, and the rain that falls is cleaner and grows the land faster than in this soggy country. The traders that came on the second Sunday of each month brought news of the outside world, a world which I could not imagine, having never travelled more than a day from my place of birth. And – "

Melville turned to see Avis' eyelids drooping, and chuckled.

"I weary you. Forgive me."

Avis forced her eyes open, and returned his laugh.

"My apologies, my lord. Your story is most interesting, truly. Tell me: what did the traders sell to you?"

Pleased to see that Avis had indeed been listening to his words, Melville continued. He painted her a bright and yet menacing picture of his childhood and early youth, full of misadventure and cruelty – but also of freedom and laughter with his mother, who he evidently cared for a great deal. Avis tried to picture a younger Melville, to see him as a young child, but was surprised to find that her imagination offered her a smaller version Melville with a shock of golden curly hair – just like her own. She shook her head as to push the disturbingly attractive image out of her mind, and paid closer attention to what Melville was saying.

"Being of my low and relatively unknown birth, I was restricted from many ways of earning food and shelter." Melville had not noticed the momentary lapse in Avis' attention. "There were certain social rules about what one could and could not do – and for me, it was more what I could not do. It was difficult to support my mother on the small amount that I could earn. And when this man William arrived, whose enemies called him the Bastard just as I was called every day, declaring that he was travelling to a land of riches and that all may join him…"

He trailed off, realising how offensive his words may appear. This land that he talked of, this wealthy land of riches, was her home – and the riches taken were stolen from the innocent. But Avis' eyes had not left his, and there was no resentment in her face, simply openness and a willingness to listen. His gratitude to her was strong, and he shuffled his legs closer towards her, so that he could feel the slight weight of her legs on his.

He had been this close to many people before, but never before this moment had he felt so vulnerable, and yet at the same time so safe. Melville slowly pushed a strand of hair behind his ear, and was surprised to find that his hand was shaking. It was difficult, being so open with another person. He had always considered it weak, a weakness that was not permissible for a man of battle. But Avis drew him out of himself in a way that no other person ever had. He felt safe with her.

"My mother did not want me to leave her." Melville said sadly. "I am her only child, and I had often to protect her from the slander and gossip of our town. Defending and guarding her had been the one constant in my life, aside poverty, and it was darkness in my soul and bitterness in my heart to abandon her."

Avis' heart softened, despite herself. He too understood the love that dwelt between a mother and her child. This explained his almost violent protection of herself and her status – being so accustomed to doing so for his mother, the other most important woman in his life. As unwelcome as it had been, she now understood it for what it was: his masculine desire to protect those that could not protect themselves.

Melville confessed, "I wanted to earn my fortune in the invasion – "

Avis could not help her retort.

"A fortune from my people!"

The words sang out in the air, cutting through the atmosphere of calm and creating jagged edges in the silence. Avis looked away, mortified that she had been so rude – and when Melville had been so polite to her when she had bared her past to him. She looked over to him, and saw sadness in his eyes.

"I am sorry," she said quietly. "Please continue."

Melville took her hand, and squeezed it.

"I wanted to be able to return to her, and make sure that she would be cared for, just as she deserved." A strong anger coloured his face as he said, almost in a shout, "but no! My King has forbidden me from returning to Normandy. He says that my place is here now, where my land is."

Avis said nothing for moment, and then lifted herself up from languishing in the comfort of the seat. She drew herself close to Melville, and leaned on him between his neck and shoulder, and spoke in a voice which was timid.

"A love of the land is something that you Normans and we Anglo-Saxons share then."

Melville dared not move, lest he shake Avis from him. He could never have hoped that being so brutally honest with his wife would have drawn her so close to him – but here she was, slowly falling asleep resting against him.

He had expected anger, and shouting, even in her tired state. But instead she had accepted his words. He could not believe that Avis, in her gentleness and power, had not risen against him, now that she knew what he was, who he was. Melville drew his arm around her, bringing her weight entirely on himself, but she was so light that it barely registered. Avis placed a fluttering hand on his stomach, and it lurched. Hers was a touch like none other: a source of warmth and comfort, but also of a heat which he now recognised as one only stimulated by her touch.

"Do you still desire to return home?" Avis asked, awkwardly. She was unsure what answer she wanted him to give, but she must know.

Melville hesitated. When he did speak, each word was carefully considered and given much weight.

"I am a Norman." He said wearily. "Normandy was where I was born, it was where I first drew breath. I learnt to walk on its soil, and its grain nourished me. I trust that my mother still lives, and that she calls Normandy home. In these ways, it will always have a pull on my heart."

Melville hesitated once more.

"But my heart is learning about this old country, and although it is not the same, its differences are certainly…alluring."

Avis smiled slowly at him. She did not really understand what he was trying to tell her, but she trusted him. She knew that it was a kind message, and a message meant definitely for her, and she was grateful to him.

But panic started to rise from her stomach. Trusting a Norman! By their very nature they were untrustworthy. They could not be entrusted with anything, let alone one's safety, one's memories, one's heart. But as she looked at Melville, gazing into the fire with the light of sparks leaping across his masculine features, she was reassured. The feeling of nausea lessened, and she could once again breathe easy. Melville was not like that. This man could indeed be relied upon.

Melville hummed under his breath. It was the same song that she had heard him singing during what felt like a different life – that day by the river bed where she had demanded that he kept his promise to her. It was the best medicine and comfort that he was able to give Avis.
She stirred, exhausted but still trying to listen to him.

"What's that?" she murmured.

"It is a song that I love," Melville replied softly. "It is a song that my mother sung to me when I had returned home, clothes torn from another beating and mud clotting in my scruffy hair. She sang it to me every day that I returned home with blood pouring from a new wound, and every night that I cried myself to sleep. It soothed and relaxed me then, and I hope it gives you rest now."

"It is beautiful," Avis breathed. "What is it about?"

"It speaks of a young man, tired of the world and unable to escape it. He decides to leave home to seek his fortune, and climbs a high mountain up into the clouds. But then an enchanter appears, and grants him the ability to alter the emotions of the people around him…"

As Melville spoke, Avis gave up in the attempt to force down the sense of safety. She could not run from Melville, and she found that now she did not want to. As much as she hated to admit it, he was not the man that she had thought he was. Avis was ashamed about the assumptions that she had made about him, about all Normans. In fact, her willingness to coat all Normans with the same tar only made her as bad as she assumed they were. How could she state that she despised all Normans when she had such a limited experience of them? In her mind she compared the three Norman men that she knew the most: Richard, Hugh le Blanc and Melville. Avis knew that if she were honest with herself, she would have to accept that the majority of Norman men she knew were indeed honourable men. Despite her sleepiness, she knew that she had been wrong.

Speaking that truth yesterday would have been death to her, but now…things were different. Something had changed. Something between Melville and herself had changed. By making herself vulnerable to Melville, and in turn hearing so much of his own life, she felt as if there had been a bond created between them that was not of their own making. One that could not easily be broken or ignored. Relaxing in Melville's presence for the very first time since they had met, Avis fell asleep.

Melville felt the tension in Avis' body leave her, and looking down, saw that she was asleep. He smiled down at her: a smile that spoke of care and affection, and a deep rooted desire to prevent any harm from coming to her. If she had seen it, Avis would have been under no illusions as to how her husband truly felt about her.

Melville looked at the fire, which had been dying away for many minutes. He calculated that, looking at the way the fire had almost gone out completely, they had been speaking for hours. He felt intensely happy. A rush of emotion filled him, soaring through his mind and reaching the very ends of his toes.

Melville looked down at his emotionally exhausted wife. His feelings about Avis had been incredibly confusing for longer than he cared to admit. With every meeting, every conversation, every day that had gone past, he learned something new, something amazing, something about her that he revelled in and completely enjoyed. Every confusing part of her personality and character was starting to fit together in a way that he had never expected, to produce this beautiful and darling creature that now lay in his arms.

He stared at her. At her physical beauty, radiating from every inch of her, and at her soul, which poured out light the more he spoke to her. He felt as if he had been walking along the cliff top of emotions for a while now, but this was the time. Time that he faced up to his true emotions. Melville didn't just fall in love with Avis. He jumped.

CHAPTER TWENTY ONE

The muffled sounds of footsteps and the lighting of a fire were the noises and lights that awoke Melville and Avis the next morning. They had fallen asleep together sitting on the seat, and were slightly embarrassed to find their hands clasped and entwined. Melville immediately rose.

"Forgive me," he said awkwardly. "I shall leave you to ready yourself for this new day."

He rushed out of the room before Avis had time to collect her thoughts, but she was sorry to see him go. She had not slept so well for days, and she had a strange feeling that his body had given her better rest than any bed she had known.

Standing, she stretched herself like a cat that had spent too much time in the sun, and made her way into her chamber. Her hand still hurt, but the pain had dulled, and the skin was already healing. Changing into her most beautiful blood red dress, Avis bathed her face in the cold water that had been brought in by the embarrassed manservant whose feet had woken the couple.

Moving downstairs to break her fast, Avis was surprised but pleased to see Melville had not left immediately as was his normal custom, but was waiting for her before he started eating. Other men in the hall had not the same courtesy, but she breezed past them without care, eyes fixed on the man at the head of the table. Avis inclined her stately head towards him, and Melville answered her with a broad smile that she laughingly returned.

Evidently the events of yesterday, and the deeply personal conversation that had gone on long into the night had changed something between them, mused Avis. Whereas before there had been nothing but resentment and cold treatment, now there was a bond between them. They, and only they knew the truth about each other's pasts – and that truth gave them something that they had not had before. Trust.

Seating herself beside him, he spoke as he piled his plate with food.

"What are your plans for today, Avis?"

Avis was only recently becoming accustomed to the use of her name by her husband, but she still did not have the courage to return the familiar gesture. Despite the openness that they had experienced the night before, she could pretend that there was something still incredibly unknown about him. Until that was removed, she could not act completely openly without fear.

"I have no certain plans, my lord."

Melville clapped his hands loudly, and a servant immediately approached.

"My lord?"

"Ready two horses, and a pack of food." Melville commanded.

The servant bowed.

"Yes, my lord."

He scurried out of the room, and Avis looked enquiring at her husband.

"Are you going somewhere?"

Melville took a large mouthful of bread, and nodded. When he had swallowed, he spoke.

"We are indeed."

Avis was startled, and lowered the handful of grapes that she had been lifting to her mouth. One fell from her palm, and rolled across the table to rest by a jug of warm ale.

"We are?"

Melville reached out a hand to place upon hers, and gently squeezed it.

"We are. Now eat! You will need your strength."

Avis shook her head, half in bewilderment and half in laughter. Who could have predicted this? Certainly not her. It was not Melville's inclination to include her in any of his activities – at least it had never been so before. Whatever it was, it was a welcome change from their stand-off under the tree or their tempestuous fight in the kitchen.

Fast broken, Avis and Melville walked to the stables – close enough for their sleeves to brush, but not close enough for either of their liking. A striking black horse was waiting, and Melville looked over at Avis, smiling.

"Do you like her?"

Avis paused, unable to comprehend his meaning.

"Is…she mine?"

Melville's smile widened, his pleasure heightened by her joy.

"Only if you are pleased with her."

Avis walked forward, timidly. The black horse was larger than she had ever ridden before, but it seemed gentle, allowing her to stroke its magnificent neck without jolting away from her in fear. Avis breathed out a sigh of contentment. Losing her horse after the invasion had meant the restriction of her freedom, a loss that had never been replaced. Richard had allowed her the use of his horses, but she had always been made to feel like an intruder. She had travelled away from her home fewer and fewer times, until eventually she rarely ventured far from the gardens and grounds. Finally, here was a way for her to reclaim her love of the landscape: by riding out into it on her new horse.

She turned around to face Melville. "She's beautiful. What is her name?"

"As yet, she is not named. I only purchased her for you two days before, and have not had time to consider it. Why don't you give her a name?"

Avis pursed her luscious lips, and walked around the mare, giving her a close examination. Melville was impressed to see that she obviously knew what she was doing. After prodding at her teeth, and checking her shoes for stones, she stroked the horse between the nose and the eyes, and smiled.

"You have a name?" Melville prompted.

Avis nodded. "Skydancer."

"Tis an unusual name." Melville had never heard a horse named in such a fashion, but Avis laughed.

"Maybe in Normandy! But we have a very different way of naming things here."

"So I am learning." Melville's smile was so complete that Avis could not help but return it. Her gratitude emanated from her elegant features.

"Thank you, Melville."

The sound of his name pouring like honey from her lips soothed a pain in Melville that he did not realise that he had. Satisfaction emanated from his face.

"I am glad," he managed. "Would you like aid in mounting her?"

Avis grinned – a wicked grin that Melville had not seen on her before. She swung round and leapt upwards, mounting the horse with an ease that Melville had seen in no other rider. He laughed aloud in surprise.

"My, you are more adept than many of the King's messengers! You have kept your talent from me!"

Avis looked down at Melville. "You have not discovered all of my talents, my lord."

And with that, she encouraged the black mare to gallop out of the stable yard, not waiting for Melville. He mounted his own horse, Storm, quickly, unwilling to let the flirtatious mood that Avis was in escape him. Two servants followed on stable horses with the food that the kitchen had carefully prepared. Melville quickly caught up with Avis, and brought his horse alongside hers.

"So what is our destination?" Avis questioned, tossing her long hair behind her as she increased the pace. Although she was still wearing her veil, she had taken to wearing a shorter version now, and it allowed the ends of her long tresses to fall down her back in natural curls.

Melville shrugged. "Where do you want to go?"

Avis brought her horse to a stop at the foot of the bridge, looking around her. Ahead of her, over the bridge, was the village that she was growing to know and love. To her left, the road to York which was dusty and uninspiring – but to her right, an unknown track that led around the edge of a dark forest, curving past it to new ground.

"What is beyond that forest?" she asked.

Melville pushed his horse forward, calling over his shoulder, "let's find out!"

Avis' sense of adventure and desire to explore was reawakened. Here truly was freedom! Pushing Skydancer into a gallop, she quickly overtook Melville who took the movement just as she intended it to be: as a challenge. Racing forward, they rode for miles, interchanging their speed but never able to converse in the rush of excitement and speed.

The cold breeze rushed past their ears and tore away Avis' veil. Winter had sunk into the air, and instead of warm wafts it brought icy gusts – but when riding as fast as they were, it was difficult to tell. It blew behind them as they laughed, Avis shaking her head to release her brilliant long hair. Billowing out from behind her, she was transformed into the image of an Old Testament angel:

beautiful beyond words but terribly powerful and not to be defied. Melville marvelled at her. She was truly captivating.

After an hour or so of intoxicating riding, they had travelled far enough along the track to see that behind the forest was another little village. Smaller than Ulleskelf, it was nevertheless formed of perhaps twenty or more dwellings, with a large church at the centre. Their two servants had not managed to keep to their frantic pace due to trying to rescue Avis' veil. Melville and Avis therefore approached the settlement alone. Small children tottered out to see them, and Avis waved. Little grins and cries of, "my lady!" echoed behind them as they passed, and Melville slowed to a placid trot. Avis matched her horse's pace to his, and they exchanged relaxed and contented looks. The enjoyment and love of riding was something that they both unknowingly shared, and their talent was equally matched.

"Now," began Melville. "Where do you want to eat?"

Avis scanned the horizon, and saw a slight hill with a strange outline at the top. It created a shadow that was unusual, but not unknown. She smiled. She recognised that shadow.

"Yonder, upon that hill. From there we shall have a wonderful view of the area." She pointed to where she meant, and Melville nodded.

After a couple more minutes of fast riding, they approached the hill. The closer they got to the summit, the more certain Avis was that the shape she had seen was what she had supposed, and when it came into clear view Melville started.

"A stone cross!"

Avis dismounted from the sweating Skydancer, and walked slowly up to it. Kneeling at its base, she dipped her fingers in the spring that she knew would be there, and crossed herself with the dripping hand. As she rose, she could see that Melville was keeping several paces back, in reverence and confusion at her actions. Avis smiled to herself. For probably the first time in their marriage, she was the one in control, certain about their situation. It was a heady, powerful feeling, and she revelled in it.

"These stone crosses were placed here by our ancestors," Avis explained. "There were many in the south also, but the Normans have destroyed them as unwanted remnants of our 'barbaric' past."

Melville looked at the stone cross. At over six foot high, it cast a long shadow across the summit of the hill. It had been carefully engraved with intricate figures and what looked like words – but not in any language that he recognised. The entire effect was heightened by the peeling paint that gave a coloured vibrancy to the grey stone. He had never seen anything so beautiful caught precisely between nature's hand and man's intent.

"It is incredible." Melville breathed.

Avis smiled, happy that he appreciated a part of her heritage. She had always been afraid of the stone crosses as a child and their majesty, but since they had been removed from her home, she had missed them terribly.

"Are there not such things in your land?"

Their conversation the night before had awakened Avis' interest in the land that had raised her husband. Her home had had such a strong impact on her, it was difficult for her to imagine the landscape of Melville's childhood.

"No, indeed." Melville returned her smile. "Such a thing is unknown to me."

Melville moved forward, and copied exactly the symbolic ritual that Avis had just completed in respect to the holy place. She marvelled at his attention to detail, and his ability to understand something so quickly. There was a reverence in his actions that she was beginning to care for. When he had finished, he turned back to Avis.

"Food?"

Avis nodded, and the two servants who had watched their master and mistress in awe immediately began laying out covers onto the ground. Although not beyond comfort, the temperature was not high, and so the servants laid out some furs for Avis and Melville to wrap themselves in as they sat down.

Once the ground had been prepared, the servants began to take out various packages of different foods. Once again Melville had acted to please her, ordering her favourite foods to be included in the picnic meal, and making sure that she had everything that she would have – or could have – desired. The scent of the food wafted in the warm autumn breeze, and Avis' mouth watered. The moment in the morning when they had broken their fast seemed a long time ago.

Settling herself down, Avis spread her gown around her, brought a large fur over her shoulders, and sighed happily. For her, there could be no greater joy than this: food, and the little sunshine that winter afforded, and the company of…she could not exactly discern her feelings for Melville at this moment, but she knew that the hatred that she had been clinging on to was irrevocably gone. She could not hate this man, any more than she could hate the sun for shining, or the wolf for hunting. What he did was from his nature.

Melville could not take his eyes from Avis. The sun glanced down on her hair, releasing a light from it that dazzled his eyes. The small space between them seemed enormous, and he dared not cross it. He was still unsure about her feelings towards him, and did not want to undo the good work that had hopefully been done the night before. His self-control, then as now, would be essential. Melville wished that he knew her thoughts about what he said – the words that had been so difficult to say but so necessary for her to know.

As they started to eat, Melville asked her more questions about the stone cross.

"From whence did they come?"

Avis could only relate to him the stories that her mother had told her.

"They say that giants once moved stones across the land for their own amusement, but after they left this world man tried to make their huge lumbering into beauty."

Melville looked up at the strange stone monument as Avis continued talking.

"They are now an expression not of power, but of devotion. Of our love for God, and His love for us. We claimed them for our own, as God claimed us to love. And just as love keeps us all together, so our love brings greater beauty to these stone crosses."

Melville turned to look at Avis as she spoke.

"Love is a powerful force," she finished. She gazed at him, delicate fingers absentmindedly curling around wisps of hair. Melville could not help but stare at her. She was so incredibly beautiful.

Avis saw a change in Melville as he looked at her intently. She dropped her eyes, unable to sit under such focus. She had never seen these sides of Melville – the carefree, spontaneous Melville, or the fascinated and intrigued Melville.

She looked away, and glanced at the people below. As she watched the children of the village at the base of the hill play in the sunlight, she shook her head gently. She should not have been so quick to judge him. No man is so simple as to be totally understood within a couple of months, and a couple of months at the most were all that they had had together. Avis knew that just as he had presumed to know her based on the stories and gossip told to him, she had assumed that she knew all about him from the fearful tales that she had heard. And they had both been wrong.

Turning to look around, she laughingly saw that Melville had kicked off his boots and was lying on his back, eyes closed, glorifying in the sun's warmth that would soon be gone until the spring. He smiled at the sound of her laugh.

"And what is so amusing, my lady?"

"Why you, my lord!" She returned, smiling in return. "I do not think I have ever seen you in such a state of comfort."

Melville's lazy smile widened.

"Then you do not watch me often, Avis."

"Do I not?" She replied. "Be so good as to tell me what I have missed!"

"This is how I always look when I'm with you."

Avis' smile faltered, and then broadened. She would never have thought that such words from such a man would give her such pleasure. Melville was still undoubtedly Norman – nothing had changed there. He was still abrupt, and rude, and at times completely incomprehensible. But something indeed had changed. Something was altered between them, and she was sure it was something within her. She could not find the feelings of anger, bitterness and resentment that she had grown up against this man.

Stretching her legs out in front of her and leaning backwards on her arms, Avis sighed. Her hands reached deep into the fur, and in doing so, her left hand brushed against something. It was Melville's right hand: but instead of clasping it, he reached up to push her arm off the rugs. She fell backwards about to topple onto the ground, but he caught her in his strong arms.

"Melville!" Avis giggled.

He laughed at her mock scorn, and drew her in closer, eyes still shut. Avis struggled, but only to prevent an easy conquest. She settled down alongside him, revelling not only in the meagre heat of the sun, but in the pervading heat of his body. With one arm wrapped across his waist, she allowed her eyelids to dip.

Melville opened one eye to gaze down upon his wife. She was snuggled deep into him, and was totally at ease in his presence. He let out a controlled sigh of contentment. This was exactly what he had been hoping for. He wanted

Avis to learn to trust him, to feel open in his presence. Perhaps, slowly, they could learn together.

"Melville?" Avis breathed.

"Hmmm?"

"Thank you."

Melville's heart sang. The thought that he had given Avis happiness flooded his veins with warmth and joy. Nothing could spoil this moment. Nothing could interfere with this intimacy. Nothing.

CHAPTER TWENTY TWO

The sound of a horse's hooves became faster and louder, and eventually Melville had no choice but to pay attention to their approach.

"Avis darling?"

Avis shook her head, unwilling to return to society.

"Come on." Melville gently lifted her up, and gave Avis enough time to pat down her flyaway hair before the horseman arrived.

Melville smiled at her wryly, acknowledging his displeasure that their time together was about to be interrupted – but he groaned aloud when the rider came into view, and he recognised the crest and livery. It was a messenger from King William.

"Melville?" Avis muttered quietly. His face had grown dark, and she was sure that he had recognised the loyalty of the man that approached them.

Melville answered briefly before the man was in earshot.

"The King."

As Melville went to greet the rider, he did not notice how Avis turned pale. She had not seen King William since that day, that day when her entire life had changed.

Although it was obvious that this rider was not the King, she could not help but feel that her privacy was once again being attacked by that unwanted warrior. Would she ever be free of him?

The rider dismounted, and walked straight to Melville, who recognised him at once. His horse shook itself after a long and difficult ride, and began to lazily eat the luscious grass that surrounded them.

"Jean?"

The rider nodded, and then stumbled. Melville caught him, and immediately helped him to sit on the pile of rugs beside Avis, who shrunk back in fear. The man was clearly exhausted. Melville's thoughts immediately exploded, imagining all manner of different scenarios, each with terrifying consequences. The King captured, the King in hiding, the King back in Normandy…

But then he noticed Avis. She was clearly uncomfortable with this man here, and it was unlikely that the rider would speak in her presence. General disdain for the intelligence of women led most men to conduct their business away from the gossiping ears of women. And besides, despite his posturing, he knew that Avis was still considered by most to be an Anglo-Saxon. Someone not to be trusted. He knew that for both Avis and Jean, it would be easier if she were not here.

"Avis." He spoke gently, and she turned to him, trying to ignore as best she could the panting man whose presence had put her so on edge. "Would you do me the courtesy of going to speak to the villagers below? I would know that they are being fairly treated, and want for nothing."

Avis smiled at him. She knew that the request was merely a pretence to remove her from this difficult situation, but she was relieved. The presence of this unknown Norman had taken from her all of her calmness, causing tension to run throughout her body, and there was no other polite way for her to simply leave them. Avis was only just beginning to trust Melville – a new stranger, a Norman stranger, was too much.

Rising and smoothing down her skirts, she smiled shakily.

"It shall be my pleasure, my lord. I shall not be long."

Avis did not want the rider to see her relief at leaving, but it was all she could do not to run down the hill towards the welcoming familiarity of the Anglo-Saxon village. Children scurried out to greet her, and chattered away in her own language. She agreed to join their game, and within moments was lost in the innocence of their cares and quarrels.

Melville watched her descend down the hill, making sure that she was out of earshot before he turned to Jean.

"My man!" He exhaled. "It has been many moons since I have seen you. What has happened to cause this rushed journey?"

Jean had caught his breath, and slowly raised himself into a sitting position, twisting to be opposite Melville. He spoke in a deep voice with a harsh Norman accent.

"Melville. I am so relieved that I have found you."

Fear tugged at Melville's heart.

"By God, man," he said quietly. "Tell me what has happened."

Jean and he had come across from Normandy together, two young men with nothing but everything to gain. He had saved Jean's life on more than one occasion, and this had created a bond between them which was more similar to brotherhood than anything that Melville had ever known. To see Jean in such controlled panic was painful for Melville to see. He knew that Jean would not have ridden so fast and so hard unless a terrible event had taken place – and would not have come to him unless there was something, however unpleasant, that had to be done.

"It is the King." Jean said dully. Melville drew in breath, but did not interrupt Jean now he had managed to begin.

"He has grown angry and tired of the actions of the ætheling Edgar."

Melville heard the unusual Anglo-Saxon word, and tried to remember its meaning. He recalled that it described a prince that could inherit the crown. There had been many æthelings after the invasion, but not many now. With the name Edgar, he began to understand.

"You remember Edgar?" Jean asked.

Melville nodded. "He resided with our King at his court after the invasion. He is part of the royal line of this country. Young stupid fool, as I recall."

Jean barked out a laugh.

"Young fool indeed. He has been rallying a group around him. An army. Anglo-Saxon noblemen and those traitorous to our people."

Melville blew out of his teeth.

"More fools."

"Fools gather." Jean said darkly. "They are marching down to the South. Towards William, determined to depose him and take the country from us Normans."

Melville was stunned. He knew that there were those who disliked the Norman presence. Avis' reactions to him, and the stories that she had told him about the invasion were enough to tell him that there was a line of bitterness deep within these people, and it would take much time for that to be removed. If it ever was to be removed. He knew that William was a difficult master, demanding much and praising little. But he never imagined that they would be so stupid as to try and force William's hand. From his understanding, it would take a whole nation to rise up to destroy William's army.

Melville did not want to enter war again, but he knew his duty. He knew that he had no choice before his King.

"When do we ride to battle?" He asked Jean sadly.

Jean shook his head.

"It is much worse than that."

Melville sighed. He glanced to check that Avis was still playing with the children. This terrible news could do nothing but force them apart by reminding them of their differences. And just when there was beginning to be an understanding between them. He raised a hand to scratch at his dark hair, and sighed again.

"Tell me the worst."

"He's marching on the North."

Jean's statement did not make sense to Melville.

"William's marching towards the North?"

Jean smiled wryly, but with sadness in his eyes.

"No. He's marching *on* the North. At the North. He plans to destroy the North. To burn every town, ransack every home, murder every man, salt every field, slaughter all cattle. He intends not to destroy the North, but to make sure that it can never be inhabited again."

Melville sat. There was nothing to say. He could not comprehend such destruction. William's anger was famous throughout his lands, but never before had such vengeance been seen. It would make the invasion look tame.

Jean watched Melville as he tried to understand what he had been told. He owed a great debt of friendship to this dark and serious Norman, and nothing that his friend could say would alter that. He would have given much not to relay such terrible news.

Avis threw the ball over to the tallest child, clapped as she caught it wildly, and quickly scanned the top of the hill. She could still see Melville and the rider sitting, facing each other. But as she watched, Melville dropped his head, and the rider reached over an arm to console him.

Avis bit her lip. Whatever news the strange rider has brought, it was clearly not good. Despite her desire to run up the hill and comfort her husband, she knew that until he beckoned her to return, her presence would not only be unwanted, but unhelpful.

At the peak of the hill, Melville collected himself, and placed his hand over his friend's that rested on his shoulder.

"What does my King want from me?"

Jean withdrew his hand, and avoided Melville's eye.

"What are you not telling me, Jean?"

Jean shifted himself, uncomfortable and unwilling to speak.

"My friend, you must tell me." Melville spoke calmly, but it was a front to cover the panic that was rising in his throat. "There have never been lies between us. Please. Tell me the truth, however bad it may be."

"It is bad." Jean spoke hoarsely, his emotion overcoming him. He played with the ends of his left sleeve, unwilling to look up, but he could not avoid Melville forever.

Melville waited, more patient than he had ever had to be in his life.

"The King wants nothing from you." Jean muttered.

Melville's forehead crinkled in confusion. "Then…"

And then the truth poured into his mind. He realised what Jean was trying to say – why he was finding it so difficult to say, and had ridden so fast with no rest to reach him.

Melville spoke in a dry voice.

"The King does not want my aid. He plans to destroy me and mine as part of the North."

Jean nodded. "You are in great danger," he said gruffly. "I have had to leave his court at night to reach you, but I am not sure whether my presence has been missed. But I could not let you be unable to prepare for this great onslaught."

Melville smiled at Jean. "My friend, you have risked much to warn me. I thank you." His smile faded. "But I am unsure as to what path to take. There is no clear way to safety."

Jean nodded. "It may be…" his voice faltered, but he continued resolutely. "It may be that there is no clear way to safety."

Melville tried desperately to picture this country's geography in his mind. There seemed to be no way to remove his household out of the way of William's murderous path – and as William seemed determined not to call him to his side, it seemed that he did not care whether Anglo-Saxon or Norman died in his vengeful path. He certainly did not consider Melville important or valuable enough to save.

Jean's voice broke into his reverie.

"Melville. You may have to accept…you may need to send away your wife to her people."

"She has no people," Melville replied. "You know that as well as I."

"In that case," Jean sighed. "You have no choice whatsoever."

"I shall send her to Ulleskelf."

"Where?"

"The village by my manor. It is underneath my protection and lordship, but not directly on the road from the South." Melville pictured the route that William would take. "She should be safe there."

But Jean sighed sadly.

"You do not understand. You may not be able to prevent William from taking Ulleskelf."

Melville stared at him in horror, but Jean did not look away. Eventually, it was Melville's gaze that faltered.

"I hate the thought that I cannot protect them." Melville murmured. "But I must return. I must prepare."

Jean nodded. "I must return to the King, before I am missed."

The two men rose, and embraced. Melville did not know if he would ever see his friend again, and he could not bear it.

Walking over to his horse, Jean mounted and looked down at his friend.

"Be strong."

"Be careful." Replied Melville. He watched as Jean encouraged his horse to gallop faster and faster, hurtling down the hill and past waiting Avis. Waiting to hear the news.

CHAPTER TWENTY THREE

Avis saw Jean ride past her, and after a few quick words of farewell to the children, began to walk towards Melville. He had dropped onto the ground, once again lying on his back, but Avis could tell that this time it was not in relaxation but in troubling contemplation. She sat down beside him, and waited for him to speak to her.

As the silence lengthened, she could not help but ask.

"My lord. What news?"

Melville sighed sadly, and did not answer.

"Melville!"

The sound of his name awakened energy in him, and he sat up, reaching an arm around Avis and pulling her towards him. He exhaled deeply, and Avis realised that he was drawing strength from her. Something had clearly happened to rock Melville's very core.

"Tell me," she said softly.

Melville looked at her. Everything in him was desperate to protect this creature from all of the concerns that Jean had brought. He wanted to carry these burdens alone; but he knew for their relationship to be based on trust he had to be open. Even if that meant he had to expose her to yet more pain.

"Avis." He pushed her slightly away so that he could see her face completely. "I want you to remain calm."

"Can I be honest, Melville?"

"Please do."

Avis smiled. "There is little you can say that can scare me more than I have been scared before."

Melville chuckled sadly. "I wish that could be true, my dear."

The affectionate term would usually have grated on her, but now it seemed perfectly right. Avis pushed a falling lock of hair away from his eyes, and smiled.

"Whatever it is," she said softly, "you need to tell me."

Melville sighed. "William is tired of the restlessness of the North. Edgar your athing – "

"Æthling." Avis smiled.

"Æthling." Melville tried to return the smile, but could not. "Edgar and noblemen from both our peoples are rallying against William. The King has decided to ride on the North and destroy it."

Avis did not understand.

"William is to destroy Edgar and his army? That surely does not concern us – unless, you are to join William's army?"

"No." Melville tried to explain the situation without terrifying her. "He plans to destroy every home, person, and animal in the North. He plans to kill everything."

Avis immediately rose. She could not even sit, she could not stay still, she could not rest.

"Such a thing – what sort of man could order such a thing, think of such a thing? It is impossible to think about even more pain and destruction in my land! This violence against my people has to stop!"

Avis was pacing up and down as she spoke, throwing her hands up in the air and gesturing wildly. She broke into a tongue that Melville did not recognise, but assumed was her natural Anglo-Saxon. Clearly, shouting in one's mother tongue was a lot more releasing than having to do it in translation. He rose and tried to calm her.

"Avis," he began, but he could not stop her speaking.

"You don't understand! I have already seen obliteration of life. I cannot, I will not see it again. What are we going to tell the villagers of Ulleskelf? How can we protect them?" She stopped walking and glared at Melville. "How can you protect us? Few men survived from that village – only you and your men stand between us and death. What are we to do?"

Her fear was tangible, and Melville tried to calm her.

"This is not the end. There is much that we can do…"

But his voice trailed away. Although he did not want to admit this to Avis, Melville was not sure whether there truly was anything that he could do. William had given him land after the invasion, but he was not part of the King's inner circle, and he was owed no favours or gratitude. There were no family ties or important friends that he could call on to protect him or plea on his behalf. He was alone. Even Jean could not stay with him. He had risked so much merely to warn Melville, but still could not remain by his side. Would there be anyone who would risk all to stand by him?

Avis had resumed pacing, muttering under her breath in phrases that Melville did not understand but could guess at. Melville stepped in front of her, and grabbed her flailing arms.

"Avis." He held her close to him, and he could feel her shaking. "Avis, you need to stay calm."

"How can I be calm?" She whispered erratically. "The world is ending."

"Oh Avis," Melville clutched her more tightly towards him. "The world is not ending."

"You can't promise me that."

Melville could tell that Avis was crying, but did not want him to know, and so he did not comment on her wet cheeks.

"I promise you that I will do anything I can. Anything."

Avis pulled away from him, and smiled through her tears.

"What are we going to do then?"

Melville gestured towards the food.

"Come and sit with me."

The two of them sat down, but Avis was still shaking slightly. Melville passed her some fruit, and she reached out for it with a trembling hand. Melville could see the burnt and blistered skin on her wrist where she had burnt herself in the kitchen, and berated himself for putting her through so much pain.

After Avis had begun to eat, Melville took advantage of the fact that Avis could not speak – or argue.

"I plan to travel to meet William. To beg for protection."

Swallowing fast, Avis spoke quickly and in anger.

"Protection? William knows nothing about protection."

"What other option do I have?" Melville retorted angrily. "I cannot just wait here, watching for William's army to begin destroying my land, killing my people."

"That's what we had to do!" returned Avis. "That is all we can do! We had no choice but to wait and watch the army end our lives."

"Oh Avis!" Melville spoke angrily. "Can you ever forget what has happened?"

"No. It is who I am now."

Melville stared at the ground angrily. Even within this moment, when they should be working together to protect each other, she could not forget that men who were born of his country had hurt her. She could easily ignore the truths of his character in favour of her bitterness against his home country.

"What do you suggest then, my lady?" He said bitterly. "Which friends shall we flee to? Which country will offer us protection?"

"Your sarcasm is unnecessary, my lord," Avis replied. "If not for your people, I would have family throughout this land."

Melville's patience was completely used up, and he finally snapped.

"Grow up, Avis! What has been has been, and now you need to face up to the fact that our very lives are threatened. Reminiscences of the past will not save you."

Jumping up, Melville quickly mounted his horse, and began giving instructions to his servants to protect his wife.

Avis also rose.

"Melville?" She said uncertainly. "You're not going?"

"I will not remain here to speak nonsense." He said tersely. "I will see you tonight. We shall speak then."

Melville rode away, and Avis watched him astounded. She could not believe that he had just left her. Perhaps she had finally pushed him just that little bit too far.

CHAPTER TWENTY FOUR

Avis strode into the hall, but her temper had diminished during her long and slow ride back to the place that she now termed as home. During reflection whilst riding, she had swung from incredible anger towards Melville, to shame at the way that she had retaliated. It was not his fault that King William had decided to obliterate the value of human life. It was not his fault that they had no one else to turn to for protection. And it was certainly not his fault that she had panicked.

As she looked around, Avis' heart sank. He was not there. Seating herself at the top of the table, she tried to ignore the pointed stares of those around her. Voices muttered, and even a direct glare to the speakers from Avis could not quieten them. It was evident to all that another argument between the lord and lady had occurred, and though the two servants who had travelled with them that day knew better than to gossip, it would only take a few glances to tell the household whose fault they thought it was this time.

She began to grow hot. She could not bear the thought that all of these people around her could at any moment be under siege from one of the most powerful armies her world had ever seen.

Avis shut her eyes, trying to drown out the fear, but it merely increased it. Behind her eyelids she could see the flames that had destroyed the village. She was a child again, hiding from the men that she knew would return. The shade of her old home could no longer protect her, and neither could her brother or father. Her mother had gone and there was none to comfort her here –

"Avis!"

Melville's deep voice rang out across the hall, and Avis jerked to attention. She opened her eyes, and saw her husband striding towards her from the opposite end of the hall. She rose, but he paid little attention to her.

"Robert."

Melville's man stood immediately and rushed to his master's side. Frantic orders were issued from him to many others, and Avis could not but help admire the way that every man accorded Melville such respect. It was clear that before she had even met him, he had earned their respect, and had never acted in a manner to lose it. She regarded him; saw the way that he held himself, strong and determined. She smiled.

Robert nodded, and strode away, with several men and the stable boy Felix following him. Edith watched them go, and began talking quietly with her neighbour.

Melville continued up the hall towards Avis, and with a heavy sigh sunk into the seat next to her.

"Wine, my lord?" Avis offered timidly. She had not forgotten the angry manner in which they had last spoken, nor the abrupt way that he had left her. She certainly did not want to rile his temper once more.

Melville finally looked upon her, and his wild gaze softened. He saw Avis' slightly fearful look, and internally berated himself. Every step forward was followed by a push back it seems, and always due to his temper.

"I thank you," he replied uncomfortably.

Avis poured the wine, and the two of them ate in silence, until Avis could hold her tongue no longer.

"My lord."

Melville pointedly ignored her, until she spoke with a slight smile.

"Melville."

With a much broader smile her husband turned to her.

"Yes, Avis?"

Avis nudged him playfully, and then continued with a more sombre expression.

"We must decide what is to be done."

Melville's face dropped. "I agree. But this is not the place in which to have that conversation."

"Later then?" Avis pushed. "Despite my actions today, I…I don't want you to keep me out of this decision. This is our land, and our people."

"And our lives," Melville reminded her. "We are in just as much danger as all of them."

He gestured around the room, and passed some more food up to his mouth. He chewed contemplatively, and then spoke again, very quietly.

"What would you do?"

Avis was stunned. She had never been asked such a question of such responsibility before, and she had not expected Melville to value her ideas so highly.

"I had not perfectly considered," she replied awkwardly. Avis did not want to venture her thoughts quite yet. At least, not until she had considered everything properly.

Melville nodded appreciatively. Here then was a woman that did not speak without due thought.

"I am glad of it." He spoke aloud unconsciously, picking at a pastry pie with his knife and not eating.

"Hmmm?" Avis probed, swirling her wine in her goblet.

"I am merely impressed that you do not offer an opinion without thought." Melville confessed. "It is not a female quality that I usually discover."

Avis laughed, and her elegance caused many to glance her way admiringly. Melville could not help but smile at seeing her so happy. But then Avis' smile disappeared when she remembered what they were talking about.

Melville noticed her uneasiness, and took her hand in his.

"Would you rather retire?" He asked her. "We can have food brought to another chamber, and we can openly discuss everything there."

His eyes glanced around the room, which was filled with those longing to know what conversation was holding their attention so fully.

Avis nodded her assent, and Melville gave orders to the waiting servant. Within moments they were alone in Avis' private chamber, surrounded by food and in front of a warm fire. The servant had created a picnic similar to their luncheon before the hearth, and Melville and Avis sat with their backs to a trestle facing the warmth of the fire.

"So," Avis began, "how much time do we have?"

Melville flinched at the harshness in her tones.

"Must you be so direct?" He asked her, picking up an apple and cutting it in half.

"Better to be prepared, is it not?"

Melville nodded, and handed her half of the apple.

"You are right." He cast his mind back to his time at William's court, and tried to estimate how long it would take them to move this far.

Avis watched Melville think, and marvelled at the handsome face so troubled. In all of the turmoil of their marriage, she had almost forgotten that Melville was an incredibly attractive man. She remembered the kind teasing she had received from the kitchen staff, and blushed. Hoping that he hadn't noticed, she looked him up and down. His greatest asset, she decided, was his humility.

With his muscles and his power, he could easily overpower many that he spoke to. But he was tender with those that were loyal to him, and though abrupt with others, it was not from a place of rudeness but of discomposure. Avis thought about their conversation the night before. Melville had not been raised for this sort of life. She had been taught how to speak to servants; how to command a room; how to dress for particular company. These skills were normal to her, and yet alien to him. Perhaps it was wrong for her to expect him to be so at ease in all of the situations that she was. It was here, in times of fear and battle, that he was in his element, and could offer her assistance and aid. This was his territory.

A spark crackled in the fire, causing them to jump. Melville reached for another leg of chicken.

"I believe it will be no longer than a week before William and his army are here," he confessed to Avis as he ate. "William is known for his speed across ground, and we are one of the earliest places he will reach. Even with a large army, it will not be long."

Avis nodded. "And is there anyone that will help us?"

Melville considered aloud.

"Hugh le Blanc was planning to return to Flanders when he left us. Many of the new Norman lords in this area are no friend to me because of my background – something that I have somehow managed to have kept hidden from William. I know that few Anglo-Saxon lords remain here at all."

He turned shyly to Avis, uncomfortable at the question he was about to ask, but he knew it had to be done.

"Do you know of any Anglo-Saxon noblemen in hiding here?"

Avis had known that the question had been coming, and could only wish that she could give a different answer. She shook her head, brushing the bread crumbs off her lap.

"None. My cousin in Ireland is too far from here. My uncle was the only kin I had this far north, and I am not child enough to think that he survived."

Melville shifted his body weight to move slightly closer to his wife. At first she stayed stock still, unwilling to accept this infringement into her personal space, but his reassuring presence was something that she had longed for ever since he had ridden off without her. Avis slowly leaned into him, and he took her slight weight.

"And so what is to be done?" She asked.

"We have two options." Melville thought aloud. "Wait. Run."

Avis was shocked at how little hope he had.

"That is all?"

"What do you expect from me?" Melville replied testily. "I have no army. My men are not nearly enough to fight the horde that will come with William. Even if every woman and child were given arms, it would not be enough. Either we continue as if nothing has happened, and beg for the King's mercy when he arrives, or we take the fewest people possible and leave tonight."

Footsteps in the corridor punctuated the silence as normality continued behind the door. Little did they know that Avis and Melville were but a few steps away planning for their lives.

"Fewest possible?" said Avis slowly. "Why? Cannot we take them all?"

"Avis," said Melville gently. "We would be on the run. We cannot take all the servants with us. They would slow us down."

"I don't mean just the servants!" Avis said. "I meant everyone. What about the villagers? We cannot abandon them to this terrible fate!"

Melville tried not to scoff at her naivety, and reminded himself that she had never gone on patrol, or marched for days upon days with no food to speak of.

"Only so many can be protected, only so many can be saved! You and I – we are the ones that need to survive this attack!"

At his words, Avis rose angrily.

"Really? And what makes us special, Melville? Wealth, title? That should not mean the others should be condemned to die!"

She began to pace up and down the room, whilst Melville watched her from the floor. It seemed to be her favoured method of releasing stress, but it bore down on Melville like a mill stone. He was becoming incensed by Avis' lack of understanding, but he tried to keep the irritation out of his voice. Rising, he stood in her pathway and stopped her in her tracks.

"Must you pace?" He said, trying to make her smile. "Can you not stay in one place and think?"

Avis' fearful eyes met his, and his smile faltered. She was clearly terrified. He lowered his voice.

"Avis," he said affectionately. "I promise I will not let anything happen to you."

"Just like you promised to honour me?" She returned, almost laughing but with sadness in every word. "Don't make promises that you can't keep Melville."

Melville snorted, angry that she still refused to trust him.

"Avis, you don't know what we're facing!"

Avis laughed a dry and humourless laugh.

"Melville, I have been in this position before. I have waited for a marauding army to destroy everything that I know and love. I have had to plan escape routes and hide supplies and after it was all over, count the bodies. Don't insult my intelligence by saying that I don't know what we face."

Avis remained in front of Melville, but avoided his eye. She took in a deep breath and stared seriously into the embers.

Melville had never felt like such a murderer in his entire life. Here he was, knowing exactly what Avis had suffered and seen in her short life, and he was forcing her to undergo the exact same circumstances! It was a miracle that she survived the first time, and her chances now were even less certain.

"Avis," he began, but she interrupted him, dragging her eyes away from the fire.

"Melville," she said softly. "There is nothing more to be said. Tomorrow we decide. Fight or flight."

Melville stared down at her, his beautiful intangible infuriating wife. Their faces were but inches apart. Avis' clear eyes met Melville's dark ones, and instinctively she knew what he was going to do. Tilting slightly down, he lowered his face until his lips were mere seconds away from hers. Unbidden, Avis moved forwards and their lips met.

Her arms left her sides and reached around his neck, entangling his hair around her tender fingers. She leaned into him. Strong arms encircled her, and held her tightly. The kiss was slow and passionate, and reached deep inside her heart wrenching her apart – but it was not pain she felt, but intense pleasure.

And as quick as it had begun, it was over. Melville pulled back, but did not release Avis. He stared into her eyes with a smile on his face, and she returned it.

"And now sleep," he whispered.

He withdrew his arms swiftly, and without another word exited the room.

Avis sunk down onto the rugs by the hearth, stunned. She could still feel the fire of his lips upon hers, even above the heat of the flames. Never before had she been kissed in such a fashion. The memory of his delicacy and yet power burned right through her, and she shivered.

Melville lay in bed, staring at the ceiling. The day's events passed through his mind, and he marvelled that so much could occur in such a short time. The passionate kiss that he had shared with Avis was uppermost in his memory, but he tried to quell the rising emotion to consider the problem that faced him.

William and his army. Melville could not ignore the fact that if he had been better born, or richer, with a more noble family or powerful friends he would not be in this dangerous situation. He turned onto his side. Nothing could be gained from counting what he did not have, he told himself. What do I have?

Hours passed and it was nearly morning when Melville made his decision. Whether or not it would be successful, it was the only thing he could do.

Although it could mean his death, it should mean Avis' life.

CHAPTER TWENTY FIVE

A faint strand of sunlight wafted into the room, and fell onto Avis' cheek. The brightness awoke her, but it was several minutes until the events of the day before rushed into her mind. If there was sunlight pouring through into her chamber, it was later than she had hoped to rise. She sighed sadly, and pushed back the coverlet that had kept her warm. Toes curling on the rushes that lay on her floor, she fidgeted with her hair and wandered around the room, unwilling to dress and commit herself to a day in which only pain could be experienced. Today was the day that she and Melville had to decide whether or not to stay and wait for William to enter their lands, or to run…where?

There was nowhere to go, Avis reminded herself as she began to dress. Melville had offered her servants, but she had grown so used to putting on her own clothes during her time of near imprisonment with Richard that she had refused. As she carefully laced the front of her bodice, she considered the terrifying world that she was now living in. When she had been under Richard's protection, for want of a better word, she had not been aware of what was going on in the country, but now she was a married noblewoman. The affairs of state were now her business, and they were interfering with her life in a way that she could not have predicted.

Her hands shook as she finished the careful and intricate knot. Now all she had to do was slip on her shoes, and find Melville. They had to make a decision, and they had to make it soon. Every moment counted, and could make the difference as William marched towards them, vengeance in his heart.

The cooling air lifted her spirits, and Avis tried to smile as she passed servants on her way to the Great Hall. Neither she nor Melville had told anyone else the terror that was approaching their quiet country. They did not want to cause panic, but as Avis walked into the loud room where many were breaking their fast, she could not help but look around and try to imagine these people fighting for their lives. There was Edith, still young, but eternally scarred by the wars of their land. Felix was running around with a gaggle of Anglo-Saxon and Norman children, not knowing the hatred that was felt between their elders. The Norman men that Avis was beginning to recognise on a daily basis had fought many times for their King. None of them could be thinking that they may soon be fighting against that very monarch that they had sworn to protect.

Shaking her head to rid her mind of such malevolent thoughts, Avis went to her usual place at the top table, and began to pile her plate – but the absence of Melville, usually eating well before her appearance, troubled her. Where could he be?

Avis gestured, and immediately a servant appeared by her side.

"My lady?"

"Please bring Robert to me." Avis gave the name of the only retainer that she had seen Melville trust totally. The servant scurried down the hall. Avis expected him to go straight to Robert himself, but the servant unexpectedly left the hall. Craning her neck to try and see where he had gone, within a moment he had returned and hurried back to Avis.

"Well?" asked Avis, sharply. She was not accustomed to her orders being disobeyed, and surely this one was not difficult.

The servant was clearly nervous. He licked his lips, and pushed back his dishevelled hair.

"My lady," he began, "I am afraid my lord Robert is unavailable."

"Unavailable?" repeated Avis, haughtily. "Just what exactly can keep him from his lady's bidding?"

Avis knew that she was being unreasonable, but the whole world seemed unreasonable today. Why would Robert not come, and where was Melville?

The servant's eyes were scanning around the room, but could see no one to rescue him from Avis' ire. She sighed.

"Tell me the truth. There shall be no retribution for the truth."

This calmed the servant, who finally explained.

"Robert left early this morning, without breaking his fast, with my lord Melville and several others."

"Left? I was not aware of any judicial court meetings that required my lord's presence this day."

"That is because there aren't any, my lady."

Avis blinked. She nodded the servant away, and then turned to her food.

Melville was gone. And clearly no one was entirely sure where. At this time of danger, he had left her unprotected, and without warning her that he would be absent. What could be so important? And when would he be returning? An angry flush rose throughout her entire body. Melville was so volatile – how could she ever learn to truly trust him?

Avis worried in the only way that she knew how; by pacing. As soon as the morning meal was over, she left the hall intending to make her way across the bridge to her favourite tree. Passing the stables, she noticed that the majority of the horses were no longer there – and none of the packs, which contained the belongings of the riders and were always strapped carefully to the side of their mount – were in their boxes. They had all gone.

But there was no time to wonder about such things. Increasing her pace, she raced across the bridge until she reached the tree. She immediately began pacing, pulling off her veil and running her hands through her long hair. Recollections of her conversation with Melville underneath the same tree kept crowding her mind, but she pushed them away as she tried to concentrate.

Melville had gone. That much was certain. But to where? There was no business to be taken care of, and no news from York that had to be addressed. York, then, was not his destination. What about the village they had passed the day before on their ride? Avis was almost tempted to saddle a horse and ride to the hill that they had been to yesterday, but she knew deep within herself that he would not have returned there without her. There would be nothing to be gained. But then where could he have gone, and with so many people?

And the majority of the horses. And with so much supplies. Avis, with a flash of horror, realised why so many horses had disappeared, and why there were no packs left. Melville had left for a considerable amount of time, taking as much food and water with him as he could carry.

Her mind worked hard, and she thought. She tied it all together, and was devastated at the conclusion that she had no choice but to come to.

Melville had not waited to discuss the matter with her. He had made his own decision – and he had decided to run without her.

Tears crept to the front of her eyes as she tried to argue against this dreadful idea. But the trouble was, it made too much sense. Had not Melville himself told her that taking too many people would slow them down? She herself was not a long-distance rider, and he had seen many examples of that on the long trip northwards after their marriage. He had asked her whether she knew anyone in the area, and she had been honest and said no! Perhaps he knew a local Norman lord; a man who would be willing to protect Melville and a small retinue, but would not want to shelter an Anglo-Saxon woman from the anger of his King.

Despite the valiant fight that Avis gave them, the tears won and they fell across her face, staining it white with salt. Unable to continue walking, she threw herself down on the ground and stared into the river, full from the snow that had melted in the highlands of Scotland. Melville had abandoned her, right at the moment when she had most needed him. And she did need him, she realised. As much as she was strong, and proud of that strength, she was not this strong. Once again, she had trusted. Once again, she needed a protector. Once again, she was left alone.

Avis surrendered herself to tears for several minutes, but after a while she calmed herself. If her experiences had taught her anything, it was that nothing could be gained from self-pity. And she was not alone. The entire village had remained, and they were Anglo-Saxon. They were much more likely to help her than Melville ever was.

Avis rose determinedly. Whether Melville was scared enough to run away or not, she would not run so easily. She knew what she had to do.

Picking up her skirts, she flew down into the stable yard almost as quickly as she had previously left it.

"Listen, everyone!" Avis cried. "Everyone into the Great Hall, now!"

The stable men turned around, shocked at the impressive tones from their refined lady. But with a glare from Avis, they began to move.

A message was sent down to the kitchens, and out into the grounds, and within minutes the Great Hall was filled with muttering voices, unsure why they had all been sent for but fearful of something that they had all done that required punishment. Clusters of Norman retainers and Anglo-Saxon servants carefully avoided each other. Avis marched to the front, and without any aid, stood on the large table.

The room quietened at the unusual sight of their lady standing on a table. Every man, woman and child turned to Avis, and she swallowed. This was it.

"My people," she began in Anglo-Saxon. "I feel that it is only right to warn you of a terrible event that is soon to happen."

She spoke the same words again in Norman, so that all of her people could understand her. The silence that had heralded the beginning of her speech gave way to murmured panic as they waited for the terrible news that she was about to bring them.

"Please!" Avis tried to keep them calm in both languages. "Please let me finish, and then I will answer any questions that you may have."

The room became soundless once again, and Avis took in a deep breath. Her skin was pale, and those closest to her could see her rocking slightly on her toes as she tried to take her own advice.

"King William and his army are on their way." Avis was trying to be as brief as possible – she knew that any extra details would merely increase their panic. "Not to visit us, but to visit death upon us. Others have displeased him, and he has decided to punish all."

The differing reactions of the people in the room did not surprise Avis. The Anglo-Saxon servants began to well up but did not allow the tears to fall; they knew exactly what type of punishment William would bring to them. But surprisingly it was the reaction of the Normans that wrenched most at Avis' heart. Their eyes were wide open, and their mouths agape. They could not believe that their King, their William, the man that they had sworn to honour and protect, who they had already fought for and defended, was now coming to destroy them. This was betrayal, on a royal scale.

"Please," Avis began again, "please do not be afraid."

"Easy for you to say!" shouted out Bronson, his face red and oil dripping from his hands. "My lady," he added hastily. "You will be protected!"

"I am to have no special treatment!" Avis spoke over the uproar. "I am one of you."

"Where is my lord Melville?" called a Norman man whose name Avis did not know. "Where is our lord?"

That is a good question, thought Avis. She hesitated. She had not considered what she was to tell everyone about Melville's apparent disappearance. With no wish to lie, it was not possible for her to tell the whole truth. Though her blood boiled against him, she could not dishonour him in front of his people. She was his wife, and she had a duty to him – even if he had ignored his duty to her.

"My lord Melville has departed," she said slowly, "to fulfil a promise. He has not forgotten us, and," her voice caught in her throat, "he will return to us."

All of the people in the room gazed on her suspiciously. If Avis did not convince them of her honesty soon, they could rise up against her. She would be powerless against such hordes. But there was one more thing for her to say.

"The village."

This simple phrase from Avis wrought a silence that she had never heard before. The Anglo-Saxons immediately fell quiet, and their sombre faces fell even further. The Normans too became quiet. They may mock the simple village folk, but they had grown to know them, to recognise them. They had become part of the landscape, necessary to their existence.

Avis saw the sadness, and it strangely raised her hopes, low as they were. Perhaps they would agree to her plan.

"I want to protect the village," she continued. "This place is more than big enough for us all. I intend to clear chambers, and invite the villagers in. They will be safer here. We can all face this together. Anglo-Saxon and Norman."

Avis was not sure what she was expecting, but she had certainly not expected the silence to continue unabated. All seemed unsure whether to trust the other side.

And then Edith stepped forward. She left the close circle of Anglo-Saxons, and walked across to the Norman men, who took a pace back away from her. A couple of the Norman women chuckled, and Edith coloured.

"I know that you despise us." Edith said quietly in Anglo-Saxon. Avis began to translate for the Normans, as Robert had disappeared with Melville. Their faces turned white at Edith's words, but none of them interrupted.

"I cannot quite say that I do not despise you," resumed Edith in her lilting tones. "But if we are to survive this, we must survive together."

Her eyes lifted from the floor, and gazed sharply at the closest Norman man. He blinked repeatedly, as if to wipe her image from his eyes. But she would not disappear. He turned to Avis.

"We will help," he said gruffly. "We must protect each other."

Avis translated his short speech to the Anglo-Saxons, and a few of them nodded in appreciation.

Avis breathed out a sigh of relief. This may even work.

Hands from both sides pulled together throughout the day, and shouts across chambers were always followed by a brief translation from Avis. Never before had she felt the lack of a translator so much, but signs were created to indicate basic ideas, and a couple of the cleverer among them had learned a few important words.

Noise and dust and the sweet sound of working songs from both Anglo-Saxon and Norman tongues filled the building. Avis had no time to do anything herself as she was constantly needed to translate between the two groups. She smiled, watching the kitchen women scold Felix as he dropped a tray of bread. There were chuckles behind her, and when she turned she saw that Edith and another Anglo-Saxon girl had been trying to lift a table – now carried on the back of a Norman retainer, who was strutting around to the amusement of many.

There were still arguments: all had the perfect plan in which to make living quarters, and no one seemed particularly happy with compromising. A few of the Normans had originally refused to help, but had been shamed into clearing a chamber of armour after a tiny Norman boy of about five years old had tearfully asked for assistance. As Avis left to go down to the village, she smiled. Her desperate speech from the table had been the only point of action that she could think of, but she had secretly never expected it to change things this much! Everything had worked out better than she could have ever expected, and been more successful than she could ever have hoped.

As she closed the heavy entrance door in the surrounding wall, snow began to fall. Avis shivered; rushing without thought, her cloak had been left behind. Quickening her pace away from her home, she rubbed her hands to keep warm and tried to imagine where Melville was at that moment. Probably warm, and filling his belly, she thought bitterly.

She strolled down the path. Birds were singing in the trees, unaware of the fear and commotion beneath them. One of the birds Avis did not recognise. Perhaps it is one of the birds from Melville's homeland, she mused – but the remembrance of that intimate conversation with

Melville increased her anger. How dare he leave her! What sort of a man would open himself up to her, and then just when she needed him most depart without saying a word or leaving a message? It was incomprehensible.

By this time, Avis had reached the outskirts of the village. Cries of, "*éadesburg*!" or 'lady' from the children rang out as they ran towards her, beaming. Barefoot, they didn't seem to notice the cold. She was always welcome with them because few people took the time to play with them. There was always so much work to be done, and little time for frivolity.

"*Gambeóda*!" She replied, dazzling them with a broad smile. "Children!"

They swarmed around her, hugging her knees, and she giggled. Instructing them to gather their parents and all the other big adults here, she watched them scamper off, and her smile faded. Avis would do anything to prevent those children from suffering the way that she did. For some of them, it would be a return of the same pain.

The villagers began to appear, dragged by the hand by the children. They looked confused, but fearful. Being summoned by the lady could never mean a good thing. Dirty hands mopped sweating brows, and some women were bringing their suckling children. They could guess that the only reason for Avis to gather them all together was to relate bad – and dangerous – news.

Avis looked out at their faces – the faces that she had grown to recognise and to love during her time at Ulleskelf. Every eye was on her, waiting for the news, and she could almost hear their silent prayers that it would not be as serious as the situation seemed to suggest. The children weaved between the legs of the waiting adults, and Avis took a deep breath. She would not frighten them unduly. Not yet.

After sending the children to play and promising to join them as soon as she had finished talking to the adults, Avis briefly explained the danger that was to befall them all.

"The King is coming," she said, no smile resting on her face. "He comes to destroy us all."

"Why must we Anglo-Saxons suffer?" cried the priest, an elderly man who had lost his brother and nephews in the last battles. Many people around him nodded, and a woman began sniffing, trying to hold back tears.

"It is not only the Anglo-Saxons," Avis said quietly. "William plans to destroy all. Anglo-Saxon and Norman, rich and poor. There are no privileges, and no exemption."

This stunned the crowd. Never before had such brutality been heard of. To kill one's own, as well as one's foe? To destroy an area because of one rebellion?

Cries and panic began to fill the air, but Avis quickly described her plan.

"If we are condemned together, we must stay together." People were already shaking their heads, but she persevered. "All at the castle have been organising everything for your arrival throughout the day – yes, Hilde, the Normans too," as a woman about her age wrinkled her nose in disbelief. "You are all to come with me, into safety."

"How safe?"

The question rang out from a small voice from behind the crowd, and it parted to reveal – the children. They had stopped their game, and crept towards the sounds of fear, only too used to such a terrible situation. All of the children had sombre faces, but none of them were crying. Fear pushed people to panic. This was not fear. This was acceptance, and it tore at Avis' heart.

"Everything is prepared," she concluded. "All you need to do is come with me."

Avis gazed around the terrified faces, and with a sinking feeling realised that many of them were not convinced.

"And leave our homes?" said one man. "Everything that I own is in that place."

"Will they be there when we return?" asked the woman to his right, pushing a baby up from her hips. Her child had been born after the last war, but she had lost two daughters to the marauders who had followed. The distress in her eyes was evident for all to see.

"I know that you have seen your belongings taken once before. All the keepsakes and memories of your lost ones, taken – just as your families have been." Avis looked around the small group, huddled together, and remembered her home village. There had been gaps in the families there, and if she had known these people before 1066, she would be looking for people that no longer lived. "But you have to be strong. The most important thing is that we survive. For them."

She pointed towards the little group of children. Mothers smiled, and the few fathers that lived looked proudly upon their sons and daughters.

"For them," Avis repeated. "You must come with me for them."

Slowly, all of the villagers nodded. They would do anything, just as Avis would, to protect the innocent. Within an hour every person had a bundle of belongings, down to the smallest babe who clutched theirs in podgy fingers. In a wretched but determined line, they walked towards the manor.

The atmosphere at the gate was abysmal. All of the servants, Anglo-Saxon and Norman, had come outside to welcome the villagers, but the sight of such a large group of Norman men had caused many of the village children despite their courage to cry, hiding behind their parents. Even the adults were wary. But Bronson stepped forward.

"Welcome," he said, in his deep and comforting Anglo-Saxon tones. "You will be safe here. We will all be safe here."

Hands reached out. Loads were taken, and arms were placed around those who were weary. A slow trickle of people moved inside, until Avis was the only one left.

Avis looked out. She could still see the bridge, and the village, though the dark night was threatening to obscure them. She could not make out the oak tree, nor the two roads beyond it. Which road had Melville taken? Where was he now?

"My lady," said a voice behind her. She turned to see Edith.

"My lady," Edith repeated. "You must shut the gates now."

Avis nodded, and Edith hurried away to settle her mother down into a large room that had been set aside for the Anglo-Saxon women.

Avis turned back towards the huge gates, and sighed. As soon as they were shut, there would be no turning back. No one would be able to get out – and no one could be let in.

With a loud screech, she pulled the gates to, and barred them with large wooden boards.

"There," she whispered. "Safe."

But not everyone. As Avis turned to follow her people inside, she knew that Melville would not be able to enter now. He was on his own. Just as she was. And she ached for him.

CHAPTER TWENTY SIX

Melville had been riding for two days now, and with every gallop of his horse his heart was wrenched further from Avis. He could feel it. Every mile was agony, and every time they stopped he was tempted to turn around and return even faster than he had left.

But he could not. He had to keep going.

Robert rode up beside him, and shouted in the pouring rain. Even when the sun had risen, the rain had not abated. They were all tired and soaked to the skin, but Melville had refused to stop all night.

"My lord!" Robert yelled. "We must rest. The horses must take time to recover, or we shall never arrive!"

But Melville had no such intentions.

"We continue," he returned. "We are almost there."

"We shall arrive in no fit state to see him!" Robert tried to talk sense into his lord, but Melville's eyes had glazed over with tiredness, and his hands kept slipping from the saturated reins. "He will not see us, I say!"

There was no reply, and with a sound of disgust, Robert dropped behind to give the message to the other waterlogged men.

Melville knew that he was not making himself a popular man. His decision not to take extra supplies at their last stopping place was another grievance he knew his men held against him. Their loyalty had always been the one constant in his life, and now he was gambling on that loyalty for the speed they needed to reach their destination. But with every second that he was away from Avis, he became more and more anxious to return to her, and if that meant travelling in discomfort, so be it.

The shy sun had risen despite the sheeting rain, but it had disappeared hours ago behind some cloud and had not been seen again. Melville and his men rode across wide open fields where harvest had been taken, and dense woodland where deer ran from them, never stopping. They all knew where they were going, and none feared their destination more than Melville. He had sworn to himself that he would never return there unless he had no other choice. He had never thought that sort of circumstance would occur so soon.

Midday would have broken if the sun was visible, and still they did not stop. Every man's legs ached from hips to toes, but still they did not demand a respite. They knew the answer that they would receive. Melville was so tired that he began to dwell once more on Avis, even though he was trying to avoid that mental subject. He cursed himself for not leaving a message for her, but he could not have entrusted any servant that remained with her with the secret of where they were going, and he could not read or write. He was ashamed of this fact and had never admitted it to Avis, but there was never a second when he didn't regret leaving. She must think I am a fool, he thought. Or a coward. Or a traitor.

He thought about her long blonde hair, and the way that she snapped at him without fear. Her love of her people, and her obvious care for others. He groaned into the wind and the rain, and wished more than anything that he could be with her at that very moment.

But instead at that very moment he saw a dim light ahead of him. It was the outskirts lantern of the place that they had been riding so hard and so fast for so long to reach. He gave a shout, and Robert was once more at his side.

"My lord?"

"Stop the men." Melville's voice dripped with tiredness as his dark hair dripped with rain. "We shall ready ourselves together before we approach."

Robert nodded. The fear that had been playing underneath the surface of his face now deepened, but he obeyed. Within seconds, Melville's small retinue of six men had come to a halt. They grouped together, and waited for their lord to dismount.

Melville slowly came down from his horse, leaned against it, willing his bones to feel strong. After a moment, he walked stiffly towards his men who had also dismounted. They stood rigidly. They knew what they had agreed to, but none of them had been truly prepared to see the periphery of their journey's end, which had so consumed them. They looked to Melville for orders and guidance, and as he looked at them he knew he had nothing of worth to say.

"Men," he began awkwardly. "You know why we are here, you know what we face, you know the consequences of our actions. There is no more to say."

Some of the men were shocked by Melville's lack of conversation, but those that knew him best were not surprised. They knew his feelings about where they were going, and all of them could guess at his emotions about the person that he had left behind. It had not been an easy decision, and now they would all pay the price.

Forming a line behind Melville, they all walked forward, towards the light. After a mile, the person standing by the light came into view, and he shouted out in Norman.

"Who goes there?"

"Melville of Ulleskelf, lord of Copmanthorpe."

There was silence. Melville and his companions continued walking forward, but more than one trembled in anticipation.

"Follow me, Melville of Ulleskelf," replied the voice, which belonged to a thin man who came into view as he stepped into the light. "You are expected."

Turning his back, the thin man began walking towards the huge building that came into view around the corner. Melville gasped. He had never seen such a thing in England, only in Normandy. The castle was enormous, and light streamed from the entrance which was already open. Many men in dark red robes lined the way inside, and as the group passed them, several of them sniggered at the sopping motley group.

Melville and his men came into an entrance hall which had a large fire in it. Desperate as they were to warm themselves at its side, they dared not without Melville's command – and he was urgently looking around the room. The man that he looked for could not be seen.

A servant walked up to Melville insolently.

"And?" He asked, with a sneer on his wide face.

"I would see your lord," Melville asked quietly. "If convenient."

"It is not convenient," the servant replied rudely. "What makes you think that he will see you?"

Melville smiled, and his men leisurely formed a semi-circle, almost enclosing the discourteous but now nervous servant.

"Because I have travelled far to see him. Because I am a lord of this realm. And because I am asking nicely."

Melville smiled broadly, but his harsh eyes never left the servant's face. The servant swallowed, and backed away. Once out of the reach of Melville's men, he muttered.

"I will speak to my lord."

He turned to leave the hall, but shouted over his shoulder.

"Though don't hold your breath!"

The servant scampered out of the hall before Melville or his men could do or say anything in retaliation to his insolence.

"I've been holding my breath ever since I left home," murmured Melville to himself. "I've been holding my breath for the last three years."

But his breath had been stolen when he had seen Avis. Avis. Even here, in the midst of all this danger, he could not rid her from his mind. Perhaps it was because he was in so much danger that he dwelled on her face. He did not want to consider that he may never see that beautiful face again.

Robert grabbed Melville's arm, and nodded towards a door. The same servant had returned, and he did not look happy.

"My lord will see you now," he said sullenly. He was evidently disappointed that he had not managed to persuade his lord to send Melville away.

"Thank you," Melville attempted to remain polite, but it was gall to his throat. Gesturing to his men that they were to follow him, he walked towards the servant.

"No," the servant held up a hand. "Just you, my lord Melville. Your men may remain here and warm their hands. They are not to come."

"I take this as an insult," Melville shouted. He was tired, and he had had enough. "An insult against my name!"

"Take it as such." The servant shrugged his shoulders. "It was meant to be."

Melville pulled his hands into fists, but calmed his ragged breathing. There was plenty of time to shout later. It would not do to antagonise his host before he even saw him.

"My men shall remain here," he conceded with difficulty. "I follow you."

The smirk returned to the servant's face, and as much as Melville wanted to punch him, he refrained.

The servant led him out of the entrance hall, through corridors lined with tapestries, jewel-encrusted candles at every corner, and gold threaded embroideries draped over every seat. The display of wealth was not subtle. Many servants passed them as they walked through, many of them carrying ornate bowls and plates covered with food or jugs spilling over with wine. Melville's mouth watered. He had forgotten how many long hours ago it was since he had eaten.

Eventually the servant led him into a small room, with red and gold coverings on the chairs. One chair was slightly larger than the others, and beside it was a small table with a bowl of apples upon it. The large roaring fire had a marble hearth, which in turn was covered in gold and silver ornaments. This room was just as richly decorated as the corridors, but Melville could not help but feel uncomfortable, surrounded by such abundance.

"My lord is on his way."

The servant exited the room, leaving Melville alone. He did not want to sit down before he had been invited to by the man that he had come to see, but tiredness ached along every bone. However, Melville was used to pain. He had fought many battles, and this may be the last he ever fought.

Trumpets sounded outside the door, and there was the sound of footsteps. Melville stood still and upright, ready. His heart pounded and the heat of the fire seemed to increase with every louder step.

The door was flung open, and in walked a burly man, tall and strong. His blonde hair was scattered with red and grey, and several scars crept up from his hands into his sleeves. He threw himself onto the slightly larger chair, and then looked straight at Melville, standing stiffly. He smiled.

"Melville." The man's voice was guttural and deep, and it threw Melville into greater fits of terror. But he knew what must be done.

Melville walked forwards and knelt on the floor.

"My King."

CHAPTER TWENTY SEVEN

It had been two days. Two days. Avis could not believe that Melville had been gone a mere two days. It felt like an age, and it felt like forever – and it felt like he was never coming back.

Our very lives are in the balance, she reminded herself. This is not the time to think about yourself, and your petty worries. Focus on the here and the now.

The here and now was the Great Hall. Avis was sitting on a wooden trestle, watching the children play and making sure that they did not hurt themselves. The first day in the manor had been a day of fear for the children, trying desperately to avoid the Norman men in the corridors, and prattling Anglo-Saxon to Norman children before they realised they were not being understood – but they had settled quickly into the new routine. Their parents had taken much longer to adjust, and there was still fear and distrust between them and the Normans that surrounded them.

Avis had thought that as each day went by, her longing for Melville to return would decrease, but she was wrong. With each passing second, her desperation to see him only heightened. Not an hour went by when she did not think about what he could be doing, and who he was with; but it was difficult to picture him in his new home because she had no idea where he was. Was he hiding in a forest? On a boat travelling to Ireland? Did he make his way to Wales, or to Scotland? Was a Norman lord sheltering him in his manor? She could not even hope to guess which, if any of her guesses were anywhere close to the truth. In all of her thoughts about him, the images had no background, and the faces that surrounded him were hazy. The idea that Melville had left to see King William had not even crossed her mind.

Her fingernails had been bitten right to stubs, and some of them were bleeding. This bad habit had been beaten in childhood, but with the uncertainty of when the attack would begin, she had returned to old ways of dealing with such huge amounts of stress. Avis did not even realise that she was doing it again until a pale female hand reached over her shoulder, and batted her hand away from her mouth.

"I do not think so, my lady," reproved Edith. "You must keep your beauty, even in this difficult time."

Avis laughed as Edith clambered over the trestle table to sit beside her mistress.

"And what use will my looks be?"

Their smiles dipped. They knew what happened to attractive women when the soldiers had killed all of the men that would try valiantly to protect them. Edith shook herself.

"No use," she said firmly. "No use thinking of such things. We do not even know if they are coming yet."

Avis smiled again. Edith had become a source of strength and encouragement over the last two fraught days, but she could not help but wish Melville had remained to be that support for her. For all of them.

"Thank you," Avis said simply.

Edith returned her smile.

"My lady."

The two women sat in silence, watching the children. The small Norman boy was also watching them. He looked nervous, but eager to join in.

"Henri!" called Avis. The boy turned to her. "You can play if you want to."

The children turned at the sound of Avis speaking such strange words, and looked at where her gaze was. They saw the boy. Henri turned red, and began to run away, but a friendly hand was put out and stopped him.

"*Tæfla*?" asked the Anglo-Saxon girl, a child called Sæthryth.

Avis translated for Henri. "Game?"

Henri smiled, and took the hand of Sæthryth. He nodded.

Within minutes, the entire assorted crew were screaming in delight and running around the room. Edith smiled.

"See what you are doing?" she said to Avis. "You are creating a new people. Anglo-Saxon and Norman."

Avis's stomach lurched against those words. It was too close to what King William was trying to force throughout the land.

"Do not say such things," she said darkly.

"I am sorry." Edith was stunned to see such a violent reaction from Avis.

An awkward silence sprung up between the pair of them, until eventually Edith spoke again, more hesitantly this time.

"You miss him."

Avis could not pretend that she did not know who Edith was talking about, and she could not lie when the truth was written across her face.

"Yes."

Edith put her arm around Avis, shyly.

"That is not a crime."

Avis broke into a short laugh.

"No. But it has been two days, Edith! Where on earth could he be?"

"Then," Edith looked confused, "he is not on an errand?"

Too late, Avis remembered the half-truth that she had told her people. No one else had asked her where their lord had gone – they had simply trusted that he would not have left them unless it was for a reason that outweighed his desire to stay. Edith was the only one that she had felt close enough to accidently reveal the truth.

"No." Avis had told no one else, but had to confide her fears to someone. "I do not know where he is."

Edith's eyes widened as she tried to take in the news that the one man who may have the knowledge and experience to help them…was missing.

"But…"

"I know." Avis nodded. "I do not understand it either. All I know is that he left two days ago with several Norman men, left no message, and has not been seen or heard of since that day."

"But what could have happened to him?"

Avis sighed, and clasped her hands together, trying not to give in to the temptation to bite her nails again.

"I do not know. Sometimes I think that the rebels have captured him – taken him to Edgar. They could kill him. He is a Norman."

Edith sat there, listening to Avis pour out her worries and fears. She wished that she could say something of comfort, but they both knew that there was little to say.

"Sometimes I think he has been captured by King William," Avis confessed. "If so, he could be forced to ride against us. To fight against his very people. And then I think, perhaps he has fled, and been successful. By this time he could be near London, and soon on his way to Normandy."

"He would not leave us."

"He may." Avis was under no illusions. She knew that even soldiers and expert men of war had fears. "He has left us. He has fought many terrible and bloody battles. It may be that he does not want to fight another."

Although it was partially relieving for Avis to be able to take Edith into her confidence, it did not stem the fresh terror that filled her every time she thought of Melville. Nothing could stop that.

"He will be fine," reassured Edith.

"You do not know that!" cried Avis.

There was silence as Edith searched the face of her mistress.

"Not," Avis said more calmly, with a delicate blush moving across her cheeks, "that I care."

She nonchalantly brushed her skirts, and fixed her eyes more firmly on the children that she was supposed to be watching.

"My lady," Edith broke into her thoughts. "I hope you do not take offence, but I have watched you. I have also watched him. I am not a clever woman, but I know people. I know the way that he looks at you, and I know that you are very much in love with my lord Melville."

Love. So that was the word that Avis had been looking for. The word sounded like a warm arm bringing her home. Of course, love. How could she have been so stupid? The rush of emotions and heat whenever she saw him; the desire that she could no longer deny when he came close to her; and the heartache now that she is without him, and he is in such danger. She was in love with him.

Edith saw the smile in her eyes, and left without a sound. Avis did not even notice her leave. She was so enwrapped in her own emotions.

Love. That was the word to describe the ache inside her very soul when she tried not to think of the possible danger that Melville could be in. That was the term to express that lurch when she saw him, and smelt him, and felt his strong arm supporting her. That was the way to tell that she was completely his. It was love.

Avis had known that her parents were in love. She could always see it in their eyes, and the way that her mother would always prepare particular food for her husband, and the way that her father could never take his gaze away from his wife. And now she could see in herself all of the signs of that deep emotion. It was not enough to say esteem, it was not enough to say admire – it was love. The feeling that she had for Melville demanded so much more than those simple sayings. She was in love with him.

As this realisation dawned on her, another thought crossed her mind, and the happiness that she had felt with the realisation of what she felt for her husband sank quickly into despondency. Melville clearly did not love her. He would not have left her if he had felt a tenth of what she felt for him. Her heart sank further, but she resolved herself. If Avis knew anything about love, it was that sometimes it was one-sided. Sometimes one person simply could not muster up such feelings for another person. Avis knew that regardless of what Melville felt for her, she could never stop loving him.

CHAPTER TWENTY EIGHT

There was not a sound. Melville's head was bowed, so he could not see King William's expression. He stared at the floor. The dried rushes that made up the covering swam in and out of focus as he tried to remain conscious, despite the exhaustion and his rumbling stomach. After what seemed like an age, William spoke.

"Rise."

Melville stood up, and faced his King. William's face was sceptical, but he did not look angry. Melville tried to breathe out a sigh of relief without being noticed, and tried to put the right words in order before he spoke.

"My lord King – "

"Sit."

The order came harshly, and Melville paused. Perhaps the idea to come to William had been a bad one. He certainly did not sound particularly happy to see him.

"Sit," repeated William in the same tone. His eyes had not left Melville, and there was little kindness there. But there had never been much expression there at all.

Melville sank into the chair that was next to him, and his aching bones cried out in relief. But he could not relax now. He shifted himself forwards slightly so that he would not fall asleep. He needed to be as alert as he could be in the presence of this mighty man.

"Thank you, my lord." Melville said. "You may not remember me, but – "

"Of course I remember you. Lord of Copmanthorpe. Ulleskelf. You impressed me on the day of the beach landing. You married."

Every word was clipped and short, giving nothing away and wasting no energy. William was clearly a man of action, and did not appreciate his time being wasted.

Melville nodded.

"I have come – "

"I know why you have come." William interrupted lazily. "Do you not think I am aware of young Jean's betrayal?"

Melville's heart groaned. The beginnings of his fears were therefore confirmed. His fingers clutched the arms of the chair, but he continued.

"Jean is no traitor," Melville said firmly. "He returned to your side. He will fight for you. He is a good man."

William reached to his left and picked up a large red apple from the bowl on the wooden table beside him. He considered it, and spoke without looking at Melville.

"He *was* a good man."

"My lord?"

"I could not allow such a man to remain amongst my retinue. He was…disposed of." William bit into the apple. Spit and tiny parts of apple flew around his mouth, and he chewed loudly, looking directly at Melville.

Melville felt sick. He had known that Jean's warning to him had been a horrific gamble, but he had never expected him to lose. Jean was a winner, a fighter. A man who had been full of life.

"You question my judgement?" William had been watching Melville's reaction with interest, and smiled cynically.

"I do, my lord." Melville knew at this point that there was nothing to be gained from false diplomacy. Honesty was his only option. "Jean was a good man. A good fighter, and loyal to you. You disadvantage yourself by ridding your party of such men."

The words hung in the air between them, and Melville swallowed. He knew that by speaking so rashly to William he signed his own fate – but then he had never believed that he was leaving this place alive in any case. It was for Avis' safety that he had come. It was all for Avis.

William considered the man carefully. When Melville swore total allegiance to his King, he became his vassal, a total servant. Melville was regarded for several moments, and then his spectator broke into a laugh.

"Your loyalty to your friend becomes you, Melville."

"My loyalty is true to all," Melville returned quickly. "Including you, my King."

"Hmmm." Another bite of the apple was taken. "Talk of loyalty is cheap, you know. It is action that I prize beyond all."

Melville nodded.

"I know. That is why I have journeyed here."

"Indeed."

"I am here to plead for my people."

William's hand paused halfway to his mouth. This, he had not expected. He placed the apple back into the bowl.

"Your people?"

"The people of Copmanthorpe. Of Ulleskelf, and my household."

"Your people?" repeated William. He looked stunned. "You are a Norman! You do not owe anything to these people, these peasants! Are they of Norman blood? They are Saxons, man! They are the ones that owe us. We have saved them from themselves."

Melville did not reply. The anger that had coursed through William had given him a blotchy complexion, and his hand flexed. But just as quickly as his fury had been roused, he calmed. William saw the internal battle, and saw it won. The King nodded, and picked up the apple once more.

"I take no requests," he said firmly. "You may join me if you wish, or you may return to your woman. I hear she is of uncommon beauty," William stuffed his face with apple once more, "though she is but a Saxon."

It was not anger, but hatred that filled Melville's body and drowned his mind. He rose to his feet and drew his sword, no thought to consequences. William's eyes widened, but he made no move to retrieve his own weapon and did not call for his guards to come and kill Melville like a wild animal.

"You dishonour me!" Melville spoke quietly through clenched teeth, but there was feeling in every syllable. "That woman who you so easily discount is one of the bravest people that I have had the privilege to know. She has faced death and she has faced fear and she has overcome. And despite the terrible life that she has lived – that we have inflicted on her! – she is kind, and caring, and delicate, and good."

Melville panted with the effort of not running through his King.

"I may have been born a bastard, but even if I had the noblest blood in Normandy I would not deserve her!"

He had run out of words to say, and stood, sword aloft, waiting for William's judgement. He could not believe that he had said such things to his King, and he knew that the consequences would be terrible. Could this be counted as treason? A bead of sweat fell from his forehead, and William sat immobile. He stared at Melville for a very long time. Too long. Melville began to sway on the spot, his fiery emotion not dispelling the exhaustion that he had felt for hours now.

"Sit." The word that William first spoke to Melville was repeated again, and this time Melville obeyed immediately.

William brought his hands together and swopped the apple from palm to palm, eyes never leaving Melville. He had neglected to sheathe his sword, which was still clutched by his right hand. More minutes passed in silence as the King contemplated his subject.

"You say you are illegitimate."

This was not at all what Melville had expected William to take from his impassioned speech in defence of his Anglo-Saxon bride, but he nodded.

"I spent my life proving that I was worth something. That is how I have come to be in England, under your orders. Because I know I am better than those who only see my birth expect me to be."

William froze. He stared now at Melville with wide eyes, apple in his left hand but not moving at all. And then he sighed.

"Apple?"

Melville was startled into rudeness.

"What?"

"Would you like an apple, my lord Melville?" William picked up the bowl, and held it out.

Melville gave a short, uncertain laugh. Nothing could have prepared him for this, and he was still not sure if he was about to be arrested.

"Should I be giving in to such temptation, my lord?"

William returned his laugh, and Melville took an apple. Biting into its sweet flesh, he almost groaned with pleasure. It was good to eat again. It was good to feel alive.

"You know of my parentage." William stated this, rather than expected Melville to respond, but he nodded. "I was unaware of yours."

Melville swallowed. The previously welcome apple now stuck in his throat.

William's eyes wandered from Melville, and stared at the ceiling.

"I, too, have spent my life proving myself to be strong and bold. I too bear what some consider a disgrace, but I consider a badge of honour."

Melville's heart began to thump loudly again.

William stood up, and walked towards Melville, who dropped to his knees in front of his King. William reached down, and pulled him up. The two men faced each other.

"Go," said William gruffly. "Return to your woman. Hold her close, and tell her from the King that she is safe. I shall not harm your land, or your people."

Melville's jaw dropped wide, and pieces of apple dropped out. He clamped his mouth shut in embarrassment. He tried to kneel again but William prevented him.

"There is no need for such dramatics." William smiled. "Take your men and depart."

Melville put away his sword, and walked towards the door like a man returning to earth after being given a chance to escape hell. But before he exited the room, he swivelled to once more gaze at his King.

"Melville?"

"My lord," Melville began awkwardly. "I cannot go without asking you…without asking you the question that many of your people are already asking."

William smiled, but his smile had no warmth.

"Ask."

Melville hesitated. Was this wise? He asked himself. Is this only going to get you into more trouble? But he could not in all honour leave the room without discovering the truth.

"Why? Why destroy the North? There are many innocents there, and people who will not know what they have done to deserve such punishment."

William stared at his vassal, this Melville who had travelled miles upon miles to secure the safety of a few peasants and a woman of low birth. And his smile wavered, and then disappeared.

"It is well for you," he said gruffly. "That it is I that is King, and not you."

"My lord?"

"It is by difficult decisions such as I have made that makes one a King," William spoke in a tired voice that Melville had not heard before. "It is for Kings, and Kings alone that such decisions must be made. It is not for the likes of you, and it is the burden that I bear. And I bear it for my people, so that they do not have to bear such things. For it is a heavy burden, and I ask no one to carry it for me. Now take your men, and go."

Melville looked at his King, and felt pity for him for the first time. He bowed to William, who inclined his head and gestured to the door. But Melville had not reached it before he heard his name once more.

"Melville."

William's voice halted his path, and he turned to look at his King again.

"Take *all* of your men."

Melville nodded, but he did not understand. All he wanted to do was be away. William smiled, and gestured that he could leave.

The same servant was waiting outside the door, and stared at Melville with a newfound fear and respect.

"Well," he said in shock. "It appears that my lord approves of you greatly."

The man must have been listening at the door, but even this act of rudeness could not dim the smile in Melville's face.

"Take me to my men," he replied easily. "And be quiet."

The man snorted at Melville's sudden bravery, but sullenly led Melville back to the entrance hall that he recognised. The majority of his men were standing around the fire, their clothes steaming, but Robert had been pacing up and down. He had just thrown himself into a chair when Melville turned the corner and strode into the entrance hall.

"We return home," Melville called out to them.

"What, immediately?" asked Robert, hauling himself out of the chair and looking disappointed at having his brief moment of rest interrupted.

"This very moment."

"My lord," begged another man, "we are exhausted."

"And so is every single person that we left behind," returned Melville in a strong loud voice. King William's servants paused to listen to him. "Exhausted of not knowing whether they are to live or die. We must ride to give them the news."

Melville's men exchanged glances with one another, unsure what the news was.

"News?" ventured Robert.

Melville smiled. Smiled at his brave men, who had undertaken so much with so little hope of success.

"The King will not be taking Ulleskelf. We are saved."

There were no hurrahs or shouts of joy from his retinue. Just sweet relief.

"Then home," smiled Robert. "And the sooner the better."

Footsteps behind Melville sounded, and his men saw a figure approaching behind him. With gasps, they threw themselves to the ground. Melville spun around to see King William once more, looking angry.

"Did I not tell you to take *all* your men?" He asked furiously.

"I…" Melville could not think what to say, but then cried out, "*Jean*!"

A shape had appeared from behind the King, and Jean rushed towards Melville. After they had embraced, Melville remembered William's words, and turned to him.

"My King – you told me that you had Jean killed."

William smiled.

"I told you that I could not allow such a man to remain amongst my retinue. I told you that I had disposed of him. Consider him at your disposal."

He swept his robes around him as he turned, and as he left the room shouted, "*All* of your men, Melville."

CHAPTER TWENTY NINE

The look-outs that Avis had stationed along the roof of the manor had not given a sound since she had put them there, and for that she was prayerfully thankful. Another day had gone past without a sign of Melville, and Avis had finally accepted that he had truly gone. Under no circumstances could he have been delayed for so long in York. He must have reached London by now, she thought dully as she pummelled some dough in the kitchen. Soon he shall be back where he always wanted to be. In Normandy.

The days had passed in slow monotony, and Avis began to hope that the King had decided not to destroy the North. Perhaps any moment now, she thought as she ate in the Great Hall alongside a pack of children and a sweaty Norman, a messenger shall reach the gates with news that the King has changed his mind. Her imagination ran wild, including Melville riding towards her on a large horse, ready to sweep her off her feet and console her with news that everyone was safe…

Henri ran into the room, and made straight for Avis. No one noticed him at first, but his panicked expression caught the attention of many, and by the time that he reached her, silence had fallen as they waited to hear what news he brought.

"Men," he panted, crawling into Avis' lap. "On horses."

Melville's eyes filled with tears. He had not cried for years – could not remember the last time that he had cried – but he had never seen such a sorry sight in all of his days. On their way back to Ulleskelf, he and his men had reached the village by the hill with the stone cross. Avis had played with the children there, while he had been warned by Jean of the terrible plague of death that William was bringing to this land. And it had reached this village.

They had seen the smoke for miles, despite the twilight. Now that they were closer, they could smell the awful odour of burnt and rotting flesh. Most of the buildings were torn down, and there was no one living to be seen.

"Hello?" called out Melville hopelessly, without any expectation of a reply. He forced his horse into the centre of the village. The carnage that he saw repulsed him, but he could not bear to leave without checking whether anyone had survived.

Robert wandered from home to home, shouting out in Anglo-Saxon. Jean had dismounted, and walked towards Melville with despair in his eyes.

"How?" he whispered in his deep voice. "How could William do such a thing?"

Melville had no answer. He just looked at Jean, whose eyes were brimming with tears. He was not a man to hide his emotions, and he spoke again.

"I do not understand."

"Neither do I," Melville replied slowly. "But if there are any survivors here, they are not likely to reveal themselves to us."

"Why?"

"We are Norman. Like the men who have just destroyed their lives."

Melville's simple pronouncement had a huge effect on Jean. He spat on the ground, and almost shouted at Melville.

"Not like William! It is disgrace to our name, what he has done here!"

"It is indeed," agreed Melville, sadly. "The title of Norman shall no longer be the same again."

Robert joined them, shaking his head.

"I find none alive."

Melville sighed.

"Then onwards. We have no time to lose. William's men have obviously been here, which in my mind is too close to our home for comforting thoughts. We must be quick."

The nods of his men displayed that their fears were just as his own. What would they find when they reached Ulleskelf?

With a final push of their horses, which were just as exhausted as they were, they circled the forest and knew that within moments their destination would be appearing on the horizon.

Melville and his men had ridden hard, and they had ridden far to protect the village by their manor and to make sure that none of the household would be harmed. But now they had reached the outskirts of the village of Ulleskelf, a terrible sight filled their vision, and Melville cried out in horror.

The village was empty.

As he reached the church, he dismounted. His men watched him, unable to speak.

"Avis," Melville called out. He had not eaten a full meal for almost a week now, and he was growing confused. "Where is Avis?"

Robert carefully got down from his horse, and walked towards his lord.

"She is not here."

"Why?" Melville's tears did not shock his men, but instead warmed them to him. It took a brave man to cry in front of his retinue. It took a strong man to admit defeat.

"This is the village," Robert reminded him, concern covering his face. "Avis does not live here."

Melville made no reply as tears streaked down his dirty face, leaving a line of glittering salt.

"Jean," Robert turned to the newest member of their party. "Take care of our lord."

Jean helped Melville to stand as Robert went from dwelling to dwelling, calling out in Anglo-Saxon for anyone who was hiding themselves to come out, just as he had done at the previous village. But no one did.

"I cannot find anyone," he called back to Melville. "But…" Robert looked around at the intact buildings. "I do not understand. Fire has not consumed this place. Something is wrong."

"They are all gone." Melville muttered, half to himself, half to Jean. "I should not have left them."

Jean tried to console him, but did not know how.

"You did not have much of a choice, my lord," he said. "You had to see the King."

"Yes, the King," Melville repeated. "I had to see the King."

Those words recalled him to himself, and he straightened up.

"What has been will be," he spoke with a stronger voice. "We have conquered this land, and now our King sees fit to conquer it once more."

His men looked at him silently. None could deny the truth in his words.

Melville spun around to gaze towards the place that he now called home.

"Onwards," he called. "Onwards, to whatever there is to find."

The panic that had spread through the room at Henri's words was violent. Men grabbed swords, and women began to gather the knives that were strewn along the table. It took Avis several attempts to gain their attention in the chaos.

"Please!" She shouted, and she stood once again on the table. Those who had heard her turned to face her, and people started to notice the strong and silent woman standing once more on a table. Eventually, all became quiet.

"We must remain calm," Avis could hear the tremble in her own voice, and so knew that all could hear it too, but she continued speaking. "Nothing can be gained from panic."

Climbing elegantly down from the table, she walked slowly across the hall.

"We do not know whether these men are messengers, or warriors. Until then, no one is to hurt them. I will not have innocent blood on my hands."

Though some looked reluctant, people throughout the room nodded. There had been enough innocent blood spilt. No more.

Avis led the people into the stable yard, where the gate was barred and a harassed look-out called down to her.

"Several men in the distance!"

"Open the gate."

Everyone gasped at Avis' words. They had been spoken clearly, but no one obeyed her terrible command.

"My lady!" Edith pushed past people so that she could stand by the side of her mistress. "You cannot mean to go out there! To face them!"

"If that is what it takes," Avis spoke steadily, belying the fear fluttering against her ribcage, "then that is what it takes. I will have no one else be taken from me, or stand between me and death."

She turned to the look-out, and repeated her words.

"Open the gate."

The poor man looked nervously at the crowd behind her, but none challenged her. Her bravery gave them all hope. Swallowing down his reservations, he took down the planks of oak that prevented the gate from being opened, and gingerly pushed it ajar. Avis walked forward, through the open gate, and then turned. She looked at her people – Anglo-Saxon and Norman – and she knew what she must do.

"Bar it behind me."

"No!"

But Edith was held back by caring hands.

"Let her go," Bronson said calmly. "She will defend us. She will not be harmed."

Edith struggled against Bronson's grip, but she was not strong enough, and none came to her aid. Many had recognised in Avis' eyes the flash of a fighter. There was none that was brave enough to stop her.

The gate was securely shut, and Avis suppressed the bile that was rising up in her throat. There was no turning back. Once again she was to face the Norman blade. With luck, once again she would escape its cold death.

She squinted into the distance. Avis could see the horsemen that the lookout had espied, but she could not make out exactly how many there were. Bracing herself, and gathering her skirts around her as the breeze played with them, she began to walk forward.

As Melville rode, he could see a lone figure stumbling towards them, skirts gathered around her with trembling arms. One survivor then, he said to himself. Rage entered his heart against the unknown perpetrators of this terrible crime. Increasing the pace of his horse, he sped on towards his home.

But then the woman fell. The breeze caught onto her hair, and long blonde tresses were blown about in the wind.

Avis.

Melville gave out a cry, a cry of relief and the release of pain. Avis heard the noise from the ground and screamed, curling herself into a ball. She knew that she could not escape the attack that approached, but acted instinctively, tucking her legs underneath herself and covering her head with her hands. Her hair flowed about her, preventing her from seeing her attacker. As the hooves stopped mere feet away from her, she shouted in a strong but frightened voice.

"Leave me alone!"

But the hands that grabbed her were not coarse, violent ones, but caring and strong hands. She heard a voice. A voice that she knew.

"Avis!"

Taking her hands away from her eyes, she turned towards the speaker. She knew that voice. But it could not be.

"Avis, look at me," Melville spoke in a whisper. "It is I. Melville. I have come back."

Avis was stunned, and could not take it in.

"Back?"

"Yes."

"But you went away."

"I was always coming back."

Avis threw her arms around Melville, who took her into his embrace. She nuzzled into his neck, his reassuring scent mingled with sweat slowing her heart and giving strength to her legs. The feel of her, her intensity and her delicacy almost caused Melville to groan aloud. He had missed her more than he had realised, and he shuddered to think what may have occurred if William's actions had not been as unexpected as they were.

Melville refused to let go of Avis for several minutes, by which time the other riders had reached them. They saw the couple's embrace, and tried to look uninterestedly around them, but it took a loud cough and throat clearing from Jean to bring them to their senses.

Melville eventually released his wife, who smiled at him shyly.

"You can tell me where you have been later. Before then, you are in sore need of a bath!"

Melville joined in her laughter.

"I dare say you are right – we have not rested since we left you."

Avis' smile faltered.

"And where did you go?"

Melville did not have the energy to explain in full, standing here in front of his own gate, but he knew that she needed to hear the good news of their safety – even if she was the only one left to hear it.

"William has assured us protection," he said hastily. "We are no longer in any danger."

Gratitude flowed throughout Avis' body, giving her the greatest relief that she had felt since that awful day when Jean had brought them the terrifying news.

"Truly, we are safe?"

"We have nothing to fear."

Now a full smile could grow upon Avis' lips, and it gladdened Melville's heart. It was an amazing thing, to cause someone that he cared for so deeply to be so happy. But then his own smile fell.

"I just wish there were more of you for me to tell," he said sadly. "You were right. We should have stayed to protect everyone."

Avis looked puzzled, and once again her nose had scrunched into a state of confusion.

"What do you mean?"

"We passed the village on our way here," Melville told her, lifting her to her feet. "I wish that I did not have to be the one to bring you the news. It has been taken. But surely you knew that. They must have taken the house also. How did you survive?"

Avis did not reply, but called out in a loud voice.

"Open!"

Melville looked confused at her wild cry, but suddenly the huge gate began to creak open. He opened his mouth in shock as people poured out from its mouth: Anglo-Saxon and Norman alike.

As the men that had travelled with him loudly greeted their friends, Avis looked bashfully up at Melville.

"I hope you don't mind. But I kept them safe," she told him. "I kept them all safe."

Melville drew her once again to his side, and placed a slight kiss upon her now muddy golden hair.

"You continue to surprise me, you know."

She smiled cheekily. "I know."

Raising her voice, she called out to the crowd thronging around them.

"My lord Melville has news for us all."

Avis turned to face him, and looked innocently expectant. Melville chuckled, and his feelings for her grew even more. He mounted his horse so that all could see him, and spoke in a loud, clear voice.

"I have been to see the King! He is grateful for our service, and so has extended his peace and protection over us. We need have no fear of his army. He will not harm us. We are safe."

There was a stunned silence after this pronouncement. No one could take in the news that they had nothing to fear, nothing to arm themselves against. And then a cheer was heard – Avis had thrown her arms up in the air, and shouted with a smile on her face with total abandon. Those around her giggled, and before long shouts and cheers joined hers, and echoed around the valley.

Melville spoke over the hubbub.

"And now everybody inside! We must bar the gates once again, in case of bandits returning from the North. There are going to be many desperate people in the coming days."

All obeyed him, chattering with each other excitedly, the men that had travelled with Melville relaying their tale to a rapt audience.

As Avis turned to go, her husband snatched her by her waist.

"And where do you think you are going?" He breathed into her ear.

Avis shivered with anticipation.

"Where everyone else is going, my lord," she replied in a whisper. "We owe them our presence at the feast. There will be a celebration."

"I would rather have you to myself."

"Well then," Avis escaped from his clutches and smiled wickedly at him as she walked away. "You should not have left."

Melville laughed, and followed her into the Great Hall. Orders were being shouted out in broken Norman and Anglo-Saxon across the hall as people from both races joined together to create the feast of all feasts. The musicians stuck feathers in their hair as they played, children dancing before them. Avis and Melville took their places at the head of the top table.

Throughout the long meal, Melville tried to take Avis' hand in his, but she playfully always kept her hand just out of reach.

"Avis," Melville muttered longingly.

"Melville," she stated plainly, smiling, clearly enjoying how easily she could tease him. This was something that she had missed, and had never before supposed that she would even care about.

"Avis," he repeated, but was interrupted by a loud voice. It was Jean, who repeated each of sentences twice; first in Norman, and then in Anglo-Saxon. Melville raised his eyebrows in surprise. He had not known that Jean had taken the time to learn the native language, and he saw that Robert's look had darkened. He chuckled to himself. Rivalry already then!

"Friends!" Jean said in a clear voice, quietening the musicians and the people around him. "We celebrate not our own deeds, but the bravery of our lord Melville. He travelled far and in dangerous lands to secure for us all our safety. Without him and his loyal men," bowing to Robert and the other men, who nodded graciously, "we would not be able to feast so happily. Melville is our lord, and he protects us. Let us honour him."

Cheers rang out, and Robert gave a rueful smile to Jean, who returned it. Melville smiled appreciatively at the friendship that was being made between his men. It was well to see such things in his household.

He rose, smiling at the respect that he was accorded from all sides. Putting his hands up for silence, he spoke.

"I will be honest," Melville said with a smile, "I was not entirely sure whether I would return from my journey to the court of King William. All I knew was that I was ready to give my own life in return for the safety of my people. You, all of you. You are worth more to me than jewels and gold, because you are my family."

Another set of cheers filled the hall, and Melville looked around at them all with a grin on his face.

"But," he continued, "I must say I am both shocked and pleased to see the work that the lady Avis has done in my absence."

This pronouncement caused many heads to nod, but Avis gave out a quiet gasp of surprise.

"There is not a single person in this room who I think could have predicted just how my lady could have acted."

As Melville spoke, a blush covered Avis' cheek. She pulled at his clothes.

"That's quite enough," she hissed, embarrassed at such public a display of praise, but her husband ignored her, his smile widening.

"Avis did not sit at home, waiting patiently for me to solve the problem – and that speaks highly of her character, and of all our women!" Men around the room laughed, and women looked proud. "She acted not out of fear alone, but of love and kindness for the people that she has claimed for her own."

Avis could not bear to hear such phrases from Melville's own lips. It was too much, too wonderful and yet too dreadful at the same moment.

"And so raise your goblets and tankards, friends," finished Melville. "Raise them to the wonderful lady Avis. Long may she live, and long may she live with us!"

Hands throughout the hall were raised, brimming with ale and wine and thankfulness to the woman that had been their protector, even when she herself had been afraid. Melville smiled down at the mortified woman beside him, and sat down.

"Did you not like my speech?" He teased.

"Melville!" Avis remonstrated. "There are countless others here who have done more than I! Where are their thanks? Where are their rewards?"

"Hush," Melville said carelessly, piling his plate with food as if he had not eaten for an entire year. "They shall receive their rewards when I have power of mind enough to do so."

Avis smiled, in spite of herself, watching this tall solid man consume his food like a starving child. She had her Melville back, after a time when she thought that she would never even see him again.

Without considering her actions, she placed her hand tenderly upon his knee. Melville almost cried out, the reaction to her touch was so strong. He had never known the touch of any other person to have this devastating effect on him. As much as he wanted to lift her bodily and carry her out of the room, he had to control himself. He carefully lifted her hand away from himself and placed it on the table.

"I do not think so," he said gruffly, before turning away from her and speaking to Bronson who had finally come up from the kitchen to enjoy the feast.

Avis' eyes filled with humiliation. He did not want her. His speech had seemed to give the impression that he truly cared for her, but this must be out of relief for his people. Of course he could not care about her, let alone be in love with her.

Rising suddenly, she strode away from their table, and walked down the room. Settling herself next to a servant girl who Melville thought was called Edith – or something of the sort – the two women began talking away.

Melville watched her go. Avis had given no indication of becoming tired of his company. He must have done something, said something, to upset her. He sighed. Was he ever to understand this complicated woman?

CHAPTER THIRTY

It was many hours before the festivities had come to a conclusion, and only then could Melville in all politeness manage to drag himself and Avis to a more private room. She had wanted to stay, and speak to their people, but Melville eventually could not wait any longer. He had to have her to himself. Grabbing her hand, he pulled her away from a gaggle of Norman and Anglo-Saxon women, and practically dragged her behind him.

"Melville!"

As Avis tried to rush apologies to the people that she was speaking to, they smirked as they watched their lord haul his stunning wife out of the hall. There was no need to guess what was on Melville's mind.

As they turned around a corner in the corridor out of the eyesight of the feasters, Avis wrenched at her wrist, trying to break free.

"Melville, where are you taking me?"

Without releasing her, Melville stopped and pushed her against the cold stone wall, leaning towards her with deep emotion. Avis gasped at the intensity in his eyes, and revelled in the feeling of his strong body against hers.

"How could I leave you?" He whispered.

Avis' breathing had become irregular, and she found it difficult to speak. She was extremely aware of his dominating arms keeping her against the wall – not that she would choose to be anywhere else. The coldness from the wall contrasted with the heat from his body, and her head spun.

"I don't know," she replied huskily. "You chose to go."

Melville groaned, and dipped his face closer to hers, but just far enough away for him to look her straight in the eyes. Her clear green eyes were transfixed upon his dark turbulent ones, reaching deeper and deeper into his very soul.

"I was a fool," he whispered. "I should never have gone."

"But then who would have saved us?"

"You can save us all."

"Do not be ridiculous."

"You saved me."

Avis was startled at his words, but Melville could no longer keep up any sort of pretence. She stared into his eyes, and leaned towards him. With a sigh of relief Melville moved, closing the distance between them, desperate for her kiss, desperate to end the torture of being so far from her.

A noise caused Avis to stop, and then turn her head. Robert had come around the corner, and frozen, seeing the two of them in such an intimate position. He had obviously tried to retreat without being noticed, but had not managed it.

"Forgive me," he muttered and fled in the opposite direction.

Melville let out a dry laugh, and rested his head against the wall beside Avis'.

"I was not quick enough," he breathed, and moved away from her. She remained, as if still pinned, by the wall, breathing deeply. She could not move, she could barely think.

Melville held out a hand to her.

"Come," he said, raggedly. "Let us talk."

"Talk?" Avis replied, confused, as he led her towards the outer chamber in which they had had some of their most intimate conversations. The last thing in the world that she wanted to do right now was talk. It was the last thing on her mind – although to be fair, her mind seemed to have little control over her actions at the present.

"Talk." Melville sat her down in what was becoming her seat of choice, and placed himself beside her. It took every effort in his muscular body not to throw her over his shoulder and carry her into his bed chamber, but now was not the time. Before they became that physically intimate, they had to take down the emotional barriers. Trust was everything.

"What do you want to talk about?"

"Do you not have many questions as to where I have been?"

Avis nodded, slowly.

"Well, yes. But I did not think conversation was at the top of your mind."

Melville laughed quietly.

"You know me well – or, which is more likely, I am not as subtle as I think I am." His eyes twinkled as he looked down at her, and she snuggled closer towards him.

Avis sighed, contentedly. He may want to talk, but she was content just feeling his proximity, and knowing that he would never abandon her again.

"Questions…" she pondered.

Melville watched her, determined never to leave her again.

"First question," she announced. "Why did you not tell me where you were going? Why leave without saying a word?"

Melville nodded.

"And 'tis a good question."

"Do you have a good answer?" Avis asked coyly.

He laughed. "I do indeed! There did not seem to be anything to gain by telling you of my plan. I did not expect to be able to return, and so there was little point in worrying you."

"But I was worried," Avis countered. "As soon as it was discovered that you had gone, and without leaving a message. If anything, not knowing where you were made me more anxious."

"I had not considered that."

"Do not do that again." Avis commanded, but in a quiet, soft tone.

"I promise."

Tiredness was catching up with Melville, and he struggled to stay awake – but he was enjoying the feeling of Avis nestled up against him so much that he was loath to send her away so that he could sleep.

"What did William say?" Avis asked quietly.

Melville sighed.

"He was very strange."

"Have you not spoken much with him before?"

"Goodness, no. I am but a small fish in the large ocean of noblemen that William has under his command. Indeed, I was surprised to find that he knew who I was."

Avis smiled. "You are more memorable than you think."

Melville returned her smile, and began to stroke her hair. It still had small clumps of mud in from their embrace earlier that day, but it reminded him of how real she was. How brave, and how delicate.

"He was very abrupt. He confused me with strange riddles about the fate of Jean, and then he tried to insult you."

Avis wrinkled up her nose and forehead in the way that was becoming most endearing to Melville.

"What do you mean, tried to insult me?"

Melville swallowed, knowing how the next sentence could sound – knowing that he had done the same thing to her that he now reviled in his King.

"He used the word Saxon in order to offend. I took it as it was meant, although," and he really spoke in earnest here, "you have altered my perceptions of your people greatly."

Avis looked up at her husband, and marvelled at the change that had been wrought, both in him and in herself. Who would have thought that a Norman and an Anglo-Saxon could be at such peace with each other, in such intimacy. She herself would never have guessed at such an occurrence, but then here she was. But then she frowned.

"At that point, William's favour must have felt very distant."

"It did," confessed Melville. "I drew my sword against my King, the very man that I had sworn to honour and protect. I thought from that point that I would never escape with my life, but after I had told him about my parentage and my childhood, he looked on me very differently."

Avis was astonished.

"Your childhood changed the mind of a great King?"

"Yes!" Melville laughed. "He too had fought against discrimination due to his parentage, and so could understand my desire to prove myself. For that reason," he shrugged his shoulders, "and seemingly for that reason alone, we are safe."

Melville fell silent, and Avis considered him. This man had borne his very soul to his King, a man who had threatened to destroy him. He had gone, willingly, almost hoping to die if it would protect those that he left behind. Avis swelled with pride for him, and love radiated from her every pore. She could care for this man for the rest of her life.

After several minutes, Melville shifted himself.

"And now," he said, pulling himself free of Avis' embraces, "time to retire for the night."

"No," began Avis, but he cut across her.

"Yes." And with that short tone, said in kindness, Avis knew that she would not be able to dissuade him. She wanted to continue talking, but knew that he was covering his exhaustion better than she could imagine. Walking hand in hand with him, they reached the door of her chamber. Before Avis could even consider what she may or may not say to Melville, he had gone.

CHAPTER THIRTY ONE

In the days that followed, Avis and Melville settled into a routine around the numerous others that they were now sharing their home with. Despite King William's statement, Melville did not consider it safe for them to return to their homes, and Avis was inclined to agree with him. Although they continued to sleep in different chambers, they spent every evening together, talking and laughing – though neither had been brave enough to try once again for that elusive kiss.

Avis continued to work with and support all of the servants, teaching the different languages and helping in any misunderstandings, but Melville never chastised her for it. He had learnt the value of letting Avis do as she pleased, and he watched as the manor became a place of laughter, and of mingling words.

As he watched Avis teaching some of the smaller Anglo-Saxon girls how to bake bread in the tradition of their ancestors, Melville ruefully regretted the day that he had shouted at her for lowering herself. His servants weren't below him. Most of them were richer than he had been when he was a child, and he could not blame them for that. They were good, honest people. Melville could see that by keeping these customs alive, they in turn kept alive the memories of those who had originally taught them.

"Melville!" A voice that he did not recognise called him to attention. It was one of the small Anglo-Saxon girls – Sæthryth, that was her name. She was beckoning him to join them, flour smeared across one cheek and a bright smile lighting the room.

Melville gestured, trying to indicate to the child that he was not going to join her, but Avis leapt up and grabbed his arm, covering him in flour, and pulled at him, giggling.

"Come on Melville!" She dragged him over to the others, who chuckled at the sight of the huge man being pulled unwillingly towards the baking.

As Melville followed Avis' simple instructions with the dough, he could not help but marvel at her. Here she was, born and raised as a high-born lady and now married to the ruling class, a Norman – and she had goose fat in her hair and stains all down the apron that she had donned before starting in the kitchen. No pretended graces prevented her from enjoying the activities that she loved, and she was not self-conscious enough to feel in any way embarrassed by her flamboyant pleasure. He revelled in her delight.

"There!" Avis' voice broke into his thoughts. "Done."

She lifted the various breads onto a tray, and carried them off, shouting over her shoulder.

"I shall return shortly!"

Melville was left with the Anglo-Saxon girls, who became less giggly now that they were left with their lord. They looked at him with awe, remembering the words that their parents had spoken to them about respect and honour. Only the small girl who had invited Melville over seemed content with his company. Sæthryth rose and walked around the table to the trestle that he was sitting on, and raised her arms.

Melville knew what she wanted. Reaching down, he lifted her up and sat her on his lap.

"*Þancede*," said the girl, who rested her head against Melville's chest. "*Þancede…*" Within moments, she was asleep.

Accustomed as Melville was with talking to children, he was not really sure what he was meant to do with a sleeping child. The other girls giggled quietly, and slipping down from their wooden trestle, they scampered out of the kitchen.

"Wait," called Melville quietly, not wanting to wake the child but not wanting the others to abandon him. The servants around him smiled to see their master helplessly trapped to the trestle.

"Don't worry," said Bronson, whose Norman had greatly improved in the week of trying to converse without Avis' constant translation. "She will return soon."

"Thank you," smiled Melville.

"*Þancede*," replied Bronson.

It was the same word that the girl had muttered to him before falling asleep.

"What does that mean?" asked Melville.

"It means, 'thank you'," Bronson translated. He shook with laughter. "It's time you learnt your wife's language."

And with that, he turned away to yell at the spit boy, Ælfthrup, who was slumbering by the hot fire.

Before Melville could think about Bronson's chastisement, Avis sauntered back into the kitchen, arms crossed.

"Miss me?" She mocked, and then grinned despite herself when she noticed the child safely sleeping in Melville's arms.

"Oh Melville. Who do you have there?"

"I am not entirely sure," Melville confessed. "Sæthryth? She seems to have adopted me."

"That does not surprise me," Avis said as she lifted the sleeping girl out of Melville's arms and balanced her on her left hip.

"Why?"

"Because she has no parents."

"What, none?"

Avis shook her head. "You have much to learn, Melville. There are many children without mother or father here in this land. After all, you are married to one."

She turned her back, taking the child with her. Melville cursed under his breath again. He and his stupid questions! Would he never remember that the wounds in this land were still raw?

It was not long before Avis could barely remember not having such a large group of people sharing her home. It felt almost natural, this full and vibrant home, and she could see that Melville was becoming accustomed to it also. Together, they had created a community that broke their fast together sleepily before dawn, toiled hard in the fields to prepare them for the spring – though with many lookouts in case of attack – and shared in the profits of their labour in the evenings, with minstrels serenading them and children darting between people's legs. It seemed as if life had reached normality. Even if it was a different type of normality than they were used to.

About two weeks after Melville's return, as the crops in the ground were shooting forth and the snow had finally melted for good, a man was spotted on the horizon. The lookout's cry brought many to the front gate, and once again fear flooded their hearts. Melville pushed his way to the front of the crowd, Avis at his side.

"Could William have renegaded on his promise?" Avis hissed to Melville so that no one else could hear.

"Never," said Melville, but his heart sank as he looked out at the figure.

"William promised to treat all of his vassals with kindness!" Avis returned with fire in her words. "And see how he is repaying them!"

With one look Melville quieted her.

"This is not the time to frighten our people," he said calmly. "For all we know, it could be a messenger from the King."

In a louder voice, he called out.

"Let him in!"

The man that entered the gates was certainly not there to rob them. He was young, but looked as if he had lived a hundred years. He lay on his front over the thin horse that was struggling to carry his meagre weight. The man's skin was hanging off his body, and dirt covered the little flesh that he had. Avis rushed towards him.

"Are you hurt?"

The man didn't reply, and Avis tried in Anglo-Saxon.

"*Bealusið*?"

The man's eyes flickered open, and his dry chapped lips moved. No sound came out.

"Get this man inside," ordered Avis. Her heart had stopped, and although she tried to quash the feeling, revulsion had spread through her heart. She had not seen any man in such a terrible condition since…

Hands reached for the man, cautiously helping him down. He was heaved over a strong servant's back, and hurried inside. Murmuring broke out in the crowd, and Melville pulled Avis towards him.

"Get them inside," he muttered. "I will see to him."

That day, the fear that had been lost was found again in everyone. Tension filled the manor, and nothing could abate it until they heard for themselves the story of the strange man on the horse.

It was not until that evening that the entire household heard the man who had arrived in such a dramatic way speak his tale. He sat beside Avis, nervous around the Norman Melville who had tried but failed to speak to him through Robert's translation. He had refused to say anything, apart from telling them that his name was Tilian.

The man motioned to Avis that he was ready to speak, and stood up on shaking legs. Avis arose to translate for him, and offered him her arm to lean upon, which he gratefully accepted.

"My friends," began Tilian, speaking in the traditions of his people, "O, hear me."

There were nods and smiles throughout the crowd, as people heard the customary opening to a heroic tale, full of epic and exciting adventures, although this one was doomed to be filled with sadness.

"I tell you a tale of great suffering, and of bravery, and of great men that we have lost."

As he told his personal story of how he had seen William and his army approaching his village, there were shudders and tears privately spent.

"I was forced to kill my own animals," Tilian spoke with a great melancholy in his voice, but no tears fell. "I saw children, who were wandering from village to village, searching for their parents. Our land, destroyed – salted so that nothing will grow. And the flames…"

Tilian's voice trailed off, in the same way that Melville had seen Avis' eyes glaze over when she thought about the horrors that she had witnessed. Melville put a gentle arm on Tilian's shaking one, and helped him to sit down. Nervous murmuring filled the hall. Avis knew that she had to say something, before real panic gripped them once more.

"My friends," Avis continued in the same style as Tilian, translating as she went. "We must be grateful that we are safe here. William has promised not to harm us." She glanced at Melville. "And I trust that promise. We are safe here."

There was a tangible relaxation amongst the people after her strong words, and Melville nodded approvingly. Once again, she had stepped in to protect the people – this time, from their own anxiety.

The gratitude of the people became much more tangible after the arrival of Tilian, and of the other stragglers that made it to the safety of the manor from their homes without detection. Their coming had increased the thankfulness of all, reminding them of their lucky escape that many outside did not have.

Another morning dawned, and another call from the lookout. Avis hurried from her room, dragging on the last piece of her clothing to see if it was another Anglo-Saxon who had managed to stay alive – but it was not an Anglo-Saxon survivor. It was a man on a horse who she did not recognise, but he was clearly a wealthy Norman nobleman. He had a bushy beard that was unkempt, and probably grown during the weeks of warfare. Covered in dirt, Avis thought that she recognised something about his look, but had no time to wonder.

"My lord," she said stiffly. "To what do we owe this pleasure?"

The man smirked down at her, and ignored her question.

"Where is Melville?"

"I…I do not know," admitted Avis.

The man's smile increased, and he chuckled nastily.

"He didn't just leave you again, then?"

Avis coloured with anger, but knew better than to lose her temper.

"What mean you with my lord?" she asked coldly, but the man did not answer her.

"Melville," he repeated sternly. "I must speak with Melville."

Avis gave a brief nod, and called to Felix the stable boy to retrieve his master. Within minutes, Melville strode into the stable yard, his linen shirt roughly thrown across his wide muscular chest. Avis' breath caught in her throat, and she watched as Melville's face darkened. When he reached Avis' side, he suddenly fell to his feet and kneeled.

"My King."

Avis gasped. The King? William had altered much since she had last seen him, though it was but three years ago. So much so, that she had not even recognised him – the man that she had sworn to destroy.

William laughed.

"What, no courtesy from you, fine Avis?"

Melville saw his wife's fists clench, and pulled her down.

"Do you value your life?" He hissed to her.

"It is my life to risk!" She replied angrily, and pulled herself upwards. Staring directly at the monarch, she said, "and to what do we owe this pleasure?"

William guffawed.

"Clearly no pleasure for you, my lady!" he said with outright honesty.

Melville rose, nervous about what this visit entailed. Could William be betraying his bargain that allowed them his protection?

William continued.

"I came merely to tell you that I return south. My time here punishing the North is over. And I hope that they have learnt their lesson." He smiled nastily.

Melville's arm was the only thing preventing Avis from flinging herself bodily at William. How dare he? How could he speak of her people in such a manner?

"I am glad to hear of it, my lord," Melville said stiffly, before Avis could begin speaking her anger.

William watched him, and grinned.

"I will not trespass on your time any longer." He turned his horse around, but could not resist a passing shot. "I'll give your regards to your mother, my dear."

Avis ran forward with a shout, but Melville grabbed her by the waist.

"No," he whispered into her ear as she struggled against him. "Do not give him the pleasure of seeing you fight. Do not give him that satisfaction."

Avis' exertion only ceased as the sight of William disappeared, and the gate was once again barred. Melville finally released her, and she turned on him angrily.

"How could you stop me?" She shouted bitterly. "You know what he is!"

"Exactly," Melville replied calmly. "And I know what he's capable of."

Avis sighed. She tried to calm her beating heart, but it would not.

"You're right," she admitted. "But I don't like it."

Melville revelled in her retort. That was his Avis: someone who hated the system, but knew not to fight it if it may cost the lives of those around her.

She shook herself, as if ridding her clothes of William's stench.

"I suppose it is therefore safe for the villagers to return to Ulleskelf," Melville mused.

Avis nodded.

"Spring is coming. The fields will need to be tended."

"We had better give them the good news."

It was a triumphant and yet sad day, the day that Ulleskelf once again became alive with the voices of its inhabitants. It took little more than an hour for the villagers to carry their possessions and children down to their homes, which were untouched. It had been as a ghost village, as if the previous occupants had been stolen away by the wind.

The household servants had helped them move back into their village, but now stood awkwardly. This was not their territory, and although they did not want to leave, it was difficult to stay. They had no place there. The tiny

Norman boy Henri was the only one who seemed comfortable, tottering on his little feet, wandering in and out of various buildings, chattering away in a mixture of Norman and Anglo-Saxon.

Eventually, as the sun set and the cool descended, there was nothing more to say. Melville, Avis, and their servants returned home. The manor seemed unbelievably empty that night, and the Great Hall had many empty seats. Voices seemed to echo much louder than ever before, and so all spoke quieter, leading to an ever emptier feeling.

Avis picked at her food unhappily. Melville watched her.

"It was hardest for you to see them leave, I think," he said.

Avis nodded.

"They are my people."

"But they are safe." Melville put his arm subtlety around her shoulders. "You saved them."

"Yes," Avis agreed. "We are safe."

Melville's arm dipped, moving past her intricate shoulder blades and hooking around her waist. He leaned in towards her, and whispered.

"And we shall shortly be alone."

CHAPTER THIRTY TWO

But Avis squirmed unhappily underneath his touch.

"I am tired," she said, distractedly. "I think I shall retire early."

And with that, she rose and left the hall.

Melville sat there, shocked. He could not believe that she had just…left. The last few days had been of unbearable tension for him – constantly surrounded by people, never having a single moment to themselves. As welcome as the villagers had been, he had been waiting for the opportunity to have Avis to himself. He had thought that now the place had been emptied, they could leisurely enjoy the time that they could devote to each other. But Avis had startled out of the room like a frightened doe.

His appetite for the celebratory feast was gone, and after playing with his food for several minutes, Melville left for his chamber in a terrible mood.

The bad mood did not lift over the succeeding days. There was now a distinct awkwardness between Melville and Avis, now that the large multitude had left their home. With no distractions, no worries about calls from lookouts, and no children to care for, they were left almost exclusively to themselves. The corridors, once ringing with laughter and shouts, were now empty, save for the lonely steps of the few servants. They could not avoid each other, although Avis was doing a very good job of it.

She felt the tension strongly. It haunted her in her dreams, when she awoke reaching out for him. She was constantly aware of his presence, and had to stop herself from leaning towards him when they sat together during meals, or walking down the passageways and corridors that she knew he frequented. A fit of tears overtook her when she couldn't decide whether to go down to the kitchens or not; one half of her arguing that Melville would look for her there and so she shouldn't, and the other half saying that was exactly the reason that she should. Ridiculous woman! She chastised herself. This should not worry you, you must not let this consume you! But what probably hurt the most was that as she watched Melville, he seemed completely unaware of her.

Melville felt no such thing. The breeze that Avis brought into his life had never felt so lovely as now, when he could spend more time alone with her. He put off necessary visits to York, trying to convince himself that such business could wait another day. And another day. Perhaps even a week. Anything to be able to stay, to stay here, with the hope of seeing Avis before his fast was broken. To see her wandering around, speaking to servants. Maybe even to speak to her himself. But Melville knew that to truly win this tantalizing creature, he could not force his company upon her. He desperately wanted her to seek him out, but all she seemed to do was blush and leave a room each time he entered it. This was so unlike Avis' character that he marvelled at it, wondered at what she was thinking. Whether she wanted him to follow after her.

A bright, shining morning brought news to Melville that the villagers had requested his presence in Ulleskelf. Although loathe to leave Avis, he admitted to himself that since their departure, he had been remiss in his care of his people. Every thought had been taken over by his wife, and now it was time to face up to his responsibilities as a landlord and master. He could not ignore his people forever.

At the breaking of the fast that day, Melville mentioned his intended journey to Avis. He finished with an invitation.

"Will you accompany me?"

Melville had been sure that Avis would jump at the chance to visit her fellow Anglo-Saxons, but he was surprised.

"I am sorry, my lord," Avis replied with a cheery but hollow smile, "but I have business of my own to attend to here. I wish you a pleasant journey."

Turning resolutely to her other side, Avis began a conversation with Jean, pointedly turning her shoulder slightly so that Melville could not join in.

Faint anger rose throughout Melville's body. He had waited too long for this woman, too long! No one, no man could be expected to be so patient. But as he gazed upon her, his heart softened. She was worth this wait.

Avis watched her husband saddle his horse, and ride off with Robert as his translator, sending Jean down to the kitchen to give out his new orders, and she shook her head. She should have gone with him. The strain between them should not have come between her duty as his wife. But he was gone, and she would not demean herself by catching up with him.

Avis wandered listlessly to the entrance hall. That stupid comment that she had made to Melville about 'business of her own'! Avis was bored, once again, but this time it was a self-inflicted boredom. She had decided against going down to the kitchens, for fear of meeting

Melville there, and so she had spent the majority of her time sitting in the entrance hall. This was the place where many of the servants exchanged their gossip, and she found that sitting quietly by the fire meant that she overheard much of the goings on of her own home. These tales and pieces of news livened her day, and more than once she had had to stifle her giggles at the most ridiculous scandals that were suspected of down in the kitchen.

Today, she wrapped herself in a luscious rug, and opened up her favourite book. Texts were incredibly valuable, and very few people had any. This one had belonged to her mother, and had been Avis' sixteenth birthday present. Within moments, she was lost in the tale of warriors and great ladies, dragons and loot. But far off footsteps drew her attention, and she partially closed the book in the hope of hearing the next instalment of the saga between Jean, and young and pretty Edith.

But it was Edith herself who walked across the hallway, and a male servant whose voice Avis did not recognise that stopped her.

"Heard the news?"

"I can't stop," returned Edith. "I've got no time. I've got to take these loaves down to Ulleskelf. Master's orders."

Avis' heart swelled to see that Melville's concern for her people had not stopped after the danger of William's army had ceased. But there was more to be heard.

"So you haven't then?"

Edith sighed.

"You clearly have to tell me, so you may as well say it."

"I heard tell that mistress is thinking of running away."

Avis froze. The thought had certainly struck her mind when she had first come here as Melville's new bride, but after all that had happened between them, nothing had been further from the truth. She had heard some strange gossip before, but this was the most ridiculous that she had ever heard! Who would believe such a thing?

Edith laughed.

"Avis – run away? You must be joking. She knows that her place is here."

Avis was relieved to hear that her friend would put an end to such fanciful rumours.

"Anyway," Edith continued, "where would she go?"

Not a sentence that Avis particularly wanted to hear, but one that she could not deny. She prayed that the man would accept Edith's response, but he pushed it further, unwilling to pass up the opportunity to talk to one of Avis' few friends.

"Then how come they are how they are, eh?"

"I don't know what you mean," Edith answered carelessly.

The man giggled.

"Of course you do. You've seen them, just as I have. How long have they been married? Months. And still separate bedchambers. If that's not a marriage gone sour, I don't know what is."

"Hush with your talk," Edith said crossly. "You speak of matters that do not concern you!"

"She's one of us." The man said proudly. "If she wants to leave the sorry Norman beggar, that's fine by me."

A loud clatter filled the room as Edith dropped the loaves that she had been carrying – but the man cried out in pain. Edith hadn't dropped the bread then; she'd allowed them to fall as she attacked the man, with such force that Avis gasped. No wonder Edith had survived the coming of the Vikings and the Normans!

"You can stop your mithering," Edith said angrily. "Whether you like it or not, we are one people now. Didn't having the Norman lot around here with the Ulleskelf people teach you anything? What happens to them, happens to us. Same for master and mistress. Now get about your work, can't you?"

Edith stalked across the entrance hall, and Avis chanced a look. She saw her friend leave the room, head held high. The man muttered as he left, but had clearly been cowed by the passionate Edith.

Avis remained stock still on the chair. So this was what many thought of her. It was definitely a conceivable thought; not an unfair assumption. She herself had come into this marriage, and into this house, hating the very man that had brought her here. But all of that had changed, a long time ago. She had changed. She only wished that he had changed just as much as she had.

Another loud noise caused her to start, and Avis dropped her book. Turning around quickly to see what had caused such a bang, she noticed a man, dripping wet, who had come through the door out of the rain. He was evidently a messenger, and was looking around for someone to speak to.

Rising, she walked towards him, smoothing down her skirts and smiling.

"My lady," the messenger bowed as he recognised a wealthy woman, and she acknowledged this courtesy with a nod of the head.

"Welcome," Avis said. "Come, towards the fire. You must be cold."

"Bone wet," admitted the man, who was shivering. She led him closer to the warm flames, and beckoned him to sit.

"No, thank you my lady," the messenger said in a grateful tone. "I have further business in York to complete before I can rest, and I will not take too much of your time. Is your lord presently here?"

Avis shook her head, almost embarrassed that she was not with Melville.

"I'm afraid you may have passed him on the road. He has not long left for Ulleskelf."

The messenger bit his lip.

"I have an urgent letter for him. Would you be so kind as to take it for him?"

Avis smiled. "It would be my pleasure. And may I offer you some sustenance before you return into the bitter winds?"

"That would be most appreciated, my lady."

Reaching into his leather satchel, the messenger handed over a large piece of parchment, folded over several times and sealed with a wax stamp that Avis did not recognise.

"Thank you," she said. "I shall make sure my husband reads this as soon as he returns. And now, if you would follow me."

Avis led the messenger to the kitchen, where Tilian was following Bronson around like a puppy.

"…and that is where the oil is kept. Make sure that no one steals it, worth its weight in gold during the winter months. And here we have – "

"Bronson!"

Avis' greeting stopped the man's words in his tracks.

"My lady!" He came towards her with open arms. "I am instructing young Tilian here. He is to be my apprentice."

Bronson beamed upon his new pupil, and Tilian nervously returned the smile. Unwilling to return to his destroyed home to see whether any others had survived, Tilian had remained with them, and had proved to be a wonderful addition to the household. His life and vigour had returned to him, and he had proved to be an excellent cook. Bronson grew prouder of him with every passing moment.

"I am glad to see so," Avis replied with a smile. "Could you please feed and water this man, before he leaves for York?"

"It would be my pleasure, my lady," Tilian stepped in, and ushered the messenger towards a table.

Avis nodded her thanks to Bronson, and then left the hustle and bustle that she loved, back to the entrance hall and her book.

The letter that the messenger had given her was still in her hand. Picking up her discarded book, she pondered. Who could the letter be from? Avis turned the letter over to have another look at the seal. The red wax had imprinted upon it the impression of two crosses, one overlapping the other. As hard as she thought, she could not recall who used such a seal, although it was a common enough symbol.

At this moment, a terrible thought struck her heart. What if this letter was from King William himself? What if the King had once again changed his mind, or had another duty for Melville that he would not be able to talk himself out of? What if this letter contained vital news about an invasion by the Scots, and they were all once again in danger?

Avis could not wait for Melville to return. For all she knew, it could be hours and hours before he had finished at Ulleskelf – and even after that he may decide to travel on to York. If this letter did indeed carry bad news, there was no time to waste. She would have to open it herself.

But just as she was about to rip open the seal, she stopped herself. Another servant walked past her, and nodded. She returned the courtesy. She could not open it here. Anyone could enter at any time, and she could not risk revisiting the horror and fear that for so long was the normal emotion here in the manor.

Avis picked up her skirts, and half walked, half ran to her outer chamber. Not until she could be sure that she was alone did she take her small knife, and carefully prise apart the seal from the parchment. With shaking hands, she opened the letter, and began to read.

Her eyes darkened as they moved down the page. The letter was in Latin, and was not from King William after all. It was from a papal legate in Rome. One particular paragraph caught her attention, and she read on, horrified.

We have considered your application to annul your marriage carefully, as marriage is a holy contract, entered into in the sight of God. However, the circumstances of your marriage certainly do speak of a couple who should no longer be forced together. Her inheritance portion, though small, is nothing compared to her inability to support you as her husband and provider, and her resistance to consummating the marriage speaks of a wilfulness unattractive in a spouse. The fact that your wedding has been unconsummated leads us to regretfully accept your request. If you return an answer to this letter requesting that the marriage be ended, we consider it a duty as your spiritual Father to accept your desire, and consider your marriage to have never been formed.

Some of the inked words on the page were melting. Avis could not understand how, until she realised that she was crying.

And so, this was how it ended. Not with an argument for all to hear. Not with hissed bitterness across their plates. Not with one person storming off, and the other letting them go. No. Their marriage had ended with secret letters, and whispered lies to men thousands of miles away, who had never laid eyes on her.

How could he write such awful things? She re-read the last paragraph again, desperately trying to find something within it that did not tear at her soul. Inability to support. Wilfulness unattractive in a spouse. Avis bit her lip, and thought back over her time with Melville. She had certainly been wilful. She had told him on their wedding night that she hated him – had tried to spit at him. She had pushed him into a river, and mocked him about his prayers. Avis raised her eyes to the ceiling and shook her head. The words hit home, and hurt her deeply, because they were just that much too close to the truth.

But then Melville had been no angel either. He had bullied her, taunted her, chased her in the kitchen and berated her, about everything that she was. He had thrown her heritage in her face, tried to keep her from those that would make her happy, and shouted at her when he should have comforted her.

Avis threw herself into a chair. They were as bad as each other.

But as she lay on that chair, she remembered the conversations that they had had in that room over the last few evenings. Dark, and deep, and meaningful, and intimate conversations. Avis had told him things that she had never been brave enough to tell anyone else, and she had assumed that he had done the same. Or maybe he spins the same tale for every girl, she thought bitterly. Perhaps I am one of many who have fallen for his good looks and his charm and his winning manner and his strong physique.

I cannot stay here, she resolved. I cannot just sit here and wait for him to return. She stood up briskly, and stuffing the letter within her bodice, strode out of the room.

Within two minutes Avis was in the kitchen. After a quick word with Bronson, in which she impressed upon him that she wanted to be alone, she set up her work on a lone trestle table and began to pummel some dough. With every push of her knuckles, Avis imagined Melville's smiling face beneath them. How dare he write of his marital anguish to another. How could he try and be rid of her. Norman.

CHAPTER THIRTY THREE

In Ulleskelf, Melville shook hands with the last of the men who had lined up to see their lord, a smile on his face. It had been wonderful to see them again, the people that had become part of his family and his landscape over the winter. A small child had grabbed hold of his left leg, and he had to prise a chubby hand from his knee. She raised her head and beamed at him.

"Melville!" she said, trying out the new word that he had just taught her.

He smiled back at her, and lifting her up, handed her over to a grateful mother.

"Home?" Jean was sitting on his horse, and raised a quizzical eyebrow.

Melville nodded. He was anxious to return to Avis, anxious to discover what had caused her to act so strangely over the last few days. He shook his head. All women were unpredictable, but Avis was unlike any woman he had ever known.

It only took a couple of minutes for Melville and his men to saddle up their horses, and soon the sound of hooves filled their ears. Melville was impatient to arrive home, and pushed Storm, his horse, faster and faster. It was not long before he had entered the stable yard, and Felix came to take the reins from his master.

Melville dismounted hastily, almost catching his heel in the saddle.

"Where is my lady?" he asked the servant. "Where is Avis?"

Felix was unsure and could not say for certain. Few had seen her all morning. And so Melville entered his home in search of his wife. It took him a long hunt before he realised the first place that he should have looked: the kitchens.

As he walked down the steps, he could hear the clattering of platters and the aromas of sizzling meats filled his nostrils. Some of the new Anglo-Saxon dishes were beginning to become normal to his Norman palate, and he looked for them every evening, hoping that Bronson had chosen them to prepare. Melville sighed. This place was finally coming to feel like home.

His entrance was heralded by his booming steps, and as soon as Melville entered Tilian rushed towards him, looking nervous.

"Tilian!" grinned Melville, happy to see the usually anxious man so at home, but Tilian did not return his smile.

"My lord," he said, quietly. "Perhaps – "

But Melville interrupted him.

"Where is my lady?"

Tilian did not reply. His eyes fixed on a point just past Melville's shoulder, refusing to meet his eye. His fingers fiddled nervously, and he shifted from foot to foot. Melville's smile faded.

"Tilian?"

But Tilian was working himself into a state of panic, and started to mutter underneath his breath. Melville could not make out his words, but this was characteristic of Tilian. When he became nervous, he returned to the worried and delicate state that he was in when he had first arrived, and muttered to himself in Anglo-Saxon quickly, words that Melville did not understand.

"Calm yourself," Melville reached an arm out, and clasped Tilian's shoulder. Behind the young man was the head of the kitchen, and Melville beckoned him to approach.

Bronson bustled over, a dead chicken over his shoulder and strings of herbs in his hands.

"My lord?"

"Avis," Melville was brief. "Where is Avis?"

As Bronson shifted from foot to foot, he opened his mouth – but no sound came out. He could not think what to say.

Melville had not expected his servants to be so unwilling to reveal Avis' location. His gut clenched. Maybe she had suffered a terrible accident. Why would no one tell him?

Eventually, Bronson pointed nervously over to the other side of the kitchen. Melville craned his neck, and made out a lone figure that was standing past two scullery maids that were flicking flour at each other: Avis.

Avis was standing at a trestle table, pounding at a mound of dough, full of seeds and flavourings. Her veil had been folded carefully and placed beside her. Long blonde hair trailed down her back and over her shoulders, and it was tangled with oil, flour, and spices.

Melville's heart sang. She was beautiful, and elegant, and ridiculous, and she was all his own. He picked his way through the crowd of busy servants, and as he passed them they stopped their work. Wiping their hands on aprons or sweat from brows, they exchanged glances. From what they had seen, Avis did not want to be disturbed. They knew better than to stay for the inevitable argument that was to follow. One by one, the servants quietly left the kitchen, hurried along by Bronson, who was anxious to get away. Before long, Melville and Avis were the only two left in the kitchen.

But Avis had not noticed. She was completely transfixed with her work, releasing all of her anger into the unfortunate dough.

Melville reached Avis' trestle. Standing on the opposite side, he watched her knead the dough with her graceful fingers.

"Avis."

It was as if she could not hear him, for all of the reaction that Melville received. As if she had lost the power of hearing. Her eyes were down, and she began to form the dough into the baking shape that she had chosen.

"Avis?"

There was no reply from his wife, and Melville was hurt.

"Why do you not speak to me?"

Avis sniffed, and pushed a strand of hair behind her.

Melville laughed harshly, in disbelief.

"What is this? Ignored, by my own wife?"

A flash of anger passed across Avis' face, but she still refused to speak to him. She would not give him the satisfaction of seeing how much she had been hurt by him.

Melville breathed out a long and dejected sigh.

"Avis." He placed his fists on the table, and tried to remain calm. "Is there anything that I have done to offend you?"

Avis paused at her work, but then continued. She had not spoken a single word, and had given no sign that she had noticed her husband at all.

Melville stepped backwards, frustrated.

"How am I to discover what I have done wrong if you will not speak?" He burst out. "I cannot read your mind, Avis."

It was Avis' utter refusal to speak to him that finally pushed Melville to lose his temper. Leaning forward, he swept his arm across the trestle table, pushing everything onto the floor. Pottery cracked and spilt flour across the floor, and the dough that Avis had been working on fell in a heap into the rushes.

Silence filled the kitchen. Avis finally lifted her eyes to look at Melville, and he stepped back. The rage that filled her face alarmed him. There was only one other person whose eyes had been filled with such thunder, and that person had conquered a country to prove his worth.

Avis slowly wiped her hands on her apron. When she spoke, her voice seemed calm. It was only the slight shake in each word that revealed how deeply she was feeling, how much effort it was to keep a semblance of calm.

"How could you do this to me?"

Melville opened his mouth in surprise. He racked his brains, but could not think of a single thing that he had done that could provoke such a response from Avis. Had he not been doing everything he could to please her?

"What are you talking about?"

Avis pursed her lips.

"What am I talking about?" The rage that she had been supressing began to escape from her control. "Does any word you say mean anything?"

Melville rocked backwards and forwards on the balls of his feet.

"I have no idea where this barrage of anger has come from?" He returned irritably.

"You honestly don't know?"

"No!"

The two faced each other, both angry, and both hurting.

Avis exhaled. "How can I trust anything that you say?"

"Because you can!" Melville argued. "Because I have given you absolutely no cause to doubt me, or my character."

Avis laughed bitterly. "You can lie to my face in such a way, with no shadow on your face. I could never have believed it until now, when I see it with my own eyes."

"I am not lying!"

"I thought we were building something – "

"We are!"

"We were." Avis' deadpan response stopped Melville's protestations. He stared at her, unable to believe what she was saying.

"I cannot believe this," he almost whispered. "I cannot believe that you would give up on this so easily."

"Why have you?" yelled Avis. "I am not the one who decided that this marriage was over. You have betrayed me in the worst way."

"Betrayed you?"

"In a way that I could never have expected, Melville." Avis took a deep breath, trying to slow her beating heart. Everything in her wanted to push past the trestle table and enfold herself in his arms, but she knew that was not possible. Melville had ruined any hope of them being happy.

Melville began to reason with her, but Avis had not finished speaking.

"If you had spoken to me but days ago, Melville," she said sadly, "I would have said that your traitorous streak came from your Norman blood."

Melville stiffened, but waited for Avis to finish.

"But now…" Avis' eyes flickered across Melville's body, and he felt himself reddening. It was as if she was looking straight beneath the linen covering his broad chest. "Now I know you. I *know* you, Melville. And whatever I understood or thought I understood about the Normans that I have met…you are not the man I thought you were, and as much as I would like to blame it on your heritage, I think this is all you."

Melville reeled back at her hurtful words.

"I cannot believe that you are saying these things!"

"And I could not believe that you would do this to me!" Avis shot back.

Melville's frustration burst. "I do not know what you are speaking of!"

"This!" Avis pulled the letter from the papal legate from her bodice, throwing it down onto the trestle table, smeared with dough and flour.

Melville stared down. He saw a large piece of parchment with curling writing in a script that he did not recognise. A large wax seal was attached at one end, and his stomach tightened as he recognised the coat of arms. The seal of the Pope.

"Where did you get that?"

His voice was harsh, but he whispered the words. Ignoring his question, Avis picked up the letter and began reading it aloud.

"My dear son in Christ, Melville, lord of Copmanthorpe…"

"No – " Melville tried to stop her, but she merely raised her voice.

"In reply to your letter…"

Melville tutted through his teeth, angrily. He turned his back on her, and hung his head. He could not even look at her as she read those awful words out in her clear, but sorrowful voice. He could not believe that this was happening. How could a decision that he had made on the spur of the moment, months ago, destroy something that was becoming so beautiful, so sweet? He cursed himself for not sending another letter, to negate the first – but he had had other, more pressing matters on his mind over the last few weeks. And so his mistake went unchanged, and now he was facing the consequences.

"…we consider it a duty as your spiritual Father to accept your desire, and consider your marriage to have never been formed." Avis finished. Her voice finally broke, and tears were streaming down her face. She lowered the letter to look at Melville, who had refused to turn around and look at her as she read out the letter.

Avis waited in the silence, but there was no sign that Melville was going to turn around to face her. Silence filled the empty kitchen.

"How could you do this to me?"

Melville finally turned around to face her, and Avis gasped at his face. He was devastated. The words that she had been throwing at him had had more of an impact than she could have had imagined. And finally he spoke.

"My letter," Melville shouted, "my letter was written months ago – before anything changed, before I really knew you!"

"I cannot understand what possessed you to even write it!" returned Avis, angrily.

Melville took a step forward towards his furious wife.

"It was sent when you and I…it seemed like the best thing for you."

Avis scrunched her nose in confusion.

"Since when did you consider what was best for me?"

"Since…since…" Melville spluttered. "I cannot put a time on when you became such an important part of my life!"

This was not something that Avis had expected. Melville was breathing deeply, clenching and unclenching his fists – but his face was serene.

"Avis," he said, and his voice seemed to caress her name. "You cannot know what it is to marry someone that you despise, and then to realise that you have fallen in love with them. My feelings for you…they are deeper than anything that I have ever known. Deeper than any ocean and farther than any land. You…you are everything."

"I cannot listen to this." Avis turned and began to walk away. Melville was hurt, and he begged her.

"Will you not stay?"

"No."

Melville hurried around the trestle table to prevent her from leaving.

"Why not? You begged me to speak the truth, and now I am! Why will you not hear it?"

There was hurt in his voice, and a confusion that tugged at Avis' heart – but still she would not stay, she would not listen to this.

Avis had almost reached the kitchen door when Melville cried out in agony.

"Why are you trying to leave me?"

The pain in his words had now reached a crescendo, and they stopped Avis in her tracks.

Without turning to face him, she spoke. She could not speak and look at him – that would be too hard. And these words needed to be said.

"I do not want to leave you. But it's too much, Melville. Everything is crowding me, and I do not know what to believe and what part of you to trust."

A hand reached out. Melville touched Avis' shoulder, and she recoiled at his touch. This apparent disgust spurred him on, forcing her to turn around, and pulling her violently into his arms. Avis struggled, not only against the strength and the warmth of his body, but against the emotions that welled up within her, crying out that this was right, that this was where she belonged. Melville's hands were around her waist, and every breath that he took reminded Avis just how close they were.

A loud resounding noise reverberated around the stone kitchen, and Melville's face recoiled in pain. Avis' violent slap began to colour his cheek, and she gasped at the force of her own anger.

Melville looked down at Avis, his passionate wife.

"I probably deserved that," he whispered to her.

Avis could not help herself. A slow but glorious smile spread across her red lips. Reaching up on her toes, she leaned closer and closer towards Melville – who could not believe what she was about to do.

The kiss was long, and ardent, and unlike anything they had ever known. As soon as their lips touched, Avis stopped struggling in Melville's arms, and he tightened his grip around her tiny frame. His lips parted, and she welcomed the new intrusion with a quiet moan of delight.

After the kiss ended, Avis stared into her husband's eyes with wonder. This man, this wonderful man. He was hers, and hers alone.

"I suppose," Melville spoke in a shaking voice, in a state of wonder at the hunger and desire emanating from his delicate Avis, "that I probably deserved that as well."

Avis laughed, awkwardly, suddenly aware of the very wanton behaviour that she had just displayed. Pulling away from the intimate embrace, she walked past Melville towards the trestle table where she had been working. She leaned down, and began to tidy the mess that he had made in his previous bout of anger.

Melville smiled in wonder. It would take Avis some time to become accustomed to the affectionate manner that he intended to treat her with, but she would learn.

He watched the elegant slope of her form as she leaned across the table, and admired her. Another rush of love flowed through him, and he slowly began to follow her. When he had reached her, an adoring hand reached up and moved away the wash of hair that flowed down her back. Avis stiffened at first, unsure as to what Melville was doing, but as he lowered his lips upon her neck, she shivered under his touch. Melville placed his arms around her waist while he continued to nuzzle at her neck, and before Avis could anticipate his plan, he turned her around to face him.

The desire on her face told him exactly what he needed to know. Hungrily, their lips met, and abandoning all fear they gave themselves up to their mutual love.

CHAPTER THIRTY FOUR

Avis wriggled, delighting in the way that she felt. She and Melville lay in his bed chamber, drinking in the pleasure of finally truly understanding each other – in every way. After their fiery encounter in the kitchen, it had not taken Melville long to carry his bride to his chamber, past the servants who hurriedly pretended that they could not see them, and irreversibly make their relationship undeniable. They had finally consummated their marriage. Avis was lying on her side, with Melville's arms around her. Neither of them had seen any particular reason to dress, and so they revelled in the feeling of their bodies as close as they could possibly be. Melville lay with his eyes closed, a contented smile on his face that Avis had never seen before. But then, she reasoned, I probably have the same smile. And why not? Now we are truly husband and wife. And he loves me.

She sighed, happily. She could not have imagined reaching a point where she felt so at peace, so comfortable around this tall, dark man. But here she was, as vulnerable as she could possibly be, and yet he still loved her. It was a miracle.

"Avis?"

"Hmmm?" Avis did not want to break the exquisite moment with conversation, but Melville was determined to speak. She kept her eyes closed, though a cheeky smile spread across her face.

"Avis!" Melville said cheerily. "Are you listening to me?"

"No," she returned, luxuriating in his mock anger. She turned to face him, and Melville laughed.

"Now I shall pretend listen to you," Avis smiled, and Melville shook his head at her.

"You are a heedless one. A reckless woman."

Avis nodded, but she was sleepy, and allowed her eyes to gently close.

"Avis."

She jerked back to consciousness.

"Melville."

Melville loved the way that she said his name, and he could not help but smile in wonderment that he was married to the beautiful woman lying naked in his bed.

"I think," he said carefully, "that there are some things that we need to talk about."

Avis' attention heightened as she saw how serious Melville was being.

"Talk? About serious things? Now?"

Melville chuckled to see her unwillingness.

"Now."

Avis scrunched up her nose in a way that was becoming as familiar to Melville as his own face. She was confused as to what there was to talk about.

"Such as?"

"When did everything change?" Melville could see that Avis did not understand his rather oblique question, and so tried to clarify. "Your feelings about me. For me. When did they change?"

He looked slightly bashful at the forward and direct question, but Avis smiled.

"I suppose," she said, thoughtfully, "the real moment that I realised I cared for you much deeper than I wanted to admit was when you returned after travelling to William's court."

Melville raised an eyebrow, and Avis elaborated.

"I was so concerned when you disappeared – "

"I didn't disappear!" Melville protested. "I went to protect you!"

"But I didn't know that," Avis replied calmly. "All I knew was that you had departed with some of your best men. The strongest men that could have protected us. You had left no message indicating where you were going. You didn't even write a short note to tell me that you would return."

"I cannot write," Melville confessed, with a sad look on his face. "If I had tried to leave you a message, I would have had to take another into my confidence."

Avis was stunned.

"Truly, you cannot write?"

"I cannot read," pointed out Melville. "I never had the instruction that you were given as a child."

Avis considered this new piece of information.

"I had not thought of that," she mused.

"But I interrupted you," said Melville. "Please continue."

"It was when you returned," Avis began again. "When I realised how terrified I was of losing you, and how proud I was that you had faced one of the most dangerous men in this land – all to protect myself, and the people of Ulleskelf. They are not your people, and yet you risked your life for them. I suddenly grasped the extent of your capacity to love, and…"

Her voice trailed off, her embarrassment overcoming her.

"Well, there you are," she said, confused. "Now you know."

Avis smiled nervously at him, and Melville drew her closer to himself. Kissing her on the forehead, he breathed a happy sigh. But Avis was not satisfied with this one-sided conversation.

"And how has it taken you this long," asked Avis, half-mockingly, "to admit your feelings for me? You must confess we could have reached this blissful understanding much earlier if you had been honest."

"I do not consider myself dishonest!" retorted Melville.

Avis nudged him.

"You know what I mean."

Melville stroked her hair with one hand.

"I do." He pondered her question before replying, and then answered hesitantly. "It was not that I had decided not to be honest. I did not believe you to return my love, and so did not want to place you in the uncomfortable position of knowing me to feel more than you did. Until I could be sure, until I had some sign from you that you considered me in a similar manner…I was not willing to risk the balance that we had created – even if it was a balance that was not as close and familiar as I had wanted. I could not risk losing you."

Avis nodded slowly.

"And so we both loved, and did not know how to love."

"You are as eloquent as ever," teased Melville.

They lay in silence for several minutes, basking in the love that they could now openly express. But Avis was not completely ready to end the conversation. There was one more thing that she had to know.

"Melville?"

It was he that was falling asleep now, and she flicked him on the nose.

"Ouch!"

"Ah, I have your attention," Avis laughed. "I have one more question for you."

"Is it a difficult one?" asked Melville, rubbing his nose in mock anguish.

"I think it may be."

The seriousness of Avis' tone brought him back to their conversation, and he began to look worried.

"Do not fear," consoled Avis. "I am not angry. I merely wish to know why you did not write to the Pope again, after your affections had changed, to tell him that you did not require an annulment."

Avis was worried that she had overstepped the line with this question, as Melville fell silent and pensive. She berated herself. This was a new beginning for them, and here she was, already provoking him!

"It does not matter," she said hurriedly, "I only wondered – "

"To do so," Melville interrupted quietly, "would be to admit that I could not…would not live without you. It seemed like weakness. I convinced myself that my letter did not bind me to an annulment and that when the reply finally came, I could burn it. You would never know, and I would never have hurt you." Melville laughed sadly. "That did not happen. I did hurt you. The one thing that I have always tried to avoid for you, committed by my own hand."

Avis reached her arm to encircle him, and nestled into Melville's neck.

"But all is mended now."

"All is mended." Melville echoed her happy words, and the tension in his body released. She had forgiven him his stupidity, and he would never be so rash again.

"You know," Avis mused, "It is good to talk about these things. We have been avoiding them for fear of hurting each other, but now all is in the open."

"I shall never hurt you again," Melville whispered to her, his emotions brimming over into his voice.

Avis lifted her head to look into his eyes, and beamed, seeing passion there.

"I know," she replied, briefly caressing his lips with hers, and then settling down against his warm body.

The warmth of the room and the happiness in their hearts gently pushed them towards sleep. As Avis' eyes fought against the pull to slumber, she spoke again.

"Melville?"

He grunted, and she took that to mean that he was listening.

"I have one last thing to tell you."

"It's not that you have written to the Pope too, is it?" asked Melville lazily, one eye opening to stare at her quizzically. "I don't know if I could bear that."

Avis giggled.

"No," she said. "But I have lied to you."

Melville started, and almost sat up in shock, and Avis rushed to calm him.

"Not about anything important!"

"What unimportant thing is not true then?"

"My name."

Melville looked confused, and was still anxious that Avis had been dishonest with him. Avis quickly continued, trying to reassure him, trying to explain.

"Avis is a Norman name. It means bird."

"I know," Melville mocked her. "I am the Norman one in this bed."

"And I am the Anglo-Saxon one," Avis agreed. "Did you not ever wonder why I did not have an Anglo-Saxon name?"

Melville considered for a moment. Once more, his ignorance was so obvious to her!

"To be perfectly honest, my love, I did not."

Avis smiled knowingly.

"Just as I learned the Norman language, I adopted a Norman name."

"Why?" Melville asked. "I cannot understand why you would align yourself so profoundly with a people that you despised."

"For my protection," Avis said. "It was safer for those who met me to consider me as almost Norman. Or as Norman as I could be."

Melville thought about this for a moment, and had to agree with her. Her name had probably protected her in moments of danger more than she knew.

"Why Avis?"

Avis tried to explain the complicated thought pattern that had led her to choose her new Norman name.

"When I look at the birds," she began. "They fly where they choose. They are completely free, and I envied them. In the new land after the conquest, I could not go where I wanted, do what I wanted, marry who I wanted!" She laughed. "Avis seemed appropriate. I felt like a caged bird, and I wanted to be free."

"So," Melville said hesitantly, "what is your real name?"

"It's Annis," she said shyly.

"Annis." Melville rolled the name around on his tongue. "It is a beautiful name. It suits you."

Avis laughed.

"So it should! It is my name."

"Does it have a meaning?"

Avis smiled at her husband. Her glorious, Norman husband.

"It means unity."

"Unity. It's perfect. Which would you prefer?"

After a short momentary instant of consideration, she replied.

"Annis. I think it better suits me."

Melville drew his wife closer.

"You know," he whispered affectionately. "I may have conquered your country. But you have conquered my heart."

EPILOGUE

The sun was shining, and no cloud blemished the blue sky. As a gentle breeze rustled the trees, the flags rippled from their posts and rope surrounding the village.

Ulleskelf was decorated from the top of each house to the grass beneath the feet of the villagers. Branches of blossom adorned walls, and flowers were intertwined with luscious leaves around each doorway. The smith of the village had wrought small silver bells that jingled merrily in the lilting breeze. All of the villagers were wearing their best clothes, and the children ran round in small packs, tripping up the servants that were trying to set a delectable feast on the trestle tables brought from the house.

It was a little over two years since the terrible winter that had become known as the Harrying of the North. Melville had declared that there was to be a feast held, and the guest of honour was currently toppling towards him.

Melville laughed, and continued to give out the food and gifts to the villagers that had become his friends. Although they respected him, none feared him because his fairness and his love of the land had endeared him to each that he met.

As he moved through the village, Melville found the musicians that were wandering about nibbling on sweet pastries and spilling ale from the tankards in their other hands.

"Enjoying yourselves?" Melville smiled at them.

The musicians hastily bowed, spilling even more of their beverages.

"Yes, my lord!" One spluttered. "And we are but now to play for you!"

Melville roared with laughter.

"Be at peace, my friends," he said good-naturedly. "There is no rush. This is a festival, is it not?"

They returned his smile, and made their way rather more quickly to the centre of the village where the festivities were to begin.

Melville followed them at a leisurely pace, and within moments the melody of a popular dance reached his ears, followed by cheers. As he turned the corner, the sight of a crowd dancing with smiles and laughter met his eyes. Children tried to imitate the adults, but were distracted by a man with dolls and puppets who led them to the side of the dancers. Felix and Sæthryth pulled Ælfthrup along with them, chattering away. Soon all could hear the children's roars of laughter.

Melville espied Annis in the group of female dancers, linking hands with two girls from the village. They fell about giggling as one of them tripped, pulling the other two down with her. A contented warmth spread through Melville as he watched with a smile as his beautiful wife picked herself up, dusted herself down, and re-joined the merriment with no sign of embarrassment. They had truly built a wonderful life.

He continued to walk around the gaggle of spectators, greeting them as friends and equals. Melville shook hands with a young couple that had recently become betrothed: Edith and Jean.

"We had long seen it coming," said Melville in a mock hushed tone, "but you must not tell anyone that I told you so!"

Jean laughed, joy lighting up his eyes as he took Edith's hand in his own.

"And we are grateful to you," he replied. "Without you, I do not know if we would have lived to see this beautiful day."

Melville pulled his friend into a tight embrace, and Jean returned it. Over the two years of safety they had worked together to rebuild the land that had been destroyed, and it was a wrench for them both to see Jean leave and build his own life.

Their clasp only loosened when the sound of horse's hooves startled them. Melville turned to see a rider in a livery that he recognised with horror. Running towards the man so that no one else would hear the message, Melville hoped beyond hope that it was not bad news.

"Word from the King?" He asked abruptly, before the messenger could even dismount.

"Indeed." The man hauled himself down from his horse, and looked at Melville warily. "You were expecting such news?"

Melville gave a short grunt.

"I was not anticipating a message from the King until this autumn," he confessed.

The messenger smiled uneasily. "Then you will be surprised by this letter."

Reaching into the pack on his horse, he pulled out a small piece of parchment that he handed over. Melville took it gingerly, afraid of what it may contain.

The messenger watched Melville with interest.

"Will you not open it?" he asked.

Melville shook himself, and brought himself back to his senses. Whether this was good news or bad, it would not alter for the waiting of it. But he did not want to open it before this unknown man.

"I thank you," Melville said. "If you would but follow the music, you shall find food and ale awaiting you."

"My lord," bowed the messenger, recognising the dismissal for what it was, but taking no offence from it. He went where Melville had pointed, leaving the letter to be opened.

A shaking hand broke the seal and unfolded the meagre amount of parchment. The Latin script was now something familiar to Melville. Annis had taken great pains to teach him his letters, and although it would never be something that he excelled in, he certainly had enough skill to decipher this short note.

The letter was from King William. It spoke of respect, and trust, and faithfulness. It declared his intention to give Melville more land in Northumbria – a fantastic honour. Northumbria was a large and rich land, giving a huge amount of power and prestige to the men that controlled it. And now one of those men was Melville.

His eyes narrowed in disbelief, and he went over the words again, his lips silently moving as he made sure that he got every word right. But his first reading had been correct. William wanted to reward him for his bravery and faithfulness. The letter did not bring bad news, but the best news that there could be.

Annis. He must tell Annis. Melville returned to the crowd of villagers, but the dancers had finished their gaiety and had now progressed to sample the many dishes lovingly prepared. There was no sign of Annis.

Robert wandered past him, talking with Bronson and Tilian.

"Annis," said Melville in a rush, "have you seen Annis?"

Robert and Bronson shook their heads, but Tilian smiled knowingly.

"Under yonder tree, my lord," he said, pointing at the large oak just outside the village boundary. "I reckon that would be the first place I would look."

Melville nodded his thanks, and proceeded to make his way between the houses towards the great tree that Tilian had pointed at. As he turned a corner, the loveliest sight in the world heralded his eyes.

Annis. She was wearing her gown of blood red silk, which had become her trademark, and her long hair was braided with flowers. The sunlight glistened on a familiar gold ring that she now wore on the fourth finger of her left hand. Her back was rested against the wide trunk of the tree, and she smiled lazily at the vision before her that Melville had been unable to draw his eyes from.

A small boy, of only a year, played under the soft shadow of the leaves. Dark brown curls softly fell across his ears, and he smiled to see his father walking towards him.

"Good morrow my love," Melville leaned down to kiss his wife, who met his embrace with love. "How does my boy?"

Annis gestured, amused. "How does he look to you, Melville?"

Melville sat himself down beside Annis, and looked at his son with pride. Myneas' face broke into a gorgeous smile as he beheld his parents.

"You know," mused Melville, "I still can't believe that we managed to create such a wonderful child."

"Can you not?" replied Annis. "It does not surprise me at all. He has two rather wonderful parents."

Melville nudged her with a laugh.

"Ever the modest one."

Annis watched her son pull at the grass with a look of discovery, and Melville looked at his wife. At his family.

"Myneas," he said, and his son looked up, confused at being disturbed.

"It is a good name," said Annis.

"It is the best," agreed Melville. "Myneas. Tell me the exact meaning again. It is a long one, and complex."

Annis nodded. "Our words have many layers. Myneas…it is the affection one has for a memory of what you love. Not the desire to return to it, but the wish never to forget it."

Annis' voice dropped, and Melville pulled her close.

"I know that some wounds always leave scars," he said quietly. "But I intend to keep you whole and healthy for as long as I live."

Annis snuggled into Melville, feeling his strength.

"I know," she said softly. "We shall protect each other. We shall build a world in which everyone is cared for."

Read on for the first chapter in the sequel to “Conquests: Hearts Rule Kingdoms”.

PROLOGUE

The prisoner had not spoken for weeks.

None had expected them to last this long. The journey over the wide sea, back to Normandy, had been a troubled crossing. Of the five ships that had left England's shore, only three had arrived safely, and even those had lost men to fear and sickness.

The prisoner had not complained.

Dressed in clothes that had seen better days, they had been forced upon a horse, despite their protestations that they were not strong enough to ride. The cloak had become torn and stained over the fortnight-long ride to the castle of Geffrei, and the hood was pulled across the prisoner's face, obscuring the night. Despite the cold, the prisoner was not offered a better cloak, or a kind word.

The prisoner had barely noticed.

As the sound of the horses' hooves slowed, the prisoner looked up. Through bleary eyes, only a vague impression of the place at which the company had arrived could be seen, but it was imposing even in its vagueness. A stone building with several floors, and no light emitting from the few windows to pierce the darkness of the evening. No flags hung from the walls, and the door outside which they stood was bare, save for one small handle.

The prisoner closed both eyes.

"You awake?"

The prisoner was dragged down from the horse, and made to stand, although every bone cried out for rest. The brim of the hood fell down over their eyes. The murmur that the prisoner attempted made no sense.

"Walk! If you know what's good for you."

There were almost a dozen knights that had ridden with the prisoner, but one was more splendidly dressed than the others. His cloak was lined, offering warmth against the bitter autumnal breeze, and it was he only that had been fed thoroughly during the journey.

"My lord Geffrei!"

The man with the lined cloak turned to face one of his men. The others were lowering themselves from their horses, and pulling up their belts over their empty stomachs.

"Yes?" He replied bluntly.

"Food is required," said the man, pointing at the prisoner. "If you do not want it to die."

The prisoner fell.

"Up!" shouted Geffrei, pacing towards the prisoner lying on the ground. "You'll walk, not crawl, into my home, you dirty animal!"

A hand reached up, cracked and sore, from the prisoner lying on the ground, but no hand went down to meet it. Eventually, the prisoner raised themself up from the ground, and hung their head.

"Now," breathed Geffrei with malice in every tone, "on you go. You're the guest of honour."

Cruel laughs rang out as the prisoner stumbled forwards against the door, clutching at the handle. It turned. The prisoner leaned, exhausted, against the door.

The room that the prisoner fell into was the Great Hall. A small brazier glinted at the far side of the room, and a medley of dogs unravelled themselves to meet their guests. Feet sounded around the prisoner as the men strode in, desperate for warmth.

Geffrei threw himself by the fire in the only chair in the room. He turned an eye to the prisoner, who had pulled themself up to stare into his face.

"Well," he said with a smirk. "Here we are. We have finally arrived. What do you think of your new home?"

The prisoner stood up, and with a great effort, spat onto the rushes on the floor.

Geffrei shook his head with a smile on his face. "Now, that's no way to treat your new home," he chastised. "What do you have to say for yourself?"

The prisoner pulled back the hood from their face, and shook long hair out from the mud-splattered cloak.

"Where is Annis?"

"Who?" Geffrei pulled off his boots and flung them across the room. "Annis?"

"Yes," said the prisoner, and she smiled as she walked towards him. "My daughter."

HISTORICAL NOTE

The Anglo-Saxon nation was brutally attacked during the 1066 Norman Conquest, led by William, soon to be known as the Conqueror. Many ealdorman, or Anglo-Saxon noblemen did die, and there was a systematic replacement of Norman nobles in positions of power. Three years later, just as winter was approaching in 1069, King William reacted to the growing rebellion against his rule, and destroyed the majority of the North of England. This became known as the Harrying of the North. Although I have saved Ulleskelf in my story, there is no evidence that any such dramatic rescue occurred.

The characters of Melville and Avis are not historical people that truly existed, but they typify the type of people that were trying to make their way in the new England of this time. Many men that came over the waters were not of high birth, and came to make a name for themselves. Many daughters and widows of Anglo-Saxon descent were forcibly married to these men, to create a new class of Anglo-Norman people.

Gospatrick, Avis' uncle, was the lord of Copmanthorpe. Both that town, and the village of Ulleskelf existed during this time, and you can still visit them now. My description of King William is based on historical record, but these two are the only 'real' people in the book.

As much as is humanly possible, I have tried to keep to the customs and traditions of both peoples as the story unfolds. An Anglo-Saxon betrothal and wedding ceremony is known to have existed, but we have no record of what occurred then. I have used my imagination, and my knowledge of Anglo-Saxon rituals, to create one.

Any historical inaccuracies are probably due to my ignorance.

For further reading on this period of history, look for:

Elaine M. Treharne. *Living Through Conquest: the Politics of Early English, 1020-1220.* Oxford: Oxford University Press, 2012.

George Garnett. *The Norman Conquest: a Very Short Introduction.* Oxford: Oxford University Press, 2009.

Hugh M. Thomas. *The Norman Conquest: England After William the Conqueror.* Lanham: Rowman & Littlefield Publishers, 2008.

M. T. Clanchy. *England and its rulers, 1066-1307.* Malden: Blackwell Publishers, 2006.

Donald Matthew. *Britain and the continent, 1000-1300: the impact of the Norman conquest.* London: Hodder Arnold, 2005.

Brian Golding. *Conquest and Colonisation: the Normans in Britain, 1066-1100.* Basingstoke: Palgrave, 2001.

Sarah Foot. *The making of Angelcynn: English identity before the Norman conquest.* Cambridge: Cambridge University Press, 1996.

R. Allen Brown. *The Norman conquest of England: sources and documents.* Woodbridge: Boydell Press, 1995.

David A. E. Pelteret. *Catalogue of English post-conquest vernacular documents.* Woodbridge: Boydell Press, 1990.

William E. Kapelle. *The Norman Conquest of the north: the region and its transformation, 1000-1135*. Chapel Hill: University of North Carolina Press, 1979.
John Le Patourel. *The Norman Conquest of Yorkshire.* Leeds: University of Leeds, 1971.
H. R. Loyn. *Anglo-Saxon England and the Norman Conquest.* London: Longman, 1962.

ABOUT THE AUTHOR

Emily Murdoch is a medieval historian who has worked at the Bodleian Library in Oxford transcribing documents, and designing part of an exhibition for the Yorkshire Museum. She has a degree in History and English, and is finishing her Masters thesis. Emily is currently working on the sequel to "Conquests: Hearts Rule Kingdoms", as well as working for various companies as script advisor, researcher, copy writer, and conservation assistant. You can learn more at www.emilyekmurdoch.com or follow her on twitter @emilyekmurdoch.

Printed in Great Britain
by Amazon.co.uk, Ltd.,
Marston Gate.